BROADLAND

A DI Tanner Mystery

- Book One -

DAVID BLAKE

www.david-blake.com

D1147455

BROADLAND

Proofread by Jay G Arscott

Special thanks to Lorraine Swoboda,
John Kincaid, Ali Dunn and Anna Burke

Published by Black Oak Publishing Ltd
2nd edition published in Great Britain, 2020

Disclaimer:
These are works of fiction. Names, characters, businesses, places, events and incidents are either the products of the author's imagination or used in a fictitious manner. Any resemblance to actual persons, living or dead, or actual events is purely coincidental.

Cover photograph 67723909 © Richard Bowden - Dreamstime.com

ISBN: 978-1-9163479-0-8

DEDICATION

For Akiko, Akira and Kai.

BOOKS BY DAVID BLAKE

CRIME THRILLERS
Broadland
St. Benet's
Moorings
Three Rivers
Horsey Mere

CRIME COMEDY
The Slaughtered Virgin of Zenopolis
The Curious Case of Cut-Throat Cate
The Thrills & Spills of Genocide Jill
The Herbaceous Affair of Cocaine Claire

SPACE CRIME COMEDY
Space Police: Attack of the Mammary Clans
Space Police: The Final Fish Finger
Space Police: The Toaster That Time Forgot
Space Police: Rise of the Retail-Bot
Space Police: Enemy at the Cat Flap
Space Police: The Day The Earth Moved A Bit

SPACE ADVENTURE COMEDY
Galaxy Squad: Danger From Drackonia

ROMANTIC COMEDY
Headline Love
Prime Time Love

'For from within, out of the heart of men, proceed evil thoughts, adulteries, fornications, murders, thefts, covetousness, wickedness, deceit, lasciviousness, an evil eye, blasphemy, pride, foolishness: All these evil things come from within, and defile the man.'
Mark 7:21-23

- PROLOGUE -

Saturday, 13th April

A COLD DENSE shadow fell over Jane Richardson as she hurried along the concrete towpath. To her left, moonlight danced over the River Bure's untroubled surface as it slipped silently past, heading back the way she'd come. A low-hanging branch scratched at her face as she ducked underneath. From somewhere far behind her came the shriek of laughter, slicing through the air, only to fall silent a moment later to leave nothing but the sound of her high heels, click-clacking out a stark but steady beat.

It was late. She knew it was. The sun had disappeared behind the Broads a long time before.

She always started work early and more often than not finished late, and had promised herself on numerous occasions that if it was dark, she'd take the long way home, *never* the shortcut down by the river. It might be a journey she enjoyed, one she even looked forward to on occasion, but only when it was light. What in the summer months was a relaxing carefree stroll felt more like picking her way through a graveyard at any other time of year. It may be April, and the days were stretching out, but the sun had disappeared over three hours before, leaving nothing but a cold full moon to light her way home.

From deep within the undergrowth to her right she heard something move. That was normal enough. If it had been light she'd probably have been able to see the animal that made the noise, as she often did during the summer. Sometimes she'd even see a rat scurrying about, and stop to watch as it fled across the path in front of her, diving between the riverbank and the thick line of trees.

Then she heard the hard, sharp sound of a twig snapping, just behind the treeline.

Rats don't snap twigs, she thought, with a prickling of alarm.

It only took a moment for more sensible reasoning to take over, brushing away any concern; after all, it was probably nothing more ominous than a wood pigeon. They were certainly common enough, stumbling their way over leaves and branches as they searched the ground for food, lifting their feet high as they did, before carefully placing them back down.

But pigeons didn't forage for food at night, at least she didn't think they did.

Another twig snapped. It sounded thicker than the last. Too thick to have been broken by a pigeon. A fox, perhaps?

Forcing herself along, she turned her head ever so slightly, watching the trees from out of the corner of her eye. But all she could see was layer upon layer of ever-deepening shadows. If there was a fox hiding in there somewhere, she'd never see it.

Facing forward again, she picked up her pace, moving closer to the river side of the path as she did.

There was another sound, like the crack of a branch.

That was no fox!

'Why'd I come this way again?' she mumbled to herself, as her heart began to pound deep inside her chest. 'Oh yes, that's right. Because it's a shortcut. Good choice, Jane. Nice one!'

Ahead of her she could just about see the arch of the railway bridge, under which she had to walk. If anyone was going to try and mug her, that was probably the most likely place. Maybe there were two of them; one following her through the trees, the other waiting under the arch.

She peered at it, trying to make out if she could see the outline of someone hiding underneath. But at that time of night, with no street lights this far from town, the shadow under the archway was pitch black.

Checking that her handbag was where it should be, with the strap over her shoulder and the bag itself – her favourite cream leather Gucci – wedged firmly under her arm, she plunged her hands deep into her pockets, fixed a defiant stare ahead, and ploughed forward, mentally preparing herself for the worst. If there *was* someone lurking under the railway arch, she knew to take her father's advice, and to avoid eye contact. Instead she should simply ignore them and keep walking. Once she passed under the bridge, her house wasn't too far away, and if the worst came to the worst she'd probably be able to make a run for it.

As she stepped into the shadow cast by the arch, the click-clack of her heels echoing out all around, from the treeline came the sudden sound of branches being forced apart as someone, or some*thing*, forged its way out onto the towpath behind her.

A cold hand of fear crept up her spine.

Her heart was pounding so loudly that she thought whoever, or even *whatever*, it was standing behind her must be able to hear it.

She should run. She knew she should run; every fibre of her being was telling her so. Instead she found herself turning around to confront whatever it was that had been following her.

If the idea that someone was behind her was terrifying, actually seeing someone there was far worse.

'Who's that?' she called out, bringing her hands out of her pockets, clenching them into fists. There was no way she was going to let anyone take her bag. Not without a fight, they weren't!

A sliver of moonlight caught the face of the figure, leering at her through the darkness.

Trembling, she blurted out, 'Who are you? What do you want?'

As the figure took a slow but deliberate step forward, a thin dark gash appeared as it opened its mouth, and in a voice barely loud enough to be heard, it said, 'You've got something that belongs to me.'

Doing her best to control her rising fear, with courageous resolve she said, 'I can assure you that I have *nothing* that belongs to you. If you don't leave me alone, I'm calling the police!'

It was a bluff. Her iPhone was buried deep at the bottom of her handbag, which remained jammed up under her arm. It would take time for her to find it, and she wasn't sure she had any.

The figure took another step forward.

A cold gust of wind drifted over them, moving the branches above, bathing the figure in moonlight.

Jane stopped and stared at the now exposed face.

Almost forgetting where she was, she said, 'I know you!'

'You don't *know* me!' spat back the figure. 'How could you possibly *know* me?'

'I – I meant, I've seen you before.'

Taking another step forward to join her in the near total darkness under the arch, the figure mumbled, 'I've not come to talk.'

'Then what do you want?' demanded Jane, stepping backwards, preparing to run.

As a solid black shadow rose above Jane's head, in a low harsh whisper the figure replied, 'Simple. I'm here to take back what's mine.'

- CHAPTER ONE -

DETECTIVE INSPECTOR JOHN Tanner stepped out of his car, closed the door, and stopped for a moment to gaze about. Lying before him was a wide rectangular jetty, in the middle of which was a square section of well-kept lawn surrounded on all sides by a gravel path. To the left was a handful of nearly identical motor cruisers, each one about twenty foot in length and all of which were moored in such a way that they pointed outwards, like the fingers of an open hand. To the right was an empty slipway, almost hidden from view by the heavy shade of a tree; and stretching out beyond that was a large body of water which sparkled gently in the afternoon sun.

Tanner knew he was looking at Malthouse Broad, but only because the map in the car had told him so. He'd never actually been there before.

He took a moment to breathe in slowly through his nose and mouth, tasting the freshness of the air. The scene was so idyllic, so serene; if he didn't know better, he'd have thought he was on holiday.

After consulting a piece of paper in his hand he turned to look to the left. In the far distance he could see a large thatched house surrounded by trees, all showing the first signs of spring. Beyond that, the cold stone tower of an ancient church was silhouetted against the brightness of a cloudless blue sky.

He stopped for a moment. For no particular reason, he found himself picturing his daughter, the way she used to draw her hair back behind her ear when she was reading a book. A memory came to him, of her staring down at a burnt lasagne he'd just presented her with, when he'd had a go at cooking one weekend, and how she'd lifted her incandescent blue eyes to him, asking, 'Was it supposed to look like this?'

He smiled to himself. It had taken him a long time to reach the point where he could be grateful for the many memories he had of her.

Before darker images could cloud his mind, he glanced back down at the paper in his hand. Turning the other way, he saw the single-storey brick building he'd noticed when he'd first driven into the carpark. It was a small shop that doubled up as a post office, according to a round sign drilled onto its outer wall. Beneath that was an old rectangular-shaped post box sporting what looked like a fresh coat of cherry red paint. With a delicate line of bunting strung out under the eaves, and a swing sign advertising Wall's ice cream outside the open door, the building had a quintessentially British feel to it.

Tanner used his key fob to lock his car before making his way towards the shop's entrance.

Inside he found the usual array of corner shop essentials, but unlike the average London one, the layout was intermixed with items normally associated with a tourists' gift shop, including a rotating rack of postcards, most of which featured pictures of boats of differing shapes, sizes and colours.

Behind the counter sat a plump middle-aged lady frowning through a pair of large thick-rimmed glasses at a folded newspaper lying on the counter's surface, the top of which she tapped at with a biro.

Seeing she had a customer, she set the pen down, removed her glasses to leave them hanging from a gold neck chain, and smiled up at him.

'Good afternoon,' said Tanner, stepping forward. 'I don't suppose you can help me?'

'I can certainly try.'

'I'm looking for a boat.'

'Ah! That'll be next door. If you walk around the side of the shop,' she said, pointing the way, 'you'll find the boat hire centre on your left.'

'Oh, no, sorry. Not that sort of a boat.' Looking back down at the paper that he still held, he explained, 'It's called Seascape. Apparently, it's moored up around here somewhere. I'm just not sure exactly where.'

Beaming a more natural smile at him, she said, 'I know Seascape! I must admit that I didn't know Mr Bardsley had sold her. I take it you're the new owner?'

'Er, not as such, no. Matthew, I mean Mr Bardsley, has told me I can stay on her for a while, just until I find something a little more suitable.'

'Oh, I see,' the lady said, sounding disappointed, but her curiosity was aroused and she leaned forward to ask, 'Are you moving into the area?'

'Well, I'm in the process of doing so, yes.'

The lady didn't respond to that, but instead just continued to smile at him in an encouraging way.

Tanner was not one for making small talk. Generally speaking, he was keen to tell people as little about himself as possible. However, he didn't like awkward silences, so he offered up another nugget of personal information.

'I'm starting a new job on Monday, and I didn't have a chance to find more suitable accommodation, so the idea of staying on the boat was suggested.'

'I see! Right, well, I'd better show you where she is then, hadn't I?'

She eased herself from the high stool she'd been sitting on, and shuffled her way around the counter.

Following her outside, Tanner found that she'd stopped next to the Wall's swing sign and was pointing towards the church tower.

With one arm fully extended and the other shading her eyes from the sun, she said, 'She's over there. You can just about see her bowsprit.'

'Bowsprit?'

Turning to look up at him, she said, 'You aren't from around here, are you?'

He'd no idea how to respond to that, but he didn't have to, as she took the answer for granted, looked back out towards the church, pointed again and said, 'You see that dark wooden pole sticking out from the front of that boat?'

He could, and duly said so.

'That's Seascape. That pole is her bowsprit.' Turning to consider him, she said, 'I take it you don't know much about boats?'

'Er, not really, no.'

'Well, don't worry. You'll soon pick up what everything's called. Now, to get there you simply follow the path round.'

'I see. Thank you!' After a moment he said, 'Is it all right if I leave my car here?' He looked over at his distinctly grubby Jaguar XJS. It used to be black, but it had been so long since he'd washed it, it had become difficult to tell what colour it was. Only a few months before, the car had been his pride and joy, but now it was just something he used to get around in, costing him a small fortune in petrol in the process.

'For now you can, but you'll be able to park it properly next to the marina office.'

Judging from his expression that he didn't have a clue where that was either, she added, 'If you drive out of here and take the first right, the office is just up on the left. It's called Ranworth Marina. You can't miss it. If you ask for Fred, he'll be able to hook you up with electricity and show you where to get your water.'

Turning to smile down at her, Tanner said, 'You've been very kind. I assume I can buy milk and bread here?'

'That's right. And there's the Maltsters pub just around the corner. They serve breakfast, lunch and dinner, seven days a week, and I can highly recommend them.'

Before leaving him to it, she asked, 'How long do you plan on staying on board the boat?'

'I'm not altogether sure. To be honest, I've never so much as stepped foot on one before, so it probably depends on how much I like it.'

'Well, you should be all right for the summer, although from Easter it does get very busy round here. But I wouldn't recommend staying over the winter though. Not if last winter's anything to go by!'

Seeing a couple of teenage boys approach the shop, she excused herself, saying, 'Anyway, I'd better get back, but it may be worth your while keeping an eye on the notice board.' She turned to show him a glass-fronted board that had been mounted on the outside wall of the shop. 'We often get people advertising their properties there. You can also pick up a copy of the local newspaper. There's a small lettings section in the back.'

Thanking her again, Tanner watched as she hurried back inside. He turned to look over at what he could see of the boat he was supposed to be staying on, which was nothing more than a dark wooden pole – or *bowsprit* – jutting horizontally out from the front.

Having driven all the way from London, he decided to leave the car where it was for now and walk round to take a closer look. As he did, he hoped that the boat would provide somewhere to stay for a few nights, at least, but preferably a week or two, so giving him time to find a suitable flat nearby.

- CHAPTER TWO -

BEING CAREFUL NOT to stumble over the many mooring lines that led to the quay from the boats alongside, Tanner followed the path as he'd been instructed. Every now and again he caught a glimpse of the yacht he was heading for, through a separation in the trees or over the roof of another boat. It wasn't long before he found himself rounding a turn in the path to come face to face with the yacht that was supposed to be his temporary new home.

Matthew Bardsley had described it to him lovingly and at length. According to him, Seascape was a traditional 1930s gaff-rigged Norfolk cruising yacht. It was made of dark mahogany wood and had been painstakingly painted with a smooth thick layer of varnish, giving it a warm, natural glow.

The yacht was twenty-four foot in length, excluding the bowsprit, and was covered by a large white canvas awning, which lay over the boom and cabin, all the way to the back of the boat. There, a pair of high wooden crutches supported the boom, the end of which jutted awkwardly out from the back.

From where Tanner stood, the whole thing looked like a large old-fashioned white tent, the sort of thing a troop of Boy Scouts would use for a weekend's camping trip.

Stopping about ten feet away, he spent a few moments looking over her from the smooth varnished hull which reflected the sun as it danced around the surrounding water, all the way up to the top of the mast, where a small blue and red triangular flag fluttered occasionally in the gentle breeze.

She was beautiful, but he could hardly tell which end was the front and which was the back. From where he was standing, he couldn't even see how he was going to get inside. Before he'd accepted the offer of living on board, the yacht's owner, Commander Bardsley of the Metropolitan Police, an old family friend, had emailed a picture to him, but that was of her sailing out on a Broad with all the sails up. She looked completely different moored up here, and considerably smaller.

Approaching the yacht, he rested his left foot tentatively on the side, just below where he thought the canvassed entrance might be. After testing that it would take his weight, he stepped on board. What he'd told the lady back at the shop was true; he'd never been on a boat before, at least nothing as small as this, and he'd no idea whether standing on the side would make it tip over. Fortunately, all that happened was that it rocked back and forth ever so slightly.

Safely on board, he began examining the canvas awning, trying to work out how it would open. It soon became clear that he was indeed standing beside some sort of a rectangular doorway, fastened to the deck by a couple of small elasticated hooks. Not wishing to risk losing his balance, he stepped off the boat, crouched down and unclipped the hooks. He began rolling the freed section of canvas up, much as he would have done had it been the zipped entrance to a tent. When he reached the top, he climbed back on board and discovered another couple of elastic hooks on the inside. Having used them to fasten the top, he leaned forward and peered into the gloomy interior.

There wasn't much to see; just a small enclosed area with two deeply varnished mahogany bench seats on either side. A thin long metal rod curved up from the back of the boat like the neck of an elegant black swan. At its end was a smooth cylindrical wooden handle, from which hung a neatly coiled rope. Opposite that, to the left, were two folding doors. They were only about three feet high, so he couldn't see what possible use they could be, at least not for an adult, but they were doors none the less, so they must lead somewhere.

It was only when Tanner swung his leg in through the canvas doorway and down onto the nearside bench that he saw a crisp white envelope lying there.

Retrieving it, he stood up straight, and smacked his head up against a solid-looking wooden beam which seemed to stretch the length of the yacht and over which the canvas awning had been draped. This was one part of a boat he did know something about, although he couldn't remember from where. It was the yacht's boom, and was what you had to duck under when you tacked, or gybed, or something.

Reaching up, he placed the palm of his hand on its smooth underside. It certainly felt sturdy enough, and he could see why you'd want to avoid it when it swung over your head.

Looking down at the envelope, Tanner saw that it

was addressed to him. Commander Bardsley had told him he'd be leaving him some sort of note, so finding the letter wasn't too much of a surprise.

Sitting on one of the hard polished bench seats, Tanner opened up the envelope and slid out a folded piece of A4 paper. On one side was a handwritten letter, and the other a schematic diagram of the boat.

A lot of the contents of the letter had already been relayed to him by the woman at the shop, but there were some other useful pieces of information. For example, it told him that there was a toilet at the front of the boat, as well as a basin and a gas hob. Unfortunately there was no fridge, freezer, or microwave. There wasn't even a shower.

Referring to the diagram on the back, he soon discovered the double gas hob, which was very much like a camping one. It was hidden under the front section of the bench seat opposite the one he was sitting on – not the first place he would have thought to look for a kitchen appliance. Staring down at it he raised a single eyebrow. He didn't mind so much about the lack of cooking facilities; he'd hardly envisaged himself spending hours creating culinary masterpieces: but he could see that the lack of a shower was going to be a problem, and he certainly wouldn't have minded having a microwave to hand.

Reminding himself that it was only going to be temporary, he read on, and was relieved to learn that he'd be able to use the shower facilities inside the marina building. He slid the letter back inside its envelope, folded it in half and stood up to push it into the back pocket of his dark blue jeans.

Crouching down, he lifted a small brass latch that

held the two wooden doors together, opened them up and peered inside.

'Well, that's going to be cosy!' he said.

The cabin area laid out before him was compact to say the least. From what he could see of the dark interior, it consisted solely of two long benches, each topped with a long red rectangular cushion.

Peering forward, he saw that there was another cabin at the front, but that was even smaller than this one, and the roof was so low he'd be lucky if he'd be able to kneel up in it, let alone stand.

Bardsley had written something about the roof; Tanner pulled out the letter, found the relevant section, and read it to himself again, then examined the top edge of the coach roof which, apparently, lifted up somehow.

Noticing that there were folds of canvas tucked around the inside edges, he hooked the palms of his hands around its lip and gently pushed it up. As he did so, two slats of wood swung down on either side to keep the roof in a lifted position, and he nudged the bottom of each onto a thin ledge, where the varnish had been rubbed away. He then eased the top down onto the supporting slats and stood back.

He'd successfully managed to raise the ceiling height. Once again he checked the letter, but it only confirmed what he'd already concluded; that only one end of the coach roof could be lifted. The other looked as if it was going to have to remain where it was.

With a shrug, he stepped inside and attempted to stand up straight. He couldn't. He was five foot ten, and at its highest point, the ceiling must be around five eight, maybe five nine at a push.

'At least it's a roof, I suppose,' he said. 'And it is over my head, just about.'

Easing himself down onto one of the red cushions, taking care not to bang his head on anything as he did, he stared around.

A moment later, out loud again, he asked himself, 'Where the hell's the toilet?'

Another quick examination of the diagram had him off the bench and onto the floor. There he began crawling on his knees towards the front of the boat, far along enough to be able to poke his head inside the forward cabin.

On his right he saw that there was another cushioned bench. Apparently, it was a third bed, although Tanner couldn't see how anyone other than a small child, or maybe a dog, would be able to fit into it. According to the diagram, the toilet should be on the left, but all he could see was a solid wooden shelf. Spotting a couple of hinges at the back, he said, 'Don't tell me it's underneath here!'

Lifting it up, he found that it was.

'So, emergency use only then!' he said, plonking the lid back down.

Deciding to come out for both air and space, he returned to the yacht's well, as described in the drawing – the area under the canvas where the boom was. There he resumed his original seat.

He'd already decided that he'd not be able to stay there long-term. He'd reached that conclusion when he saw the toilet. But for now he had no choice, and so began thinking about the practicalities of spending a few days on board. He'd brought a sleeping bag with him, along with his pillow, so he'd at least be comfortable at night. Food wasn't going to be a problem, as he could eat his evening meal at the pub, and he rarely bothered with breakfast. Lunch was always just a coffee and a sandwich taken, so all he'd need to buy was some milk, tea, coffee and some form of snack food. Apparently, there was a kettle knocking about the place somewhere, along with some cups. As long as the marina did have a working shower, he knew he'd survive.

So, with a plan in place, he clambered out of the boat to make his way back to the shop. There he'd check the notice board, to see if anyone was offering a flat to rent. Failing that, he'd ask for a copy of the local newspaper.

- CHAPTER THREE -

Monday, 15th April

THE FOLLOWING MORNING, Tanner awoke naturally. Instinctively, he checked the time on his phone, and was pleased to see he still had ten minutes before his alarm was due to go off.

He'd slept surprisingly well, far better than he'd been expecting. The gentle lapping of water against the outside of the hull, the same rhythmic knocking sound he was listening to now, must have sent him off pretty much straight away, as he didn't remember doing so. He hadn't been forced to spend the night fighting his way through a seemingly endless number of ever-darker dreams either, as he'd found himself having to do since the death of his daughter nine months before. Recently his dreams had become so disturbing that he'd often woken up gasping for air, desperate to distinguish between what was real and what, hopefully, wasn't.

The call of nature forced him up. Feeling brave, he successfully navigated the use of the emergency toilet services in the port bow. After that, he grabbed a towel along with a plastic bag in which he'd packed his toiletries, and set off for what he'd discovered the previous evening, the humble shower housed within the even more humble marina building.

On his return, he dressed whilst standing inside the well of the yacht, having closed the canvas doorway first. The night before, when he'd changed for bed, he'd discovered that the yacht's well was the only sensible place for doing so. Trying to undress in the cabin had felt more like taking part in a game of Twister than getting ready for bed.

Once dressed in his somewhat creased white office shirt, dark grey suit and navy-blue tie, it took him about three times longer than normal to make an instant coffee. He sat down with a sense of having achieved something, and with mug in hand, spent a few minutes flicking through the local newspaper he'd picked up the day before with the milk and coffee.

Finding an article on the third page about a series of robberies that had been taking place, he settled down to read. There wasn't much to it. Just that the person, as yet unknown, had been breaking into boats moored up in isolated locations along the Rivers Bure, Ant and Thurne. It finished with the usual local outrage that the police weren't doing enough to find those responsible, and then the obligatory comment from the police that they were doing everything they possibly could to bring the criminals to justice.

After noting that the officer who'd made the comment was Detective Chief Inspector Barrington, the man who was going to be his new boss, he turned to the classified section at the back. He'd already circled three possible flats the evening before, and read through the ads again. None of them had sounded particularly appealing, and being read in daylight didn't seem to help.

Checking his watch, he finished his coffee, placed the empty cup on the bench opposite, and folded the newspaper away so that it was ready to take with him. He slipped into his black office shoes, retrieved his phone, wallet and car keys, closed the small cabin doors and clambered out.

After closing up the awning, and with his new job now firmly in focus, he set off to begin his first day working as a Detective Inspector for Norfolk Police.

- CHAPTER FOUR -

THE FEELING OF mild anxiety that accompanies anyone starting a new job stayed with Tanner as he drove the six and a half mile route from Ranworth Marina to Wroxham Police Station, where he was to be based. It was a journey that was in stark contrast to his previous commute into London. The only section of it that could be classed as even vaguely similar was when he had to cross the low bridge over the River Bure, where the traffic was moving at what he considered to be average London speed. But even having to stop and start his way over that was hardly a burden, quite the opposite in fact, as it gave him the chance to enjoy a picture postcard view of the river. With its waterside shops, restaurants, boats and houses, it was a truly idyllic scene. There was even a gaggle of white swans for him to watch, taking it in turns to crane their elegant long necks towards a mother and two small children, no doubt in a bid to try and entice food out of them.

Arriving at Wroxham Police Station a few minutes later was another new experience. He'd had his interview for the position at Norfolk Constabulary's head office, just outside Norwich, and he'd yet to meet his new boss.

The building itself was different from any police

station he'd been to so far in his career, the most obvious difference being just how small it was. With only one ground floor level, a red brick exterior, a dark grey tiled roof with matching-coloured doors and window frames, to Tanner it looked more like a hospice, or a care home for the elderly.

Parking between a police patrol car and a Vauxhall Astra, Tanner stepped out, glanced over at the building and checked his watch. It was just gone ten to nine, making him eight minutes early.

Locking his car, he faced away from the building to straighten his tie, did up the middle button of his suit, slipped his left hand into his trouser pocket and turned to make his way towards the entrance, doing his best to look as confident and relaxed as possible.

Inside the heavy front door, he was presented with a typical police reception area that smelt of an unsubtle mixture of pine disinfectant and bleach. To his immediate right was the front desk, behind which sat a uniformed policeman who Tanner presumed to be the duty sergeant, a tired looking man with a round shaved head and a double chin covered in a light dusting of grey stubble. His eyes were fixed on a computer monitor, and he didn't even seem to notice that someone had just walked in.

Approaching the desk, Tanner cleared his throat, and with brisk formality said, 'Detective Inspector John Tanner to see Detective Chief Inspector Barrington.'

Without smiling, the duty sergeant looked over at him. 'I take it you're the new DI?'

'So I've been told.'

'OK, take a seat. I'll let the boss know you're here.'

Tanner gave him a half smile by way of a thank you. It wasn't returned.

As the duty sergeant picked up his phone, Tanner walked over to a row of blue plastic seats. He stood facing them, his hands clasped firmly behind his back, and took a closer look at some of the posters displayed on the wall, moving slowly up and down the room as he did. He rarely liked to be seated when waiting for something, especially if he was feeling apprehensive. His preference would have been to pace up and down whilst staring at the floor, which he found helped him to think. However, it seemed to give an impression of impatience, not the image he wished to give to his new boss, so he pretended to take an interest in the station's community advertising.

'Detective Inspector Tanner?'

Spinning around, Tanner saw he was being addressed by a portly dark haired man with small eyes and a rounded, puffy face; the cheeks of which were red and blotchy.

As Tanner smiled in acknowledgment, the man stretched out a welcoming hand, saying, 'Welcome to Wroxham! I'm DCI Barrington. If you follow me, we can have a bit of a chat before you get started.'

Placing a guiding hand on Tanner's shoulder, he led the way through to an open-plan office area filled with a mixture of uniformed and non-uniformed police personnel who were either staring at computer screens, or talking quietly on the phone.

As he followed DCI Barrington down past the desks, he heard one of the many phones ring. Turning his head towards the sound, he saw a non-uniformed officer with curly dark brown hair, medium build, probably in his late thirties, reaching over his desk to answer it.

Following his gaze, Barrington said, 'That's DI Burgess, but I'll introduce you to him and the rest of the team a little later. But first...'

DCI Barrington stopped beside a door into a separate glass partitioned office, and showed Tanner inside.

- CHAPTER FIVE -

THE CHIEF INSPECTOR'S office was a modern-looking room bathed in natural light from a large window overlooking the car park to the front. On one wall hung a large Ordnance Survey map of the Norfolk Broads; but of more interest, to Tanner at least, was the rich aromatic smell of freshly made coffee.

Instinctively, he glanced around, looking for its source. In the corner, beneath the glass partition that looked out into the open-plan office, sat a chrome coffee percolator on a low table, burbling away quietly to itself.

Seeing what he was looking at, Barrington closed the door and asked, 'Can I get you anything to drink? A coffee, perhaps?'

'Oh, um...' began Tanner. Normally when asked such a question he'd automatically say no, but not because he didn't like coffee. Quite the opposite; he loved the stuff, and was a self-confessed addict. However, he was also something of a connoisseur, and would only drink the instant variety that was normally offered to him, like the one he'd been forced to buy for his boat, out of pure desperation. However, on this occasion, he was happy to break with tradition, and said, 'That would be good, thank you.'

As Barrington began pouring coffee into two white china cups, he asked, 'When did you arrive?'

'Yesterday afternoon,' said Tanner.

'Milk and sugar?'

'Just milk, thank you.'

'Whereabouts are you staying?'

'Oh, er, on a boat, actually,' he replied, a little self-consciously. 'But it's only until I can find something more permanent.'

Barrington passed one of the cups to Tanner. 'A boat! That sounds very adventurous!'

With the hint of a smile, Tanner said, 'If by that you mean uncomfortable, then I'd have to agree with you.'

Barrington gestured for Tanner to sit, as he did so himself. He took a sip from his coffee, and then set down the cup on its matching saucer. 'Now listen, Tanner, I'm going to be completely honest with you. You weren't my first choice for this position. In fact, I'd have to say that you weren't my choice at all! It's nothing personal, it's just that I prefer officers with local knowledge, preferably those who've been brought up in the area, or at least who've spent a good few years working in Norfolk. I personally believe that local knowledge is the key to successful policing, especially here, and frankly, you don't have any!'

'I know, but—' began Tanner, but Barrington interrupted him. 'On top of that are the reasons you asked for the transfer.'

Tanner could feel a hot surge of anger flow through his body, pumping blood up towards his neck and face as it did. He wasn't expecting to have what had happened to his daughter brought up in the conversation, at least not in such a disparaging manner, and found himself already beginning to resent the man sitting opposite him for doing so.

Forcing himself to remain calm, Tanner said, 'And as I've explained before, the circumstances–'

'You don't need to explain, Tanner,' interrupted Barrington. 'I've read your file. What happened to your daughter was just… Well… I have children myself. I can't imagine how difficult it must have been for you. But that aside, it's hardly a reason to offer someone a job, now is it?'

'No, but–'

'I don't need a bunch of lame ducks working here whose only interest in doing so is that they fancy a cushy alternative to life in the Met. We may not be London, but the Broads can be just as challenging, especially during the silly season. I don't know if anyone has bothered to tell you, but we have over eight million visitors piling into the place every summer, which puts a tremendous strain on staff and budget alike. I really can't afford to have people stationed here whose sole interest is to mope about feeling sorry for themselves!'

From the seething look on Tanner's face, it was fairly obvious that even if someone had told him that they had over eight million visitors a year, at that moment he didn't give a shit.

Realising that he may have been a little indelicate when bringing up his guest's presumed reason for putting in for a transfer, Barrington said, 'Anyway, you're here now, and you certainly had a glowing reference. Who was your referee again? I seem to remember it was someone fairly high up.'

As Barrington took hold of his mouse and glanced

at his monitor, Tanner replied, 'Commander Matthew Bardsley.'

His referee, the man who'd offered him the use of his yacht, was one of the highest-ranking police officers in the UK.

'He's a close family friend,' he added, with deliberate intent. Tagging that on to the end would make him virtually untouchable; at least it would stop Barrington from making any more snide remarks concerning either himself or his daughter.

Barrington repeated, 'Commander Bardsley, that's right!' After pretending to re-read what *had* been a glowing reference, he added, 'Well, he certainly holds you in high regard.'

'He and my father were friends long before joining the police. He's known me all my life.'

Before Barrington discovered that they were members of the same golf club, and played together every Sunday afternoon, he clicked the file closed and said, 'Well anyway, as I said, it's nothing personal. It's just that we prefer to take on locals. And it's for that reason I'm going to put you on Missing Persons, for now at least.'

Barrington studied Tanner, trying to gauge his reaction to the news that he was going to be working on what they'd normally assign to a lowly police constable. He was even half-expecting to have to defend his decision. But all Tanner did was to stare straight back at him.

Tanner wouldn't care even if he'd been put on Missing Pets. He wasn't going to admit it, but Barrington was right; he *had* been looking for a less challenging role. He'd happily quit the Force if he had the slightest clue as to what he could do instead. He couldn't afford to retire, which would have been his first choice. Taking up a position within the Norfolk Constabulary had been Commander Bardsley's suggestion. Bardsley had grown up in the Broads, and had heard on the grapevine that Wroxham had an opening for a Detective Inspector.

Admittedly there'd been a time, and not all that long ago either, when Tanner would have laughed at anyone suggesting he'd actively seek a position in what his colleagues referred to as Holiday Land, a term they gave to any constabulary located outside of the Metropolitan Police catchment. Back then he'd thrived on working within the pumping heart of one of the world's largest cities, feeding from its energy like so many millions of others did. When he'd first joined, he'd even been naïve enough to think that he could make a difference, in the same way he thought his father had. But everything had changed when he found himself sitting helplessly by as his only child was slowly sucked ever deeper into what he now thought of as London's putrefying core, to end up half-naked in a gutter as just another discarded corpse. Only then did he understand that he'd been kidding himself. What he'd actually been doing was trying to make a name for himself. That was what had pushed him to spend an ever-increasing amount of time away from home: the pursuit of self-gratification. Nothing more! He knew that if he'd made an effort to be around for her, she wouldn't have deliberately started to hang out with boys she knew he'd disapprove of in a desperate attempt to get his attention. They were the ones who introduced her to the club scene, always leaving her to catch a cab on her own afterwards, high on God knows what. It was only after she'd been murdered that he found out about the cocaine-fuelled sex parties she'd started to frequent with the same group of so-called "friends". Not being allowed to investigate her murder had been the last straw, even though he knew it was the rule, and it left him resenting the very establishment he worked for, who didn't seem to understand that he *had* to find out who'd killed her. After all, what was the point of working for the CID if he wasn't even allowed to help?

Barrington began to feel a little uncomfortable. 'Anyway, Missing Persons will help you to familiarise yourself with the area and get to know some of the locals. It will also give you a chance to settle in and find your feet. I know it's a long way beneath your pay grade, and tracking down husbands who've left their wives, and vice versa, is going to be a little dull, but you'll have to put up with it, for now at least. One came in this morning. Someone's wife. Probably after a domestic. So if it's OK by you, we'll start you off on that.'

With still no response forthcoming, Barrington pushed himself away from his desk. 'Right then! I'd better introduce you to everyone.'

- CHAPTER SIX -

A S SOON AS they were outside the office, DCI Barrington called out, 'May I have everyone's attention, please?' He gazed around the open plan area, waiting patiently for those who weren't on the phone to turn towards him, and for those who were, to either end their calls, or at least to lower their voices.

It had been a very long time since Tanner had been introduced like this, not since he'd first started working at Colindale Police Station. He'd not liked it then, and he certainly didn't like it now.

When he was sure that virtually everyone in the office was looking his way, Barrington continued, 'I'd like to introduce you all to Detective Inspector John Tanner. He's here to replace Tommy, who as you all know is now enjoying a very much deserved retirement.'

A murmur of approval followed.

Until his retirement a few weeks earlier, Tom, or Tommy as he'd been affectionately known, had been based at Wroxham Police Station since he'd first joined the Force, way back in the early 1970s.

'Having worked for the Metropolitan Police for over twenty years, Detective Inspector Tanner brings with him a vast amount of experience, which I'm sure we're all going to find invaluable.'

The news that the DI was from London sent a series of whispered comments around the room. It was unusual for a Detective Inspector to move up from London to Norfolk, especially one who still looked relatively young, and the suspicion would be that there must be a reason behind it, other than as being part of a promotion.

'He comes highly recommended,' added Barrington. 'Now, obviously he doesn't have the local knowledge that you all have, but I'm relying on you to give him the support and guidance he'll need. To help speed up that process, I've temporarily assigned him to Missing Persons. I think that'll probably be the quickest way for him to find his feet.'

Barrington took a moment to glare around at everyone, so driving home the point of his intended remarks; that although none of them probably wanted Tanner there, especially him, the sooner they accepted the fact that he was, the sooner they could get things back to how they were before Tommy had shuffled into his office to announce his retirement.

'Good. Right! And I believe we had a report come in this morning that someone's wife isn't where she's supposed to be. Who's working on that?'

Near the door that led out into reception, a girl wearing blue jeans and a dark top raised her hand. She was slim and attractive, had shoulder-length black hair, pale skin, and sparkling blue eyes.

'Detective Constable Evans, if you could brief DI Tanner on where you're at with it. And as you know the Broads just about as well as anyone around here, it would be helpful if you could work together on

Missing Persons for a while.'

'But sir!' came a voice of protest from the other side of the room, near the whiteboard.

Tanner saw that it was the same man he'd seen answer the phone earlier, when he'd first walked in.

'Yes, Burgess, what is it?' asked Barrington, his voice taking on a distinct edge of irritability.

'Well, DC Evans has been working with us on the boat break-ins for months now, sir.'

'You've still got Cooper and Gilbert, haven't you?'

'Yes sir, but–'

'And as you said, it has been *months*!'

It was clear from the emphasis that Barrington intended it as a reprimand, albeit a veiled one, and it was enough to end the discussion. To further ensure that the subject was closed, Barrington rounded off the brief introduction by saying, 'Right! That's it for now. Carry on!'

As everyone in the room returned to what they'd been doing before, Barrington led Tanner over to the young Detective Constable who'd raised her hand earlier. She was sitting within a cluster of desks along with two uniformed officers, a man and a woman, both in their early twenties, who were now staring at their computer monitors with some intensity as the senior officers approached.

'Good morning, Jenny. I trust you had a good weekend?'

Without smiling, she stood up and said, 'Very good, thank you, sir,' stealing a quick glance at the new DI as she did.

'Detective Inspector John Tanner, this is Detective Constable Jenny Evans. So, what's this missing persons report about? I hear someone's wife has gone walkabout.'

'The person in question is Jane Richardson, sir,' Jenny said. 'Her husband is Simon Richardson. They live just the other side of the railway bridge. He called it in this morning. He'd been away for the weekend, and she wasn't around when he came back last night.'

'I assume she was supposed to be?'

'He seemed to think that she was, sir, yes.'

'Do you think it sounds serious?'

'I'd say probably not, sir, no. Not yet, at any rate. When I questioned him, he said that it wasn't the first time she'd gone off to stay with friends for a few days without letting him know. So at the moment we're rating it as a low priority.'

'That sounds about right, but you may as well head out to have a chat with him anyway, face to face. It will give you the opportunity to give DI Tanner a tour of the town.'

'Yes, sir,' replied Jenny, glancing momentarily at Tanner.

'Before you do that, if you could show him where Tommy's desk was, I believe we agreed to set him up there. And assuming the space is still free next to him, you may as well move over there yourself, when you get a chance.'

'Yes, sir!' she repeated, this time with the merest hint of a smile.

'By the way, when's your Sergeant's exam?'

'Not until October, sir.'

Turning to Tanner, Barrington said, 'Jenny's just come off one of the new trainee detective courses, and she's already eying up her Sergeant's! Anyway, I'd better leave you to it.' He headed back to his office, leaving Tanner and Jenny alone together, unsure as to which one of them was going to say something first.

With a flirtatious smile, Jenny eventually said, 'I suppose I'd better show you where your new desk is, hadn't I?'

Leading him over to the next cluster of desks along, she stopped behind a chair and rested her hands on the back of it.

'This is where Tommy sat.'

Stopping beside her, Tanner looked at his new desk, which appeared to have only just been cleared in preparation for his arrival, as it was dust free and had nothing on it but the basic essentials.

'I assume you've been set up to use the intranet?' Jenny said.

Tanner stared back down at his desk again, but this time with a tight feeling of nervous expectation. 'I've been sent a login and password, yes,' he replied. He had no choice but to look at this as being a fresh start, even if it wasn't one he particularly wanted. He knew that if he didn't, his life would effectively be over. Squaring his shoulders, he looked back at Jenny, and with a deep intake of breath said, 'Sorry, what was your name again?'

With a not very amused smile, Jenny replied, 'It's DC Evans, but everyone around here calls me Jenny.'

'Right, DC Evans who everyone calls Jenny, I suppose we'd better arrange to have a chat with that Mr – Richards, wasn't it?'

'Richard*son*,' she corrected. 'Let me give him a call to find out when he's free.'

Tanner watched her return to her own desk before

sitting cautiously down in his new chair.

Having swivelled it from side to side a couple of times he checked the eye level of the monitor, then felt for the lever to adjust the chair's height. Once it was set to his satisfaction, he peered under the desk and reached to turn on the computer that he found lurking there. When it sprang into life, he pulled out his phone to look up his login and password.

- CHAPTER SEVEN -

THE MOMENT JENNY finished arranging to meet the husband of the missing woman, she stood up from her desk, and signalled to Tanner that she was ready. Pulling on a hip-length brown leather coat, she led the way out to reception, and the carpark beyond.

It was a cold, overcast day, more like January than April. Tanner walked briskly towards his car, unlocking it with the key fob.

Catching up to him, Jenny was surprised to see the rather dated Jaguar in desperate need of a good clean. 'Is that yours?'

Feeling it was probably too early in their relationship to come back with a sarcastic remark, such as, 'Actually no. I stole it on my way over here,' instead Tanner replied, 'It is, yes.'

'And you bought it on purpose, or was it the second prize in a lucky dip competition?'

Reaching the driver's side door, Tanner paused. For someone so young, she certainly seemed confident enough; perhaps a little too much so. But at least she had a sense of humour.

'It was actually the first prize,' he said, placing his hand under the unpolished chrome handle and pulling the door open.

Jenny looked the car up and down as if it was a friend who'd made a very poor wardrobe choice, and wrinkling up her small pointed nose said, 'You don't think it's a little...*Eighties*?'

Having been about to climb in, Tanner stared over the car's low roof at her. He was used to colleagues making remarks about his car, but they were normally more complimentary. He'd had complete strangers walk up to him to comment on it, but again in more positive ways, often relating a story about how they'd either once had one, or knew someone who had. A few years earlier, he'd even had it pawed over by a group of firemen. He'd found them surrounding it after he'd left it parked on a London street. At first he'd assumed the worst, that it had caught fire somehow, but that hadn't been the case. They'd finished attending a nearby false alarm and before heading back, had decided to take a closer look. Of course, in those days he'd kept it spotless, but even though that was hardly the case now, that was the sort of reaction he was used to. The XJS was after all becoming increasingly rare, certainly ones in the condition his was in, or would be if he could motivate himself enough to give it a clean.

Caught off guard, finding he'd taken offence at the remark, and with his ego dented slightly, Tanner said, 'Not your sort of thing, I take it?'

'Sorry,' Jenny replied, feeling both stupid and guilty. The last thing she'd meant to do was to insult the man's car! But she was nervous, and had a dangerous habit of saying the wrong thing whenever she was. Making derogatory remarks was hardly the most sensible thing to do, especially when the man in question was a senior ranking officer who she was attempting to win over. 'I didn't mean anything by that. It's just that it's, well, unusual, I suppose; and the go-faster stripe down the side does have something very Eighties about it.'

Realising she'd probably done it again, she attempted to fill in the second hole she'd just dug for herself, adding, 'But it's very nice though!'

Tanner took a moment to look along the thin red and grey stripe that ran horizontally down both sides of the car. He'd never much cared for them. Neither did he like the so-called "flying buttresses", a design element unique to the XJS which consisted of two concave shapes of steel that flowed down from the low roof, either side of the rear window, only to disappear into the rear lighting blocks. He'd not thought about it before, but the girl was right; despite having been originally designed in the early 1970s, the car did have a distinct Eighties feel to it, and not in a good way. However, his ego wouldn't allow himself to agree with her, so instead he said, 'I must admit, it does look better when it's been cleaned.'

'You mean…less Eighties?' said Jenny, half frowning, half smiling.

Unable to be anything but amused by her comment, returning the smile, Tanner said, 'About a decade or so, yes!'

He opened the door to climb inside, and Jenny joined him.

As he eased the car out of the parking space, he said, 'You'll have to direct me.'

'No problem,' replied Jenny, as she secured her own seatbelt.

By that time she'd reached the conclusion that she'd better stop trying to flirt with the man who was now, however temporarily, her immediate superior. Flirting had never been one of her core strengths. Whenever she tried, she always end up saying things that in her mind sounded funny, but when heard out loud were often just offensive.

As the new DI looked over his shoulder to reverse out, she took the opportunity to steal a close-up look at his face. Despite the fact that he must be a good fifteen years older than her, probably nearer twenty, and that he could hardly be considered successful, given that he was still only a Detective Inspector, and one who'd moved up from London to the Norfolk Broads, instead of the other way round – something she'd been hoping to do herself, in the not too distant future – combined with the fact that he drove a car straight out of some sort of sad Eighties TV mini-series, she couldn't help but find him attractive. He wasn't even all that good looking; he'd have had his work cut out if he'd been a fashion model. At least he was thin, she thought. Well, thin-ish. He'd managed to keep hold of most of his hair, although there were clear signs that it had started to recede, and it was going noticeably grey. But there was something about him which she found herself drawn to. His deep-set brown eyes made him seem both intelligent and vulnerable, and the corners of his mouth turned naturally upwards whenever he talked to her, giving her the impression that he liked her. He also seemed to share her rather odd sense of humour.

As he turned back to face the front, she glanced over at his profile. *His nose is too big*, she decided, but she was being picky. For a middle aged man he was good-looking enough. *No wedding ring*, she noted, as he turned the steering wheel; but then she saw the hint of white where there perhaps had been one.

OK, I really don't need a middle aged divorcee who's probably got three teenage children knocking about the place, she thought, and put her interest in him down to the fact that he was from London, where she wanted to live at some point; that and the fact that she was currently between boyfriends.

Reaching the end of the carpark, Tanner asked, 'Which way?' and turned to catch her staring at his left hand. It was either that or she was looking at the speedo, which seemed unlikely, as they'd just come to a halt.

Feeling as if she'd been caught in the act of mentally assessing whether or not he was boyfriend material, which in fairness was exactly what she'd been doing, she snapped back into work mode and said, 'Oh, right, and then right again at the roundabout.'

- CHAPTER EIGHT -

INDICATING TO TURN right as directed, he asked, 'Whereabouts are we going?'

'It's not far,' Jenny said. 'They live in one of the new-build houses on the other side of the railway line.'

'And he's going to be home, is he, given that it's ten o'clock on a Monday morning?'

'He's an IT manager. He says he works from home most of the time.'

'What about his wife? What does she do?'

'She's the manager of The Bittern. It's a pub, just down by the river.'

'I'm assuming she hasn't turned up there?'

'He said that he had called to check, but she wasn't expected in today.'

'How about yesterday?'

'Not then either. She has Sundays and Mondays off. The last time any of the staff saw her was when she left work on Saturday night.'

'Do we know what time that was?'

'Not yet, no. I'm going by what he said on the phone. I've yet to confirm this with anyone from the pub.'

Jenny felt herself beginning to relax in the XJS's comfortable cream leather seats. It was much easier to talk to the new DI from London about work related matters than what she did or did not think about his rather odd choice of car. One thing it did offer was an ultra-smooth ride, certainly more so than hers. It also seemed to attract attention. She'd already seen one old guy turning around to look at it as they drifted past. She couldn't remember anyone having ever turned to look at her car.

As the road weaved around, up ahead she saw the Wroxham Railway Bridge, which led trains into the nearby station. Sitting forwards, she said, 'Once you're under the bridge, it's the first turning on your left. River View Lane.'

Tanner pulled onto an untarmacked track, bounded on both sides by recently ploughed fields; the one on the left led towards a small wooded area with the railway line just beyond that, whilst the other drifted away into the horizon, where it disappeared into a grey, featureless sky.

As they drove down the track, they disturbed a flock of crows which lifted off the freshly overturned earth and flew towards a dark outline of still leafless trees that lay up ahead.

'Keep going to the end,' directed Jenny. 'His house should be on the corner.'

Before long, Tanner saw that behind the row of trees was a line of pristine white town houses, set back from a wide dark river. Beyond that were more trees, which were like all the others; bare-branched but displaying the first signs of early spring.

'It's certainly remote!' remarked Tanner, as he looked around for somewhere to park.

'It's one of many new-build estates that the council has been approving recently,' said Jenny. 'Nobody around here likes them much, but there doesn't seem to be a lot we can do about it.'

Tanner elected to park on the grass verge. He unclipped his seatbelt and stepped out, and took a moment to take in his surroundings. He could see the appeal of wanting to live there. The site had a clear, unobstructed view of what looked like a quiet stretch of river. Apart from the houses, there wasn't a single other building: no shops, garages, nothing. Perhaps it was a little too quiet for his liking. The only noise was the sound of the river, and the occasional caw from the crows, echoing down from the overlooking trees.

Tanner and Jenny headed over towards the first of the houses, all of which were identical in appearance: two storeys, whitewashed walls, gleaming black front doors, and grey slate roofs.

In the drive were two cars, both parked facing inwards. One was a gleaming new silver Porsche 911 and the other an older red Audi TT.

After briefly glancing in through the cars' windows as they passed on their way to the front door, Tanner said, 'They seem to be doing all right for themselves.'

'No children, though,' observed Jenny.

'Probably not,' agreed Tanner, pleased that she'd noticed that neither of the cars had been fitted with child seats, and the insides of both appeared to be too clean to have been used as regular family run-abouts.

He pressed the doorbell.

Taking a half step backwards, they stood in silence, listening to the chime ring out inside the house.

It wasn't long before they heard the sound of approaching footsteps, and the door was opened by a well-groomed man in his late twenties wearing tanned chinos and a jumper. He was thin, but not tall, had a light tan, short sandy brown hair and wore a pair of thin rimmed glasses.

'Mr Simon Richardson?' enquired Tanner, as he retrieved his formal police identification from out of his inside jacket pocket.

'I am, yes,' replied the man, with a clipped accent that had an irritated edge to it, as if the call at the door was keeping him from something more important inside.

'I'm Detective Inspector Tanner, Norfolk Police. This is my colleague…'

Realising he couldn't remember Jenny's surname, nor her rank, Tanner stopped and glanced at her.

She must have been expecting as much, as she held up her own ID. 'Detective Constable Evans. We spoke on the phone, Mr Richardson.'

'Of course, yes,' said the man, changing his demeanour from one of mild irritation, to someone showing concern for his missing wife. 'I don't suppose there's been any news?'

'Not yet, no,' replied Jenny, and looked meaningfully at Tanner.

Assuming that was a signal for him to take over, Tanner asked, 'May we come in?'

'Please do,' said the man, and turned to lead them down a narrow hallway towards the back of the house. There the room opened up into an average-sized open-plan, ultra-modern kitchen, with bi-fold patio doors, angular cream-coloured units, a white tiled floor and a view out into a small, recently fenced garden.

'Can I get you anything to drink?'

'We're fine, thank you,' declined Tanner, with brisk

formality, as he glanced around the kitchen.

On the dark grey work surface, beside the sink, was a single white bowl with a spoon resting inside it. To his left, on a kitchen island, was a wine-stained glass sitting beside an untidy pile of letters and magazines.

Apart from the fact that there seemed to be only one of everything, there didn't seem to be anything out of place.

Tanner kicked off the proceedings. 'We understand that you think your wife may be missing.'

'That was why I phoned the police, yes,' replied Richardson, with just a hint of sarcasm.

Seeing that Jenny had taken her notebook out, and was already poised with a pen, Tanner continued, 'When did you see her last?'

'Friday morning, when she left for work.'

'But you didn't report her as being missing until today?'

'Well, no, but I've been away for the weekend, playing golf. I left on Friday evening, before she came back from work.'

'What time was that?'

'Around eight o'clock.'

'And she hadn't come back from work by then?'

'No, but she works at the Bittern. She's the manager there, which means she inevitably ends up staying late.'

'So you left for your golfing weekend on Friday evening, and you haven't heard from her since?'

'I'm afraid not, no.'

'No calls, texts, emails, messages?'

'Nothing,' confirmed Richardson.

'So you're saying that you didn't have any contact

with your wife for three whole days, and yet you only thought to call the police this morning?'

'Well, yes, but that wasn't unusual.'

'Forgive me, but it does sound a little unusual.'

'To you, maybe, but we've never been one of those couples who spend every waking hour together. We've always enjoyed a degree of independence, even after we married. We don't even share the same circle of friends; so if one of us goes away, we don't necessarily stay in touch.'

'Fair enough,' said Tanner, but he still thought it sounded odd, especially for a couple who couldn't have been married for all that long. Making a mental note to come back to it, he asked, 'Did she drive to work?'

'She preferred to walk. It's only about half a mile away. Even closer if you take the short cut down by the river.'

'And which way did she normally go?'

'It would depend on the weather and the time of year. In the winter she was supposed to take the long way round. There are no street lights along the towpath, you see, and she never felt very safe going that way. However, saying that, more often than not she'd end up walking back by the river anyway.'

'And you say she worked on Saturday?'

'According to the pub she did, yes.'

'I don't suppose they know which way she came back?'

'I'm afraid I didn't think to ask, but knowing her, it was probably along the river.'

'Is it likely she could have stayed afterwards for a drink?'

'She didn't normally, no, but again, I didn't ask. Why?'

'No reason,' replied Tanner. If she'd been drunk when she left, and had taken the route along by the river, she could have easily fallen in. He'd known it to happen often enough along the Thames.

Not wishing to raise the possibility yet, Tanner went on, 'I assume those are your cars parked on the drive outside?'

'That's correct. Hers is the Porsche. A present from *Daddy*.'

There was a definite hint of resentment there, which Tanner also noted.

Putting it to one side again, he asked, 'Have you been able to get hold of her friends?'

'I haven't, no; but I don't know their phone numbers. I've only called the pub.'

'Did they say when they'd last seen her?'

'They said she left around half past ten on Saturday night.'

'What about her family? Do any of them live nearby?'

'Her parents do, yes. Down the road in Horning.'

'Couldn't she be staying with them?'

'I wouldn't have thought so.'

'You haven't asked them?' questioned Tanner, with unhidden incredulity.

'Well, no, but I'm sure she wouldn't be there. Her car's still outside, and they live too far away for her to walk.'

'Don't you think you should have called them anyway, just to make sure?'

'I suppose, but to be honest, I didn't want to worry

them.'

'So you thought you'd call the police instead?'

'Uh-huh.'

'Leaving us to contact them?'

'Well…I…'

'And how do you think they'll react when they get a call from the police, instead of you, asking if they know the whereabouts of their daughter, who's just been reported missing by her husband?'

Shifting his weight from one foot to another, Richardson said, 'I hadn't thought of it like that. I suppose I'd better give them a call.'

'I *suppose* you had, yes!' stated Tanner, with a condescending glare. 'What about other family. Brothers, sisters?'

'She doesn't, no.'

After pausing for a moment, Tanner went on, 'Going back to her friends. You said you don't have their phone numbers, but do you think you'd be able to get in touch with them in some other way?'

'Er…' Richardson replied, gazing up at the ceiling. 'I might be able to via Facebook, some of them at least.'

'So, basically, what you're saying is that all you've done since arriving back from your golfing weekend is to phone up the pub where she works. And when you found out that she wasn't there, even though she wasn't supposed to be, given that she doesn't work Mondays, your next call was to the police?'

With a sheepish shrug, he said, 'I couldn't think of anywhere else she could be.'

'You mean, apart from at a friend's house, or with her parents?'

'You think I'm worrying too much, don't you?'

'No, Mr Richardson, I'd have to say that I *don't* think you're worrying too much. In fact, I'd go as far as to say that you don't seem to be worrying at all! You don't appear to be trying very hard to find her, either!'

'As I said, I tried everywhere I could think of!'

'As in the pub?'

With no response forthcoming, after another moment's pause, Tanner followed that up by asking, 'I take it you do at least have a recent photo of her we could have?'

'I do, yes.' Richardson turned to examine a row of family photographs lined up along the kitchen windowsill.

Deciding on one, he picked it up, and as he handed it over to Tanner, asked, 'So you think she could be with her parents?'

Taking it from him, Tanner said, 'We won't know until you ask, will we? But I suggest that's the first call you make. If she's not there, you'll have to have another think about who else she might be staying with.'

Tanner took a moment to stare down at the picture, which featured the two of them at some sort of party. The man's wife was certainly attractive enough. High cheekbones, full lips, blonde hair, steel blue eyes that had a determined look about them. Now that he knew what she looked like, he wouldn't be surprised if she'd simply run off with someone else; after all, she couldn't have been short of admirers. With that possibility at the forefront of his mind, he handed the framed photograph over to Jenny, and asked, 'How long have you been married, Mr Richardson?'

'Just over four years.'

'No children?'

'Not yet.'

'And how would you describe your relationship?'

'It's good. I mean, we've had our moments, of course, but hasn't everyone?'

Tanner gave his face one last searching look. 'OK, Mr Richardson, I think we're about done here. I suggest you give her parents a call and see if she's there. If not, you'll need to have a good think about who else she might be staying with.'

'Yes, of course.'

'In the meantime, let me give you my number.' Retrieving his police ID, he was about to pull out one of the business cards he kept inside when he remembered he only had his old ones from when he'd been based at Colindale Police Station. 'DC, er, Evans, can you give Mr Richardson one of your business cards?'

Caught off guard, Jenny said, 'Oh, yes, of course,' and tucked the picture of the missing woman under her arm to delve into her handbag and retrieve her own police ID.

Turning back to Richardson, Tanner asked, 'I assume we have your contact details?'

Jenny answered for him. 'We do, yes. But we don't have Mrs Richardson's mobile number, or her email address.'

'I can give those to you now,' Richardson said.

Leaving Jenny to make a note of the missing woman's details, Tanner headed towards the kitchen doorway and out into the hall.

At the front door he turned. 'And if you could let

us know the minute you hear any news, we'd be very grateful.'

'Absolutely,' he replied, squeezing past Jenny and Tanner to let them out.

Stepping down onto the driveway with Jenny alongside, Tanner glanced back over at the two cars before asking, 'You said you played golf at the weekend?'

'That's right,' replied Richardson, standing in the doorway.

'You took your car, I assume – the Audi.'

'I always do, yes, why?'

Looking over at the car he asked, 'Can you even get a set of clubs into the back of a TT?'

Richardson seemed to hesitate for a fraction of a second, before saying, 'Just about. The back seats fold down.'

Walking over to the car, Tanner bent over, cupping his hands around his eyes as he did so.

Peering through the small triangular rear windows he saw that the back seats weren't down, but he could see that if they had been, then there probably would be enough room to fit a set of golf clubs inside, just about.

Standing back up, he looked out towards the river.

'If your wife did walk back along the towpath on Saturday night, which way would that be?'

Taking a step out of his house, Richardson pointed over to the left.

'The path runs all the way along the river bank,' he began. 'If you follow it around, it will take you under the railway bridge, into Wroxham.'

'How long would it have taken her?'

'Only around fifteen minutes. It's not far.'

'OK, well, thanks again, Mr Richardson. Give her parents a call, and if she's not there, ask them if they have any ideas of where she could be. If you haven't worked out where she is by, say, lunchtime today, let DC Evans know.'

Having glanced briefly down at the business card Jenny had given him, Richardson looked up and said, 'I'll give her parents a call now.' He turned to head back inside the house, closing the door behind him.

- CHAPTER NINE -

A S SOON AS the door was shut, Jenny turned to Tanner. 'What did you think?'

Tanner glanced over the front of the house, making sure all the doors and windows were closed so that they wouldn't be overheard. Confident they were, in a dismissive tone he replied, 'She's probably staying with friends, and hasn't bothered to tell him.'

'Didn't it seem odd to you that he's hardly made any effort to find her?'

'A little, I suppose,' said Tanner, 'but he did at least call the police. I know one or two couples who probably wouldn't have even bothered to do that.'

'But he hadn't even called her parents!' exclaimed Jenny. 'Nor had he made any effort to contact her friends, and he wouldn't have needed their phone numbers to do so. He could have simply messaged them on Facebook.'

'Perhaps.'

'And maybe the only reason he called the police,' Jenny continued, 'was because that's what he thought he should do.'

'I see where you're going with this,' he said, 'but I don't think we can even class her as being a missing person yet, at least not until her friends and family have been contacted. To be honest, had it not been for the fact that her car's still here, I'd have thought the most likely explanation was that she's run off with someone else.'

Glancing over towards the river, Jenny said, 'I suppose she could have fallen into the Bure, especially if she'd been drinking. She certainly wouldn't be the first.'

'I was thinking something similar myself. Maybe we should walk the route, just in case there's any sign of her.' He didn't think it likely, not if she'd tripped and gone straight in; but with nothing much else to do other than to head back to the office to stare at a computer screen, he thought they may as well, and he set off in the direction that Richardson had described, with Jenny following closely behind.

Reaching the river's edge, they followed the towpath leading towards Wroxham town centre, with Jenny keeping her attention dutifully focussed on the ground, looking for anything that might suggest someone had tripped and fallen in.

Tanner, meanwhile, was simply admiring the view. After all, the Broads were still very new to him. Only occasionally did he think to look down at the ground, particularly when he came to a section of concrete that had been lifted and cracked by expanding tree roots, where someone could easily have tripped and gone over. There he stooped down, and examined the area more closely, peering from the edge of the river over to the other side, where there was a thick line of trees and shrubs; but there was nothing to suggest anything untoward had happened there.

About ten minutes later, they reached the railway bridge that Richardson had mentioned. There they stopped to consider its Victorian red-brick structure as it loomed up above them, before stepping into the gloomy damp shadow that must permanently hang underneath it.

From nowhere, the thunderous sound of a train crashed over them, startling them both.

While the train clattered overhead, something caught Tanner's eye, near the edge of the moss-covered brick-lined wall.

Heading towards it, he crouched down to take a closer look. There, on the towpath, he could just about make out a circular patch on the ground that was darker than the surrounding concrete. Pulling out his phone, he turned on its torch app and shone the light over.

As the last of the carriages rattled away, in the chill silence that followed, Jenny stepped over to see what the new DI was looking at.

As she crouched beside him, Tanner pointed at what he'd found, and asked, 'What do you make of that?'

'Blood?' she replied, but more as a suggestion than an actual answer.

Reaching out with his finger to dab at its edge, Tanner said, 'It could be. But if it is, it's dry, so it must have been there a while.'

They stared down at it for a moment longer before Tanner stood up. 'I'd better give DCI Barrington a call to update him. I'll let him decide what he wants to do about this.'

He stepped out of the archway's gloomy tunnel, turned off his phone's torch and dialled the number for Wroxham Police Station that he'd pre-programmed in the evening before.

He was swiftly put through to Barrington, and briefly explained the situation; that Jane Richardson had last been seen on Saturday night, but that her husband had yet to ask any of her friends or family if they'd either seen or heard from her. He described the route she could have taken back from the pub, and said that they may have found a patch of blood, just under the railway bridge. Did Barrington want forensics to come down to take a look?

Barrington was of a similar opinion to Tanner, that until her friends and family had been contacted, she hardly rated as being missing; and with budgets as tight as they were, they couldn't justify the time and expense of getting forensics involved at this stage.

Ending the call, Tanner returned to the corner of the archway. There he followed the brickwork up to the top of the arch to assess whether the area would be protected from the elements. Deciding that it probably wouldn't be, he turned to Jenny. 'I don't suppose you've got any evidence bags on you?'

'I should have,' she replied, and delved into the depths of her handbag.

Retrieving a rolled-up bundle of them, she separated one out and passed it over.

Tanner pulled out his keys. Selecting one, he crouched down and scraped some of what did look very much like dried blood into the bag. Sealing it up, he tucked it discreetly into his inside pocket. He then laid the same keys down on the ground beside the possible blood-stained area, to use as a size comparison, before taking a couple of pictures.

Retrieving the keys, he stood up and said, 'It's

probably nothing, but you never know, and I suspect that where it's lying it would be washed away the next time it rains.'

With that done, they spent a few more minutes examining the area under the archway, using their smartphones' torches.

Jenny saw something glinting at the other end of the archway and went over to take a look. There she found a small but distinctive item of jewellery. It was in the shape of a butterfly, with bright blue wings and elaborate gold edging.

As Tanner came over to join her, Jenny said, 'It looks like an earring.'

'I'll take your word for it,' said Tanner. 'I'd better take a photograph of it,' he added. 'See if you can bag it without touching it.'

As Tanner again took a few photographs, Jenny delved back into her handbag, looking for something that would enable her to pick up such a small item of jewellery. She eventually found a pair of tweezers, which did the job perfectly, and she tucked the bagged item into one of her handbag's side pockets.

When they were confident that there was nothing else to find, they stepped out from under the railway bridge and continued their journey along the towpath, all the way up to Wroxham.

After Jenny had taken a moment to point out where the Bittern pub stood, they made the return journey, occasionally studying the ground as they did.

Back in the XJS, Jenny guided him towards town, heading for Wroxham Police Station, briefly stopping at a garage on the way to pick up a sandwich and a coffee for lunch.

- CHAPTER TEN -

ALAN HILLMAN WAS tired. He'd been tired for months. He could hardly remember a time when he hadn't been, not since the birth of his first child, and that was over eleven years before. Since then, Kate, his wife, had had two more children, and although the arrival of the first had given him an immense sense of purpose, joy, excitement and sheer delight, it had also come with a huge sense of responsibility, both financially and emotionally. And it was a burden that seemed to grow exponentially with each baby born.

Nobody had told him how much he'd end up worrying about them all, and how anxious he'd become about being able to support them. It hadn't helped that their first child, Harry, had come at the very worst time, from a fiscal perspective at least. He'd been born in September 2007, just one month after what became known as the Credit Crunch. They'd only bought their house the year before, but that had been when they'd both been working. The intention had always been for Kate to return to work, after her maternity leave, but she was in recruitment, and when it came time for her to go back, not only was her job not there, but the company she worked for wasn't either.

Alan worked in computer sales, which hadn't been affected nearly as much as most other industry sectors; but the pressure to meet the monthly mortgage payments on just the one salary, as well as to keep up with the bills, buying the food and paying for all the nappies, bottles, milk powder and god knows what, had at times been overwhelming. The situation had become so bad that at one point they'd faced the very real possibility that they were going to have to lose their house. Fortunately, Harry's grandparents stepped in at the last minute to settle their rising debt and help cover some of their monthly expenditure. When the interest rates came down, life became more sustainable, but the pressure remained, at least it did for Alan, and money always seemed to be an issue.

After a few years, and two more children, the subject of holidays had come up. Up until then they hadn't been able to afford one, at least not a proper one. With three children to look after, Kate had been content to go without for a while, but being stuck at home with them, day after day, year after year, she began to ask if they could find a way to afford a break. Alan's idea of a holiday was to curl up somewhere and sleep for a week, but his wife had always had more adventurous ideas, which sounded as exhausting as they'd no doubt be expensive. But at least he'd been able to persuade her that they should stick to the UK for the time being.

And so, with their growing family in tow, once a year they'd taken themselves off to various places, sometimes in Devon, other times in the Lake District. This year, however, was their most adventurous to date: a boating holiday on the Norfolk Broads.

For a change, this one had been Alan's idea. He'd always had some vague romantic notion that one day he'd be able to buy a yacht and sail off around the world, leaving his cares, worries and most importantly his job behind. The chance of him ever doing so was slim at best, not with three children, a job with limited promotional prospects, and a mortgage that wasn't even close to being paid off. Furthermore, he didn't even know the first thing about boats. The closest he'd ever come to one was when he'd taken his family to the London Boat Show, but none of the boats had been in the water. They'd all been surrounded by plush carpeted platforms instead.

It was a friend who'd suggested an Easter boating holiday on the Broads, being slightly cheaper than the same thing taken in summer. The websites he'd been directed to had sold the experience as being relaxing and care-free – just the sort of thing he felt he needed. He found it easy to picture himself as a heroic captain, floating effortlessly down a majestic river, with wide sweeping views, and reeds bending gently in a soft, soothing breeze.

The reality had turned out to be somewhat different.

They'd arrived for the start of their two week holiday the weekend before the Norfolk coast was battered by a harsh and bitter storm that blew in from Scandinavia. Conditions were so bad that they hadn't been allowed to take their hire boat out for three days.

When they were eventually given the keys, Alan had no idea how challenging it was going to be to take a boat out on a river that was swollen to near bursting point. The wind, which was still blowing hard, didn't help. With frequent bouts of heavy rain to add to the fun, for the first four days they ended up being stranded up against an isolated bank, just past Upton Dyke on the River Bure, with nowhere to buy even the most basic necessities. They weren't even able to find a tap to fill up with water. Even when the rain had passed, the wind was still blowing so hard from the east that it kept them pinned up against the mooring. Every time Alan attempted to motor off, the wind just blew the boat back again. Either the engine wasn't powerful enough, or more likely he just didn't know how to do it. Whenever he'd tried, all that would happen was that they'd be carried still further down river, with the bow of the boat being constantly pushed in towards the bank.

So for the first few days they were forced to put up with each other inside a boat that seemed to grow smaller with each passing day, Kate constantly blaming him for wanting to take them boating, in Norfolk of all places, and the children forever moaning that they were bored and taking out their frustrations on each other. And all the while, Alan was desperate to do nothing but sleep, which he could have done at home, and without costing him a penny!

A bitter tension soon followed, leaving Alan and his wife only speaking to each other when they had no other choice, and his children permanently sulking.

It wasn't until he woke up on Wednesday morning that he found that the wind had finally dropped, switching from an easterly to a south westerly. The river's flow had also eased, becoming more manageable, and the combination of the two made motoring off the bank they'd been stuck up against seem as straightforward as steering his car out of his drive at home.

Once they set off, almost immediately relationships on board began to warm, at least to the point where he and Kate were talking again. The children were now content enough to spend their days waving at every boat they passed, or when they were moored up, playing at fishing off the bow with a few pieces of old rope they'd found. Even Alan began to enjoy the holiday, demonstrated by the fact that he'd begun cracking the odd joke every now and again, a clear sign that his mood had lightened.

His boat handling skills also improved. After a while, the only remaining challenges were mooring and setting off again; those, and working out what to do when they had a sailing boat tacking into the wind towards them. In those instances, he just did his best to try to keep clear.

Sunday saw them spending the day exploring the River Thurne, where they motored up as high as Potter Heigham. There they found an ancient medieval bridge, one that is well known locally for being a challenge to navigate under due to its restricted height. Originally they'd hoped to be able to motor underneath it, but that was until they saw first-hand just how low it was, leaving them content to watch other boat users having a go, some with more success than others.

That evening they decided to moor up just past Thurne Dyke Mill, an impressive white windmill that used to pump water out of the surrounding marsh land into Thurne River, but which was now redundant, and served only as a tourist attraction.

After the family ate dinner at the nearby pub, they returned to their floating home. With the children in bed, and with his wife lying down with them, Alan enjoyed a quiet couple of hours sitting in the wheelhouse, doing nothing more than enjoying a couple of glasses of wine whilst listening to the gentle sounds of the Broads, as dusk slipped into the dark peace of night.

The following day they spent a leisurely morning exploring the village of Thurne, along with some of the idyllic countryside beyond. They had lunch at the same pub they'd dined at the previous evening, and decided they'd motor over to Horning for the afternoon, as it wasn't too far away. From the pictures they'd seen, it was definitely worth a visit.

As they all began clambering back on board, Alan asked Kate, 'If I start the engine, do you think you'd be able to put their life jackets on?'

'Of course I can!' she snapped back. 'I'm not completely stupid!'

With an exasperated look, desperate not to have yet another argument, Alan said, 'I didn't mean that you couldn't, I was just asking if you could. That was all!'

'Well, it's not as if I haven't done it before!' came her response, as her head disappeared down into the front cabin.

'*Thank you!*' replied Alan, loud enough to ensure that she would hear him.

Shaking his head in disbelief that his marriage had reached the point where he wasn't even able to ask his wife to do something without having his head bitten off in the process, he pulled out the boat's keys from his jeans' pocket and climbed onto the high seat behind the wheel. Inserting the key into the ignition, he turned it all the way around and held it there for three seconds, as he'd been instructed to. That was supposed to warm up the diesel's engine's heating element. He then let go of the key and placed his finger over the black engine start button. Pausing for a moment, he said a silent prayer that the engine would start. It had always done so far, but he wouldn't have known what to have done if it hadn't. Depressing the button, he held it down for a few moments, patiently listening to the engine whir around a few times before chugging thankfully into life. The moment it did, he removed his finger from the button and turned to look behind him. There he saw a thick cloud of exhaust smoke billow over the stern of the boat to begin heading in his direction. A moment later it engulfed the cockpit. He closed his mouth and held his breath. He'd no intention of breathing in the noxious fumes.

With the engine started, it was time to cast off the mooring lines, but he was going to need help to do so. Assuming he'd either said, or maybe not said something that had upset his wife, he'd have preferred not to ask her, but he didn't have a choice. He couldn't do it on his own. Leaning over towards the front cabin entrance, he called down, 'Honey, I don't suppose you could give me a hand casting off?'

'I'm a bit busy at the moment,' came her muffled response. 'Can't Harry help you?'

Harry was now nearly twelve, but Alan still didn't think he was old enough. Although mature for his age, he lacked the upper body strength that would be needed, especially if something went wrong.

'I'm not sure he's quite ready yet,' replied Alan,

which was exactly what he'd said the last two times she'd suggested it.

Harry's little blonde head popped itself out of the cabin, and with imploring blue eyes, said, 'I can do it, Daddy! Look, I've even put on my own life jacket!'

'I'm sure you can Harry, but I'm not convinced you're strong enough, not yet anyway.'

'Oh, *please,* Daddy, let me!'

Alan stared down at his angelic face, and with a sigh signifying his reluctant capitulation, said, 'Very well.'

'YES!' Harry pumped his fist in the air, and with a victorious smile he scrambled over the side of the open cockpit, jumped down onto the grass verge and charged forwards, heading towards the front of the boat.

'But you *must* be careful!' Alan called out after him, somewhat belatedly.

There was no response. Harry had already reached the rope that secured the bow and was tugging at the knot in an effort to untie it.

Watching him struggle just to do that, Alan was already regretting his decision, and cursed Kate for having suggested it. Not only did Harry lack physical strength, but he could hardly swim. If he fell in between the boat and the hard wooden siding when pushing off, and if a breeze were to force the boat back against the bank, the result would be unimaginable!

Remembering something, Alan slid off the driver's seat and grabbed hold of a spare white plastic fender that had been lying on the floor. Taking it by a short length of rope that was attached to one end, he climbed out of the cockpit and carefully made his way along the narrow walkway, all the way to the front. By the time he got there, Harry had managed to untie the knot and was standing with his feet apart, holding the line with both hands held out in front of him.

Crouching down at the boat's bow, Alan said, 'Here, take this,' and passed him the fender. 'Now, remember what the man said who handed the boat over to us. If the boat looks like it's going to hit something, whatever you do, *don't* use your arms or legs to try and push if off! The boat's just too heavy. Use the fender instead by jamming it between the boat and whatever it is that it's going to hit. Do you understand?'

Taking the fender, with a serious expression etched over his lightly freckled young face, Harry looked up at his father and said, 'I understand, Daddy.'

'OK, good. I'm going to untie the rope at the back of the boat. When I've done that, I'll return to the cockpit. There's nothing moored up behind us, so I'm going to reverse out, into the river, going that way,' and he pointed in the direction he was going to go. 'As I'm going out, follow the boat down the mooring, and when I say so, push the boat off and step on board at the same time.'

'Yes, Daddy.'

'Whatever you do, don't leave yourself stranded on the bank!'

'I won't, Daddy.'

'But if you can't get on the boat, I'd rather you stayed on the bank than risk falling in the water.'

As a wave of doubt swept over Alan's mind, he said, 'Are you sure you're OK to do this? I can always get Mummy to do it.'

'I can do it, Daddy, I promise!'

Alan stared deep into his son's translucent blue eyes. Maybe it was time he stopped being so protective of him. After all, in little more than a year's time he'd be a teenager.

'OK, now remember – follow the boat down the mooring and when I give the signal, push it out and step on board.'

Seeing Harry nod, Alan turned to make his way to the back of the boat. There he jumped down onto the grass, untied the mooring line, and with the rope in hand, climbed back on board, dropping the line on the deck as he did so. He then made his way back to the cockpit, sat down on the chair and turned the wheel all the way round to the right. Checking that the river was clear of traffic, with his left hand on the wheel and his right hand on the throttle, he gradually brought the lever down towards him. As he did so, the rumbling noise from the engine increased and the boat began pulling itself backwards, away from the bank, out into the river.

Seeing Harry was following the nose of the boat up the bank, rope in one hand, fender in the other, he was just about to tell him to push it off and step on board when the tone of the engine changed from a low rumble to a much louder churning noise. Then there was a sudden jolt, after which – nothing, and instead of the boat continuing to reverse out, it began drifting along with the current.

'Shit,' he said, quietly to himself, and placed the lever back into neutral again. It sounded like something had caught in the propeller.

As half the boat jutted out into the middle of the

river, the current began to take hold of it, and with no engine to stop it, the boat was starting to drift downriver at a steadily increasing pace.

Glancing over at the bank, Alan could see that Harry was already having to walk a little faster just to keep up with it. Doing his best to remain calm, he called out, 'Hold on, Harry! The propeller must have caught on something. I'm going to try to go forward and see if that clears it.'

Harry gave him another nod, but with far less confidence that time.

Not wasting another moment, Alan eased the throttle lever into the forward position, but after a clunking sound, followed by the same low churning noise, there was nothing but a dull whine.

The boat was being swept along faster now.

From the shore, Harry called out, 'I can't hold it, Daddy!'

Alan could feel himself beginning to panic. He could see Harry was almost running along the bank just to keep up with the boat, bow line in one hand, fender in the other. It was too late for him to jump on board. It was moving too quickly. And there was no way he'd have the strength to stop it, which would leave him stranded on the bank, watching helplessly as his parents were swept away by the river. Alan wasn't even sure that *he'd* be able to stop it, but he felt he had no choice but to try.

Abandoning his position by the wheel, he leapt out of the cockpit, onto the side of the boat and scrambled forwards towards the bow, as fast as he could without going over the edge. Once there, he kept going, leaping off the end to land on the grass bank, near to where Harry was, still holding onto the bow line.

By the time Alan picked himself up, Harry was already a good ten feet away, and Alan had to launch into a sprint just to catch him up.

As he did, between breaths he said, 'It's OK, Harry…I've got it,' taking the rope as he did so.

Slowly, he took up the slack.

As the rope tightened, he pulled back on its end with all his strength, digging his heals into the grass bank as he did.

The boat did seem to slow, but there was no way he was going to be able to stop it. It was just too heavy, and the current was far too strong.

Looking further along the bank, Alan saw there was a purpose-built concrete mooring, at the far end of which was a highly polished wooden sailing boat. If their plastic boat ploughed into it, it would be wrecked, there was no doubt about that!

With rising desperation, Alan spotted a series of steel cleats lining the mooring's edge. If he could somehow loop the bow line around the nearest one, he thought it should give him enough leverage to bring the boat to a halt. He wasn't sure it would, but it was looking as if he had no other choice. It was either that, or letting go of the bow line, so allowing the boat to be sucked out into the middle of the river, adrift with no engine, with his wife and two other children still on board.

It wasn't an option. However, if he missed the first cleat he could see that looping the bow line around the next one down would probably swing the whole thing straight into the wooden yacht ahead, crushing it like an egg in the process.

When the first cleat was only about ten feet away, Alan again took up the slack, dug his heels into the grass and heaved back once more. The boat slowed; he raced forward, looped the bow line once around the cleat and pulled back on it again.

To his huge relief, the boat gradually came to a gentle halt.

Seeing that the boat's aft end was swinging naturally in towards the mooring, he called over to Harry, 'Run ahead! When the back of the boat comes in, use the fender to stop it from hitting the side. Then see if you can grab the rope I left on the deck and try to loop it around that t-shaped metal thing on the ground, like I've done.'

Without replying, Harry sprinted forward, reaching the edge of the mooring just in time to drop the fender down between the hard standing and the stern of the boat as it swung in towards him.

Harry watched as the boat forced itself up against the fender, its thick white rubber surface squeaking in protest. Without letting go of the fender's tether, Harry reached forward, took a hold of the stern line that was lying on the deck, where his dad had said it would be, and dragged it back towards the cleat. There he looped it once around, as he'd seen his dad do, and pulled back on the rope.

With the boat secure against the quay, he glanced over to the front, where he could see that his dad was busy securing the bow line around the cleat. Determined to be helpful, he peered down into the water, where the propeller was, looking for whatever it was that had caught up in it.

There, watching him from underneath the water,

was the face of a woman; eyes wide, mouth apart, hair swirling like a nest of snakes.

A cold wave of fear swept along Harry's limbs, freezing him where he stood.

The woman's eyes seemed to fix on his.

Everything stopped, everything except his heart, which pounded hard, deep inside his chest.

Then he saw her lips move, and Harry let out a terrified scream.

- CHAPTER ELEVEN -

BACK AT WROXHAM Police Station, Tanner and Jenny had only just sat down at their respective desks when they saw DCI Barrington's head poke out from his office. 'Tanner! Evans! A word, please!' he called, and disappeared back inside.

They looked at each other, shrugged and stood up to weave their way between the various chairs and desks.

Tanner whispered, 'He doesn't sound very happy.'

In a similar hushed tone, Jenny said, 'Between you and me, he rarely does.'

'I don't suppose you've got any idea what this is about?'

'Not a clue. Sorry!'

Stepping through Barrington's half-open door, Tanner cleared his throat. 'You wanted to see us, sir?'

Barrington glanced up from his computer monitor. 'Come in, both of you. And close the door behind you.'

With the door shut, and without asking them to sit down, Barrington leaned forward, and asked, 'Can one of you please explain to me why you didn't think it was necessary to tell me who that girl's parents are?'

Tanner was confused. 'You mean the missing girl?'

'Of course I mean the missing girl! Why didn't either of you tell me who they are?'

After Tanner and Jenny had exchanged similar blank looks, Tanner replied, 'The husband said he was going to call them first, so we've yet to even speak to them, sir.'

'Well, I've just had her father on the line. He's none other than John bloody Lambert!'

Tanner had heard the name somewhere, but couldn't for the life of him remember where.

'Of Lambert Oak?' prompted Barrington. 'As in the pub chain?'

Having made the connection, Tanner was still none the wiser as to its significance. Unsure how best to respond, he just stood there awaiting enlightenment.

'So?' Barrington eventually asked.

'Sorry, sir, I'm not with you.'

'Has she turned up yet?'

'Oh, the girl! Not yet, no, sir. But as I explained on the phone, her husband has hardly lifted a finger to do anything to find her, so we're still expecting her to show up at either a friend's house, or possibly with some member of her family.'

'Well, she's not with her parents, I know that much!'

'Right.'

Returning to his monitor, Barrington reached for the mouse, saying, 'I'm ramping this up to high priority. We need her found, and fast!'

'And why's that?' snapped Tanner. 'Because she's the daughter of some pub chain owner?'

'He's not just some pub chain owner!' retorted Barrington. 'Apart from being one of the most well-known people from around these parts, he's also one of the richest men in the UK!'

'I see. And that makes his daughter more important than everyone else's, does it?'

Remembering what had happened to Tanner's own daughter, Barrington strove for a little more restraint. 'It doesn't make her more important, no, but it does introduce another possibility, one that would have been useful to have known about, and certainly before now.'

Tanner kicked himself. He'd allowed his emotions to overshadow his reasoning. It was now glaringly obvious what Barrington was referring to, although there was one thing missing.

'Has there been a ransom demand?' he asked, with more control.

'Not yet,' stated Barrington. 'But that doesn't mean we can rule it out. One thing I'm fairly sure of, though, is that it's a possibility that's been playing on Mr Lambert's mind. He's just accused me of having done less than nothing to try to find her, and threatened that if we don't make a bit more of an effort, he's going to be calling my boss, Superintendent Whitaker, to demand my resignation.'

'That's a bit extreme, isn't it?' said Tanner. 'I mean, she was only reported missing this morning!'

'I suspect the man's just a little upset, seeing that he's only just found out that his daughter seems to have disappeared. I'm sure we can *all* appreciate just how distressing that news must have been for him,' he added, his eyes fixed firmly on Tanner.

At that moment there was a knock, closely followed by the man Tanner now knew to be his counterpart,

DI Burgess, peering around the door.

Barrington scowled at him. 'Yes! What is it?'

Realising he must have walked in at a bad time, Burgess said, 'Sorry to disturb you, sir, but I thought you'd better know that a body's been found.'

A stunned silence fell over the room, as everyone stared at Burgess.

With a look of pure exasperation, Barrington eventually said, 'Please God, tell me it's not John Lambert's daughter!'

'I'm afraid we don't know who it is yet, sir,' related Burgess. 'There's no ID, but the body does appear to be that of a young woman.'

Clasping his hands together, Barrington raised them up to his mouth as if he was about to start praying.

In the silence that followed, unsure as to what else to say, Burgess eventually came out with, 'I've asked forensics to go down, sir.'

As if emerging from a trance, Barrington looked up at him and said, 'Good, yes, of course; but I don't want anyone else knowing about this, not until we know who she is. Is that understood?'

'Yes, sir!'

As he turned to leave, Barrington called out after him, 'And I want Tanner to take the lead on this one.'

Stopping where he was, Burgess spun back. With an expression of near total incomprehension, he glared first at the new DI, then at Barrington. 'Tanner?'

'Yes, Tanner!' repeated Barrington, focussing on his new DI, who looked about as surprised as anyone.

'But sir,' protested Burgess. 'He hasn't been here for more than five minutes! You can't possibly give it to *him*!'

'I'm fully aware how long he's been here, thank you, Burgess, but at the end of the day, he's got a hell of lot more experience of this sort of thing than you have.'

'But he's not even from around here, sir! He doesn't know who anyone is – he doesn't even know *where* anything is! He wouldn't have a single bloody clue as to where to start!'

'And you would, I assume?'

Burgess looked Barrington straight in the eye. 'I believe I would, yes!'

'And what if it turns out to be a murder investigation? When was the last time you led one of those?'

An awkward silence followed.

Burgess had never led a high-profile case such as a murder investigation before. He knew that, just as Barrington did, but he was damned if he was going to admit to it; certainly not in front of the new DI. 'But at this point there's nothing to suggest that it *is* a murder, sir. She's probably just another stupid tourist who fell in the river and drowned.'

Barrington thought for a moment.

Burgess was right, of course. That was the most likely explanation. If it wasn't, and there was a more nefarious reason behind it, then he was going to need someone with a lot more experience than Burgess could bring to the table. Until they knew otherwise, however, maybe it would be more sensible to let Burgess lead.

Sensing he was on the verge of changing his mind, Burgess backed up his argument by saying, 'I can handle it, sir!'

With a reluctant sigh, Barrington said, 'Very well, but I at least want Tanner around to assist you.'

Looking Tanner up and down with a gleeful sneer, Burgess said, 'As long as it's clear that he's only my *assistant*, I don't have a problem with that.'

Deciding to allow the derogatory remark that had obviously been aimed at his latest recruit to slide, Barrington looked over at Tanner, still standing to attention in front of him, and asked, 'I assume that's OK with you?'

With an ambivalent shrug, Tanner said, 'I'm happy to work in any capacity you see fit, sir.'

'Right! That's settled then.'

'What about me, sir?' piped up Jenny, who until then had been happy to stand beside Tanner, keeping her mouth shut.

'You may as well stay with Tanner for now,' replied Barrington. 'At least until we know who this dead girl is, and if there are any suspicious circumstances surrounding it.'

Concluding the meeting, Barrington said, 'OK, that's it! You three had better head straight down there. And Burgess?'

'Yes, sir?'

'Report back to me the minute you find out anything.'

Delighted with the result of the meeting – that he was finally going to have the lead on what he hoped *would* end up being a murder investigation, plus the fact that the new DI had effectively been assigned to be his assistant, with a malevolent smile aimed squarely over at Tanner, he replied, 'That won't be a problem, sir.'

- CHAPTER TWELVE -

BACK IN THE XJS, Tanner and Jenny followed DI Burgess's non-descript dark blue saloon out of Wroxham Police Station, past Horning, over the River Ant, and through Ludham. After that came Potter Heigham, where they crossed the River Thurne, and took a series of ever-narrowing country lanes that eventually led into the small village of Thurne, near to where the woman's body had been found.

Driving slowly into the village, up ahead Tanner saw a row of emergency vehicles parked up on a grass verge, opposite a red telephone box that looked as if it could have done with a coat of paint. The vehicles included a squad car, an ambulance, and a police forensics services van.

Seeing Burgess reverse up onto a grass verge directly behind them, Tanner did the same.

With the engine off, and the handbrake on, he took a moment to have a look around.

They'd arrived at the end of what Jenny explained was Thurne Dyke, a short narrow channel that led out into the River Thurne, which was apparently a popular place for mooring.

They got out of the car to see Burgess beckoning with some impatience for them to join him.

As they approached him, Burgess fixed a stare at Tanner and in a condescending tone, called out, 'We'll have to make our way by foot from here,' as if walking to the scene of a possible crime wasn't something city-bred Tanner would have ever done before.

Without waiting for a response, Burgess marched off, over the grass verge, down to a tow path which led out past a long line of small motor boats moored up on the left side of the dyke.

Setting off after him, as if to excuse her colleague's rather off-hand manner Jenny said, 'He's probably just nervous. Tommy, I mean DI Mills, used to take the lead on this kind of investigation. This is Burgess's first one.'

Tanner wasn't bothered. He'd been expecting to be treated with a degree of contempt by his new colleagues, especially by those who shared the same rank as him.

As he continued to cast a casual eye over his surroundings, in a relaxed, conversational tone, he said, 'I suppose you don't get many bodies turning up around here.'

'You'd be surprised,' she said. 'Not as many as London, of course, but enough to keep Tommy busy, especially during the silly season.'

'I assume by that you mean the summer?'

'It's more from April to October. It's already begun to pick up. Next weekend is Easter, and that always brings hordes of tourists. And they'll keep coming, right up until the schools' half term holidays in the Autumn.'

Taking an interest in the many small boats they were strolling past, Tanner said, 'Barrington mentioned something about how you get over eight million visitors a year.'

'I think he tells everyone that on their first day,' Jenny replied. 'He told me something similar when I first started. It never seems quite that many, but apparently it's true.'

'And I suppose most of them take out hire boats?'

'Not as many as you might think, but a lot of them do, yes. It wouldn't be a problem if half of them knew how to use them, but most of them don't; and when you add alcohol into the mix, unfortunately the fact that one or two of them never make it home does become a little inevitable.'

'What about you? Where are you from?'

'Oh, I'm a Horning girl,' she answered, quickly adding, 'No jokes please!'

With a boyish smirk, Tanner said, 'Heaven forbid!' But he couldn't resist, and feeling more relaxed than he had in a long time, said, 'So you don't go around feeling permanently horny?'

Pretending to be upset, Jenny glared up at him. 'I said, no jokes!'

'Sorry,' said Tanner, turning away to hide his grin. 'I couldn't help it.'

'No? Well, don't worry. It's to be expected, I suppose.' She turned her face away slightly, muttering under her breath, just loud enough for Tanner to hear, 'But I do, though.'

Finding himself about as aroused by the comment as he was embarrassed, Tanner wasn't sure where to look. He'd never heard such an attractive young lady say anything quite so openly sexual about themselves, at least not when they were sober, and certainly not when the comment had been for his personal benefit.

Seeing his reaction from out of the corner of her eye, she gave him a cheeky smile and said, 'Only joking, Gov!'

Not entirely convinced that she was, Tanner looked down at the cute curve of her nose. 'I didn't think nice girls were supposed to say things like that?'

'Who said I'm a nice girl?' she questioned. 'Besides, I doubt you've ever met one from Horning before.'

'I haven't, no, but at least I now know what to expect!'

Reaching the end of the dyke, where Burgess had turned left to follow a well-trodden grass path that led down along the river's edge, Tanner stopped to look over at the wide river channel that was laid out before them, and then turned to gaze up at Thurne Dyke Mill on the right, an impressively tall white windmill with four giant blades, each one made up of white trellis-like panels.

Seeing what he was looking at, Jenny said, 'It used to be a water pump. Very popular with the tourists.'

'I can see why!' exclaimed Tanner, taking a moment to admire it before turning his attention back to where Burgess had gone.

As they followed him, heading in the opposite direction came two paramedics, and behind them a young family: two adults, presumably the parents, and three children. The tallest of the children was a skinny blond boy with a lightly freckled face. He looked incredibly pale, and was walking hunched over, clutching at a foil blanket draped over his shoulders.

Tanner assumed he must be the person who'd found the body, but he didn't stop to ask the family anything. Instead, he just nodded at the leading paramedic and continued to walk past.

Up ahead, Burgess had begun talking to a couple of uniformed police officers. The three of them were standing next to a dull white motor boat, the bow of which was pointing towards them, tied up to a purpose-built mooring platform. Beyond them was a diver clad in a glistening black wetsuit, who was busy wrestling a cylindrical oxygen tank off his back.

Drawing closer, they could see a couple of forensics officers dressed head to foot in their customary white overalls, leaning over the back of the boat, and kneeling on the mooring platform was another, staring down at something on the ground. It wasn't until they reached Burgess when they were able to see what it was.

- CHAPTER THIRTEEN -

BURGESS DISMISSED THE uniformed constables, turned to face Tanner and Jenny, gestured up towards the other end of the boat and said, 'They've only just pulled her out.'

'I assume the boy we passed on the way here was the one who found her?' asked Tanner.

Burgess nodded. 'Not unsurprisingly, he's in a bit of a state, as is his dad; but they've both been able to give statements. The propeller must have sucked the body in when they were reversing, stopping the engine. They nearly ended up floating off down the river. It was only after they'd managed to pull the boat back in that the boy saw her.'

Tanner tried to see more from over Burgess's shoulder, but the forensics officer was blocking his view. All he could see was bare legs and shoeless feet.

'Any idea what sort of age she is?'

'No idea. Our medical examiner, Dr Johnstone, is taking a look at her now.' With some reluctance, he added, 'I suppose we'd better see how he's getting on.'

Finally Tanner was able to see the girl's face. Her faded blue eyes were staring out through clumps of tangled wet hair. Her skin was sunken and white, her lips purple and still.

He stopped.

His mind drifted to another, similar scene.

He was standing under a street light in London, rain running down his face, staring at another girl, her face horribly beaten, her body twisted and broken.

Jenny looked around to see what was wrong.

Seeing the haunted look in Tanner's deep brown eyes, with natural concern she asked, 'Are you OK?'

Shaking his mind free of the memory, he focussed his eyes on Jenny's.

In that brief moment he found himself desperate to tell her what had happened, all those months before. How he'd been called to attend a suspected murder scene to find the body of a girl, sprawled half-naked in a gutter, beaten almost beyond recognition. How he'd refused to believe who she was, despite seeing the bracelet he'd given her for her nineteenth birthday. And how he'd not been allowed to investigate her death, leaving him with a shameful sense of worthlessness, impotence, and guilt.

The moment passed.

Regaining control of his thoughts with an effort, he sent her an apologetic smile. 'Sorry, yes, I'm fine. I was just…thinking about something.'

Burgess, meanwhile, had edged his way around the body.

Crouching down opposite the medical examiner, he asked, 'What do we have?'

After a quick glance up, seeing that it was Burgess the doctor said, 'It would appear to be a dead body!'

Ignoring the obvious sarcasm, something Dr Johnstone was renowned for, with less ambiguity, Burgess asked, 'Do you have any idea how she died?'

'I'm afraid I don't, but I've only just arrived myself.'

Burgess pressed him for more. 'Could she have drowned?'

'There are signs that she may have done, yes. However, there are other injuries which will need further exploration.'

From his position standing directly behind the medical examiner, Tanner pointed down and asked, 'How about those marks on her neck?'

Not recognising the voice, the doctor glanced around, and raised an eyebrow at him. 'And you are…?'

Realising he probably should have introduced the new DI a little sooner, Burgess said, 'Dr Johnstone, this is Detective Inspector Tanner. He's just joined us from London, and currently working on Missing Persons.'

'I assume you're thinking that this may be one of them?' the doctor asked.

On Tanner's behalf, Burgess answered, 'That's what we're hoping to find out.'

Returning to look at the body, the doctor began a brief summary of his findings so far.

'The bruising around her neck *could* be significant. It's certainly consistent with someone who's been strangled, but it could equally have been caused by something catching around her neck, after she'd fallen in. A loose mooring line, for example. The injuries to her abdomen are definitely post-mortem, most likely to have been caused by the boat's propeller; but there's also this.' He leaned forward, towards her face, and pointed at the top of her forehead. There, between two thick strands of hair, they could see a half-moon shaped indentation, dark purple in colour, the skin of which was broken around the top.

Having seen similar injuries before, Tanner suggested, 'A hammer?'

'Possibly,' replied the doctor. 'But it could equally have been caused by her falling onto something, like a mooring cleat, for example, or maybe a boat stanchion. It would have had to occur before she went in the water, though. A body will always float face down, so any injuries caused by passing boats would only appear on the back of her head, not the front.'

Leaning forwards to take a closer look, Burgess asked, 'Any idea of a time of death?'

'Around thirty-six hours ago, give or take.'

'So, sometime on Saturday night?'

'I'd say around then, yes, but I'll have a better idea when I get her back to the lab.'

'And no sign of any ID?'

'None that I've found, no.'

'Distinguishing marks, tattoos?'

'Nothing so far.'

Having seen enough, Tanner turned to look over at Jenny and asked, 'I don't suppose you still have that photograph?'

At first, Jenny didn't seem to hear the question, as she did nothing but stare down at the girl's body.

Since she'd first seen it, in particular the way her stomach had been ripped apart, leaving nothing but a grotesque mass of churned up flesh, Jenny had momentarily forgotten where she was, or even what she was supposed to be doing. She hadn't even taken out her notebook.

Seeing how she was transfixed by what lay before them, Tanner snapped her out of it by repeating, 'The photograph, Jenny!'

She came back with a start, and muttered, 'Sorry. Of course. Yes,' and began fumbling with the zip of her handbag.

Eventually she pulled out the photograph that Richardson had given them earlier that day.

Taking it from her, Tanner stared first at it, then down at the dead girl.

'Is it her?' questioned Burgess.

Despite the fact that the young woman beaming a smile at them from the photograph looked nothing like the body stretched out before them, Tanner said, 'I'd say it is.'

Snatching the photograph out of his hands, Burgess studied them both. But as far as he could make out, the two looked nothing like each other. One was a picture of an attractive young woman with inviting eyes and a vivacious smile, whilst the other was a half-bloated corpse that had just been pulled off the propeller of a boat.

Handing the photograph back to Tanner, Burgess said, 'They don't look anything like each other!'

'Well no, but in fairness, they rarely do. I was going more by the similarities of age and hair colouring, and that the estimated time of death coincided with the time our missing person was last seen.'

'Well, I can't say I'm convinced!'

'She was married, if that helps,' interjected the doctor.

He was looking over at her left hand where there was a gold wedding band, along with a matching engagement ring. Surrounding them, the skin bulged to the point where it looked as if it was about to burst.

Ideally he'd have removed all items of jewellery at this stage, but it was rare for him to be able to take rings from fingers. They normally had to be removed by other means during the post-mortem process.

'She's also wearing a necklace and an earring, which someone may be able to recognise.'

'Only one earring?' questioned Tanner, remembering the one they'd found under the railway bridge earlier that day, and kicking himself for not having thought of it sooner.

'Only one, yes,' confirmed the doctor. 'The other one looks like it was torn off at some point.'

Tanner and Jenny were thinking the same thing, that if the missing earring matched the one they'd found earlier, then they'd most likely have already discovered where she'd been killed. Jenny reached into the outside pocket of her handbag, took out the clear plastic evidence bag containing the earring, and passed it over to the man who she was beginning to think of as her boss.

Tanner crouched down beside the dead girl's head to compare the two items; but it was clear from the outset that they weren't the same. The earring the dead girl was wearing consisted of a simple gold spiral. The one in the bag was in the shape of a blue butterfly.

'Is it a match?' asked Jenny.

'Not even close.'

Overhearing the conversation, Burgess asked, 'Is what a match?'

Standing back up, Tanner said, 'We found an earring near to where the missing girl lives.' As he handed the evidence bag back to Jenny, he added, 'We also found what we think might be blood.'

'And where was that, exactly?'

'Under the railway bridge,' replied Jenny. 'Upriver from Wroxham.'

'And that's where you think she was killed, do you?' Burgess asked Tanner. 'Before her body was dumped in the river?'

'The thought had crossed my mind.'

'So you're saying that the body floated from Wroxham, all the way down the River Bure, where it would have popped out just over there.'

Burgess pointed downstream to where Tanner could see another river entrance, about a hundred metres further on.

'Then the body somehow managed to defy the laws of physics by miraculously floating *upstream*,' continued Burgess, 'to end up where it is now?'

Realising he'd allowed himself to be led into what was obviously a gaping hole of impossibility, Tanner said, 'I must admit that I don't know the river system around here, so I'd have to agree that that does sound a little unlikely.'

'Which is exactly why we need local people working for us, not a bunch of bloody Londoners!'

Tanner elected to remain silent. He'd no desire to engage in a discussion with this man about his ability to work effectively in Norfolk. After all, Burgess was right; he didn't know the Broads, but he didn't think it would take him long to learn their layout. Despite the area he'd covered in London being relatively small, it was vastly more complex in comparison, covered as it was by a labyrinth of motorways, flyer-overs, streets and paths, all of which heaved with humanity from every corner of the planet. In contrast, the Broads seemed to consist of just a few rivers.

Burgess gave Tanner a long provocative glare, almost daring him to come back at him.

But Tanner wasn't rising to the bait.

Feeling distinctly pleased with how exceptionally well he'd been able to prove his point that the new DI really was worse than useless, turning to face the other direction, Burgess said, 'She'd have probably gone in somewhere around Hickling Broad, or Horsey Mere. Certainly beyond Potter Heigham. She could even have gone in near Martham. It's a big area, so it will be difficult to pinpoint exactly where.'

Doctor Johnstone began easing himself up from where he'd been kneeling. After stretching out his back he handed Burgess two clear plastic evidence bags, one containing the necklace, the other the earring.

'These might help to identify her,' he began. 'As far as DNA evidence goes, I think it's unlikely we're going to find any, not with her having been in the water for so long. But I'll bag her hands before I leave, which will help protect anything that may be lodged under her fingernails.'

Holding the two bags up to examine their contents, Burgess asked, 'When do you think we'll be able to have the results from the post-mortem?'

Giving his watch a quick glance, Johnstone said, 'Tomorrow afternoon.'

'How about tomorrow morning?'

'I can try,' replied Johnstone. 'It will depend if anything unexpected crops up.'

Giving Jenny the evidence bags, Burgess looked over at Tanner. 'You may want to show those to the husband of your missing girl, to see if he recognises them. If he does, then I suppose you'd better arrange for him to come in and identify the body; but only if he does, mind! If he doesn't, then I think it would be fair to say that this must be someone else.'

Burgess was hoping that that would be the case, and that the dead girl wasn't the same as Tanner's missing person. That way he hoped Barrington would pull Tanner off what he now considered to be *his* investigation. As much as he liked the idea of having the new London DI working as his personal assistant, the novelty factor had already worn off, and it now felt more like he was there to keep tabs on him.

With a nod, Tanner left Burgess to call Barrington, and having taken one last look over the scene, he led Jenny back the way they'd come.

- CHAPTER FOURTEEN -

AT SIMON RICHARDSON'S house, Tanner rang the doorbell and waited.

As the door opened, he said, 'Sorry to bother you again, Mr Richardson, but we were wondering if we could speak to you for a moment?'

'I take it that means you haven't found her?' asked Richardson, giving Tanner a disparaging glare.

Unable to say if they had or hadn't, again Tanner asked, 'May we come in?'

'Of course. Sorry. It's been a long day.'

Stepping back inside the house, he led them down the hall towards the kitchen.

Once there, Tanner said, 'We've found a couple of items of jewellery that we'd like you to take a look at.'

On cue, Jenny removed the two clear plastic evidence bags containing the necklace and the earring from her handbag, and placed them on the surface of the kitchen island beside them.

Frowning down at them, Richardson asked, 'Can I pick them up?'

'You can,' agreed Tanner.

As he carefully lifted each one, he said, 'I assume you're thinking that they might belong to my wife?'

'We're not assuming anything, Mr Richardson. It would simply help us to know if you recognise them.'

After studying each item, Richardson eventually said, 'I'm not sure. I don't think they're hers, but then again, she does have rather a lot.'

'So they could be?'

'I suppose they could, yes. At least they look like the sort of thing she'd wear, but I don't recognise them.'

'I see,' said Tanner. He'd been hoping for a more conclusive answer, and was forced to hide his disappointment.

Remembering the other piece of jewellery they'd found, the one from under the railway bridge, he looked up at Jenny. 'DC Evans, could you show Mr Richardson the other item?'

'Of course,' she replied, retrieving it from her handbag to place down on the worktop.

After staring at it for a few moments, Richardson eventually shrugged and said, 'I'm sorry, but I don't recognise it either. May I ask where you found them?'

Tanner hesitated. Had the man been able to confirm that the items found on the woman's body had belonged to his wife, then he'd have told him, before asking if he'd be willing to make a formal identification. But with his responses being so vague, they were no closer to figuring out who the woman was. Even Tanner was having his doubts as to her identity. When he'd first seen the body he'd have put money on it being that of Richardson's wife, and that someone had killed her underneath the railway bridge on her way back from work. But with such ambivalent responses to the jewellery, combined with Burgess's comments about how she'd had to have floated upstream to end up where she'd been found, he wasn't sure any more. Until they had a more positive identification, as Barrington correctly said, they should keep quiet about the whole thing. News of dead bodies being discovered always spread like wildfire, especially in small local communities. Even more so when the body in question was that of an attractive young woman, and Tanner knew that the last thing such an investigation needed was for harmful rumours and speculation to begin circulating about a possible identity, whether or not the victim had been murdered, and if so, who the killer was most likely to be. So instead of answering, he decided to change the course of the conversation. 'I understand you were able to speak to your wife's parents.'

'Sorry, I forgot to tell you. I spoke to her father this morning, shortly after you left, but he didn't know where she was either.'

'To be honest, Mr Richardson, we already knew that. Mr Lambert called the station himself.'

'He did say that he would. I assumed he'd tell you that I'd spoken to him.'

'And you didn't think it necessary to tell us who he was?'

'No, why? Should I have done?'

'Well, Mr Richardson, when the daughter of a wealthy man goes missing, there is another possibility as to her whereabouts, other than that she decided to stay over at a friend's house and had forgotten to tell you.'

'Sorry, I'm not with you.'

'That someone may have kidnapped her!'

Richardson stared at him. 'Do you think that's what's happened – that she's been kidnapped?'

'At the moment, we're simply keeping all possibilities open, but it would have been useful to have known who her father was when we first spoke, certainly before he had a chance to put a call into the station to tell us himself!'

'Of course, yes, sorry.'

'Anyway,' Tanner continued, 'have you been able to get hold of her friends yet?'

'A couple, but they've not heard from her.'

'And what about other family members?'

'Jane's father said he was going to give them a call.'

'Do you know if he has?'

'I don't. Sorry.'

'What about male friends?'

'What about them?' questioned Richardson, in a defensive tone.

'Does your wife have any?'

'You mean - do I think she might have run off with one of them?'

'As I said earlier, Mr Richardson, we're just trying to keep all possibilities open.'

'Well, she's never mentioned any, but then I suppose if she was having an affair with one of them, she probably wouldn't, would she!'

'So you don't know of any then?'

'I don't. The only one she's ever talked about was some guy from university.'

'And what was his name?'

'Phil, I think.'

'How about a surname?'

'No idea.'

'I assume you don't know where he lives either?'

'I think she mentioned somewhere in London.'

'Well, that certainly narrows it down,' said Tanner, with a thick layer of sarcasm.

'Look, I'm sorry, but as I've said before, I don't hang out with my wife's friends, so how the hell should I know what they're all called, or where they all live?'

Tanner hadn't meant to have been quite so facetious, but he was becoming increasingly frustrated by the fact that Richardson hardly seemed to know a single thing about his own wife; what jewellery she wore, who her friends were, or even if any of them were men.

Deciding it was probably best to call it a day, Tanner said, 'OK, that will do for now, Mr Richardson. But if you do think of anyone she might be staying with, or anything at all, please let us know.'

- CHAPTER FIFTEEN -

A S THEY WALKED over to where Tanner had parked the car, Jenny said, 'I was a little surprised by his response to the jewellery. I'd have thought he'd have been able to recognise them if they had been his wife's.'

'I think it's a man thing,' replied Tanner.

'A man thing?'

'You know; like in the way a woman would see flowers in a room the moment she walked in, whereas a man probably wouldn't, even if they stood on a pedestal right in the middle, and were lit by a spotlight.'

'I thought we were talking about jewellery?'

To help clarify his remark, he said, 'I'd say it's fairly normal for a man not to be able to recognise his wife's jewellery, unless of course the item had some sort of special significance, or was something she'd wear all the time. It's just not something us men pay much attention to, I'm afraid.'

'You're saying that men aren't interested in jewellery?'

'I don't think most of us are, no.'

'I see,' said Jenny. 'So if I was to offer to buy you a really expensive watch, for example, you wouldn't be interested?'

'I don't think watches count as jewellery, so if you'd like to buy me one, feel free!'

They smiled briefly over at each other; then after a moment's pause, Jenny said, 'I've been thinking about what Burgess said earlier, about where the body was found.'

'Oh, yes. What about it?'

'You know how he said that she couldn't have fallen in the river along here, because if she had, she'd have had to have floated up the Thurne to have been found where she was?'

'And that things can't float upriver. How could I forget?'

'Well, I've had a bit of a think about it, and I'm not sure he's right.'

Reaching the driver's side door, he looked at her over the XJS's low sleek roof. 'So you're suggesting that the body *could* have floated upriver?'

'I am.'

'Even though he said it would go against the laws of physics for it to do so, which I must admit did sound like rather a convincing argument.'

'Yes, but he was forgetting that the Broads are tidal, especially at this time of year. If the tide was coming in at the right time, the body could have easily been carried up the Thurne.'

'Are you sure?'

'I'm fairly sure, but only if the tide was coming in at the time.'

'Why wouldn't Burgess have known about that?'

'Well, he's from Norwich. He's not a Horning girl, like me.'

'No kidding!'

'He's also not a sailor. And you can't sail on the Broads without knowing something about the tides.'

'And you *are* a sailor, I take it?'

'Well, yes, although I can't say I had much choice in the matter. My dad made sure of it. According to my parents, I could sail before I could ride a bike.'

'You can ride a bike as well!'

Jenny narrowed her eyes at him, before the corners of her lips creased up into an amused smile, winning her a grin in return before he ducked to climb inside.

As he started the engine, Tanner said, 'If you know so much about sailing, maybe you should come round to my place sometime.'

'And why's that?' replied Jenny, clipping on her seatbelt. 'I suppose you're going to tell me that you live on a boat?'

'Er, actually, I do!'

'You live on a boat?' she repeated, staring over at him.

'An old wooden sailing-type one, yes.'

'What, by choice?'

'Well, sort of, although I must admit that had I known how small it was going to be, I'd have found a flat instead.'

'How on earth did you end up living on a boat?'

'It's a long story,' Tanner replied. 'But for now, I think we'd better get back to the station and let Barrington know that DI Burgess isn't quite the local he thought he was.'

With that, he reversed the car off the grass verge, executed a perfect three-point turn, and drove back down the narrow un-tarmacked track, heading for Wroxham Police Station.

- CHAPTER SIXTEEN -

B Y THE TIME they'd left Richardson's house, it had already gone five o'clock. Feeling both tired and hungry, they decided to stop off at a garage on the way back to pick up coffee and a snack.

Walking into Wroxham Police Station about ten minutes later, coffees in hand, Tanner told Jenny that she'd better stick around for a while before heading for home, just until he had a chance to catch up with Barrington. He crossed to his superior's office, noting on the way that Burgess wasn't at his desk.

Before knocking, he took a quick peek through the glass partition. Inside he could see Burgess, sitting with one leg crossed over the other, chatting to Barrington. Thinking it would probably be better to leave them to it, he was about to turn away when Barrington saw him standing there and beckoned him inside.

With a reluctant sigh, he pushed open the door.

'Ah, Tanner, we were just talking about you!'

'Nothing good, I hope,' replied Tanner, which was about the only response he could think of that didn't make him sound like he was being unnecessarily paranoid.

Not getting the fact that he'd meant it as a joke, albeit a rather poor one, Barrington said, 'No, no, nothing like that. Take a seat, won't you.'

Still carrying his coffee, Tanner entered, and closed the door behind him. He pulled out the free chair, away from Burgess and the desk, as Barrington said, 'DI Burgess was just giving me an update on the girl's body.'

Sitting down and crossing his legs, Tanner suddenly found he was very curious to know what the other officer had been saying. So he looked directly at Burgess, raised his eyebrows and said, 'Oh, yes?'

'I was just telling DCI Barrington,' began Burgess, looking particularly smug, 'that at this stage, there's no evidence to suggest that it's anything other than an accidental drowning.'

'Apart from the marks on her neck and the wound to her forehead,' interjected Tanner.

'Which Dr Johnstone thinks could have easily been caused by her having tripped over and hitting her head on a cleat, before becoming entangled in a mooring line,' rebutted Burgess, his self-satisfied smile turning into more of a sneer.

Apparently unaware of the tension that had grown between his two DIs during the course of the day, Barrington told Tanner, 'And Burgess doesn't seem to think that there's any connection between the woman's body and the missing person.'

By way of confirmation, Burgess nodded and said, 'That's correct, sir.'

Turning to him, Barrington asked, 'Are we anywhere nearer to being able to identify who the dead girl is?'

'I'm afraid not, sir. As I mentioned on the phone, there was no ID found either on or about her. Neither were there any tattoos or distinguishing marks. And the photograph we had of the missing person bore little resemblance. All we have are the items of jewellery, and we're still waiting for Dr Johnstone to send back the wedding and engagement rings, which he was unable to remove on site.'

Looking at Tanner, Barrington asked, 'Were you at least able to show the other items of jewellery to the missing girl's husband?'

'We've just come back from there now, sir,' replied Tanner.

'And…?'

'Mr Richardson, the husband, said that both the earring and the necklace *could* have belonged to his wife, but he wasn't one hundred percent sure. He did think that they were the sort of thing she would wear, it's just that he didn't recognise either of them as definitely belonging to her.'

'How soon until we get the results from the post mortem?' Barrington asked Burgess.

'I was told first thing in the morning, sir, as long as nothing unexpected crops up.'

'Well, let's hope not!'

Turning his attention back to Tanner, Barrington asked, 'Any news on Mr Lambert's daughter?'

'You mean, assuming she's not the girl we just pulled out of the river?'

Burgess couldn't help himself, and blurted out, 'We've already established that she wasn't, or at least that she wasn't likely to be!'

'Well, yes,' began Tanner. 'And if it wasn't for the fact that they're both married women, of a similar age, with similar hair colouring, and the dead girl's time of death coincides almost exactly with the time the missing girl was last seen, then I'd have to agree with you.'

Acutely aware that Tanner was being sarcastic, Burgess said, 'But you just said that the husband wasn't even able to recognise his wife's own jewellery!'

'I actually said that he wasn't *sure* if it was hers. But as he'd already admitted to not having had a particularly close relationship with her, it didn't surprise me that he wasn't.'

'And the photograph of the missing girl,' added Burgess, looking straight at Barrington. 'She didn't look anything like the woman we found!'

Shrugging his shoulders, Tanner replied, 'After floating upside down in a river for two days and being sucked into a propeller, to be honest, I'd have been surprised if they *had* looked the same!'

Burgess didn't seem to have an answer to that one, so Tanner went on, 'Then of course there's the place we found the earring, under the railway bridge.'

'Which DI Tanner should mention did *not* match the one the dead girl was wearing!'

'No,' agreed Tanner, 'but as I said before, we did find what I still believe to be blood close to it, and as it's along the route the missing girl is thought to have taken on her way back from work, the time of which coincides with the time the dead girl is thought to have died, then I think there is a very strong possibility that the two are one and the same.'

Glaring at him, in an accusatory tone Burgess said, 'There's something DI Tanner has neglected to mention, sir.'

With his elbows on the desk, and his hands steepled together, Barrington asked, 'And what's that?'

'That the girl's body was found in the River Thurne, up from where it meets the Bure, where he's suggesting his missing girl went in. And that would mean she'd have had to have floated *upriver*, which I believe would be a scientific first.'

It was time for Tanner to play his trump card. After waiting for just a fraction of a second, he looked over at Burgess and said, 'But I thought the Broads were tidal?'

As Burgess exchanged an anxious glance between Tanner and Barrington, all he could say in response was, 'Well, yes, but...'

Seeing the Ordnance Survey map of the Broads which Barrington had mounted to the wall behind him, Tanner stood up from his chair, stepped over to it and said, 'Assuming they are tidal, if a body went into the river on Saturday night, here,' and he pointed at the railway bridge that went over the River Bure, just outside Wroxham, and traced the river all the way east, to where it was joined by the River Thurne, 'if it was here when the tide started to come in, then it could have easily been carried up to where it was found.'

Whilst Burgess fumed with indignation at having been made to look like a complete idiot by some London DI who hadn't even finished his first day working for Norfolk Police, Barrington meanwhile couldn't help but be impressed.

Seeing the scowl Burgess was giving Tanner, unable to suppress an amused smile Barrington said, 'You seem to have come to grips with the Broads rather quickly, Tanner.'

Feeling a twinge of guilt for having been so

successful in making Burgess out to be both incompetent and stupid, Tanner said, 'I can't take the credit. It was DC Evans who suggested it.'

'Well, I've always said that it's all about local knowledge. And you can't get much more local than Jenny, isn't that right, Burgess!'

'Yes, sir,' replied Burgess, and in an effort to hide his embarrassed indignation, forced a thin smile for his boss.

'OK,' continued Barrington. 'But all that means at this stage is that there's a slightly increased chance the dead girl is John Lambert's daughter. Even if that is the case, there's still not enough evidence to suggest anything other than she had one drink too many after work and tripped over a mooring line on the way home. And as I've no intention of launching a full-scale murder inquiry until I know otherwise, we're just going to have to sit tight and wait for that post mortem report to come in.'

- CHAPTER SEVENTEEN -

WITH THE MEETING over, avoiding eye contact with Burgess, Tanner headed out to make a beeline to where Jenny was sitting.

Seeing him approach, she smiled at him and asked, 'How'd it go?'

'They're still holding out hope that the girl's body *isn't* that of John Lambert's daughter.'

'Did you tell them about the tides, and how that could have carried her upriver?'

Sitting on the corner of the desk, he glanced casually around the room to make sure nobody could overhear, before leaning in to say, 'I did, yes, and thank you for that. But as far as Barrington is concerned, all that means is that there's a slightly increased chance that she is Jane Richardson, and if that's the case, then she's most likely to have simply tripped over on her way home from work.'

'What about the mark on her forehead, and the ones around her neck?'

'Burgess told him what the medical examiner had said about how she could have hit her head on either a cleat or a boat stanchion before becoming entangled in a mooring line, and Barrington seems happy enough to go along with that.'

'Well, it's possible, I suppose.'

'The alternative is that she was deliberately hit with something like a hammer, strangled, and then dumped in the water, and I'm not sure Barrington is quite ready to accept that as being a more likely alternative; at least not yet, he isn't.'

'So, what happens now?'

'He said that we're going to have to wait until the post mortem report comes back before we do anything else. But personally, between now and then, I think we should do a little digging of our own.'

With a suspicious frown, Jenny asked, 'What did you have in mind?'

After glancing around the office again, in a low conspiratorial voice, Tanner asked, 'Would it be possible for you to get those three items of jewellery over to forensics, to see if they come up with anything?'

Reaching down to retrieve her handbag, she said, 'Our forensics department is in our Head Office in Norwich, so it will take a while.'

'Can't you get them biked over?'

'I can,' she said. 'But shouldn't we ask Burgess before we do that?'

'Probably,' replied Tanner, before reaching into his inside jacket pocket to pull out another evidence bag which he discreetly passed over. 'And could you send this to them as well?'

Staring down at it, Jenny asked, 'What is it?'

'It's the sample of what we thought was blood that I took from under the railway bridge. If it is, and if it matches the dead girl's, then we'll have a pretty good idea as to who she is.'

As Jenny took the bag off him to place together

with the other items, Tanner looked down at his watch and said, 'Then I suggest we begin to request access to our missing girl's personal accounts, including her financial records.'

'Without asking either Burgess or Barrington?'

'Don't worry. I've a sneaking suspicion they'll be thanking us, probably about thirty seconds after that post mortem report comes in.'

- CHAPTER EIGHTEEN -

AFTER JENNY HAD quietly arranged for a police motorcycle courier to take the four evidence bags over to Norfolk Constabulary's Head Office in Norwich, they spent half an hour moving her desk over next to Tanner's, whilst waiting for Barrington to leave, which he did just before six.

Ten minutes later he was followed by Burgess, along with a number of others, which left only a handful of uniformed constables to cover the night shift.

With the missing girl's details that Richardson had given them when they'd first been to his house, only then did they begin the tedious task of contacting various organisations to gain access to her phone, email and social media accounts.

By half past seven they'd been allowed into everything apart from her financial records. For those they'd have to contact the local magistrate to put forward a formal request, and they'd definitely need DCI Barrington's authorisation before doing that. But with her mobile phone details, access to both her personal and work email accounts, Facebook, Instagram and web browsing history going back six months, they had more than enough to be getting on with; too much for them to cope with on their own.

With the feeling that they were a little more prepared for what they thought would happen when the post mortem report arrived, they decided to call it a day.

Stepping out into the carpark at the front of the building, they were met by a magnificent sunset, one that spanned the entire Norfolk horizon before them.

'That's quite something!' exclaimed Tanner, whose view of the sky was normally obscured by sprawling housing developments and over-sized concrete tower blocks.

After nothing more than a cursory glance, Jenny said, 'I'd say that's about average; but there is something I wouldn't mind seeing, though.'

As Tanner continued to take in the full panorama of the setting sun, somewhat absently he asked, 'What's that?'

'Your boat!'

Until then, Tanner had almost forgotten that he had a boat to go home to, and not a house or a flat like most normal people.

'Ah that! Yes, well, I should have told you that it's not mine. I'm just looking after it for a friend.'

'I'd still like to see it,' insisted Jenny. 'Whereabouts is it moored?'

'Er…' began Tanner, trying to remember the name of the place. 'It's Ramworth Broad, I think.'

'I suspect you mean *Ran*worth Broad,' corrected Jenny, 'although there aren't any moorings there. It's the home of the Broads Wildlife Centre. You probably mean the one opposite; Malthouse Broad, with the cute little post office and the Maltsters pub behind.'

'So you don't know it then?'

Enjoying his off-beat, bone dry sense of humour, which reminded her a lot of her dad's, she said, 'Why don't you show me?'

Glancing down at his watch, he said, 'It's getting late. It will probably be dark by the time we get there.'

'Tell you what, how about you follow me there? That way you're less likely to get lost. And if your car breaks down, or runs out of petrol, both of which seem highly likely, given what you're driving, then I'd be able to call the AA for you. And all I'd ask in return is that you buy me dinner at the Maltsters pub.'

Jenny was about as audacious as she was attractive, and Tanner was finding it very difficult not to like her, more than perhaps he thought he should, given that she must be a good fifteen years younger than him.

Attempting to keep that firmly in mind, with a warm smile he said, 'OK, you're on! But if your car breaks down or runs out of petrol before mine does, then *you're* the one who's buying the dinner!'

'Fair enough,' said Jenny. 'But that's not going to happen. I'm in the VW Golf, and I only filled it up yesterday.'

- CHAPTER NINETEEN -

ARRIVING AT MALTHOUSE Broad, Tanner gave Jenny the grand tour of his new floating home by the light of his phone's torch. As he did so, she attempted to explain to him some of the basic principles of how he'd be able to sail it, were he to ever have a go.

The conversation continued over dinner at the Maltsters pub, during which Jenny resorted to using a pen and a napkin in an effort to explain how a boat was able to tack upwind. Although Tanner got the idea that it involved a lot of zig-zagging, the principles behind how a sail worked with the keel to drive the boat forward were completely lost on him. Eventually Jenny was forced to give up, giving Tanner the chance to steer the conversation over to her.

They spent the next hour or so chatting about what life was like being brought up on the Broads; how her father had taught her to sail, and how he'd driven her around the country to compete in various national events, first in an Optimist dinghy, then in a Topper. She'd kept sailing competitively until she'd completed her A-Levels, after which university beckoned and she'd moved down to Southampton.

'What did you study down there?' asked Tanner, who'd been listening with genuine, if not jealous interest. His childhood had consisted of nothing more than riding his bike around and playing Asteroids on his Atari.

'Environmental Science.'

'And yet now you're a Detective Constable for Norfolk Police,' he observed with a wry smile.

'Yes, well, to be honest I found the subject insanely boring, and I thought that if I was bored after studying it for four years, I couldn't imagine how I'd feel if I took it up as a profession. And besides, I couldn't find a job, nothing that offered a sensible salary at any rate.'

'So how did you find your way into the police?'

'I don't know really. I'd always seen them around, patrolling the waterways. I suppose I thought that if that's all they do – drive a boat up and down the Broads – then it was the perfect job for me! I went along to one of their open evenings, and I suppose I let them talk me into it.'

'And then you decided to join CID, and become a detective?'

Jenny shrugged. 'I'd been working as a PC for nearly five years by then. It's all right during the summer, when all the tourists are here, but there really isn't all that much to do during the winter months, and I was getting bored. So I applied for the twelve week TDC course, which I enjoyed, and here I am!'

'How long ago was that?' asked Tanner, who by then had already worked out that if she was twenty-two after four years at university and had spent five years working as a PC, she must be either twenty-seven or twenty-eight.

'I finished in November of last year, so I'm still finding my feet, although, to be honest, there hasn't been all that much going on since then, not until today, that is.'

As she took a sip from her coffee, she realised that she'd spent virtually the entire evening talking about herself. Concerned that Tanner would think she was inexcusably selfish for having done so, along with being quite possibly the most boring person he'd ever had to have dinner with, she turned the spotlight back on him. 'How about you. Why did you join?'

'I'm not sure I had much choice. My father was in the Force, and I suppose it was just expected of me. I can't imagine what else I'd have done.'

'Do you enjoy it?' she asked, watching him over the top of her coffee cup.

'At first I did,' he replied, 'but it does tend to wear you down after a while, especially in London. I think it was when my father passed away that it dawned on me that I'd probably only signed up because he'd wanted me to, not necessarily because *I* did. That was about ten years ago, but by then it was too late for a career change, or at least I felt it was. My wife wasn't working at the time, so I was the sole earner.'

'You're married?' she asked, as casually as she thought possible, and stole another glance at his left hand, which was still devoid of any kind of a wedding ring.

'Divorced,' Tanner said. 'We'd been struggling for a long time, but it was when…it was when our…'

He hesitated, and then stopped to stare down at the coffee cup he cradled in his hands. He wanted to tell her about his daughter, or more specifically about what had happened to her, but now that the time had come, it felt too soon. Far too soon. He'd only known Jenny for a day, and even though it had been an unusually long one, a day was still a day, and it was hardly enough of an acquaintance to open up your soul to anyone. But despite that, here they were, chatting over dinner, like two old friends who'd not seen each other for years and were busy catching up.

'It was when something happened that, well, it changed things, and was ultimately what made me put in for a transfer.'

His reluctance was obvious, and Jenny didn't want to pry. At that stage, she wasn't even sure she wanted to know. Although they were clearly getting along, she felt there were definite limits to how much someone should know about another person's life quite so early on in a relationship. She was also afraid that whatever it was that he'd nearly told her could be something that would detract from how she was beginning to feel towards him. With those thoughts weaving their way through her mind, she decided to steer the conversation away from whatever it was that had such a troubling impact on his life. Hopefully there'd be other opportunities for him to tell her, but preferably when they knew each other a little better.

'And now you're here, what do you think?'

Grateful for having been led away from the subject, he said, 'Well, I certainly wasn't expecting to be involved with a dead body, not on my first day at least!'

'I suspect you've been unlucky – or lucky, depending on your point of view. We usually only have a couple of people drown each year, and generally it's because they've had too much to drink and either fall in or decide to go for an impromptu swim.'

'What about this one?' he asked, interested to hear her thoughts in a more relaxed, social environment.

'I'm not sure,' she replied. 'To be honest, it's usually bodies of men we find ourselves having to drag out of the water, and the incidents are normally reported immediately by someone who's witnessed the event first hand, either the victim's friends or family. This one is obviously different.'

'What's your gut feeling?'

'My gut feeling?' she repeated. 'My gut feeling is that I probably shouldn't have had the chocolate fudge pudding!'

The comment had Tanner nearly snorting coffee out through his nose. 'Surprisingly, I meant about the case!'

'Oh, that!'

She thought seriously for a moment. 'My gut feeling is that the body of the woman is our missing person, and that there's no way she tripped over on the way back from work.'

'And why's that?'

'It's the marks on the neck. It's one thing to fall over and hit your head on a cleat, but it's quite another to then become entangled in a loose mooring line. And if that blood you found does belong to the victim, then there's no way that's what happened. You can't fall over, hit your head on something hard, get back up again, wander over to the other side of the path, bleed for a bit, and then wander right back to fall in the water, somewhere where there's a loose mooring line waiting for you to become entangled with.'

After a momentary pause, she added, 'There's something else as well.'

'What's that?'

'There are no cleats under the railway bridge, or anywhere along that stretch of the river. The nearest one would be the concrete moorings in Wroxham.'

Thinking about work again, and the day ahead, Tanner checked his watch. Shocked to see that it was nearly eleven o'clock, he said, 'It's getting late.'

Looking up, he caught the eye of a passing waiter and signalled to him that they wanted the bill.

Pulling out his wallet in preparation for paying, Tanner asked, 'Shall I call you a cab?'

'To be honest, I'd prefer to be called Jenny.'

It was Tanner's turn to narrow his eyes at her.

'Sorry,' she said, in an apologetic tone. More seriously she replied, 'Thank you, but no. I'll be fine driving. I only had one glass.'

They took a moment to smile across the table at each other, each allowing themselves to entertain the same thought before dismissing it a second later. As far as Tanner was concerned, if it was too soon to talk to her openly about his recent past, then it was definitely too soon for anything else.

Their thoughts were interrupted by the waiter placing a silver tray on the table with a printed bill. Removing his credit card, Tanner glanced briefly at the total, raising an eyebrow as he did. It wasn't much less than he was used to paying in London. Somehow he'd thought that being located in the middle of virtually nowhere would mean the cost of a meal would be significantly reduced. Putting that down to his own naivety, that and the fact that he'd hardly travelled around the UK before, he placed the credit card down and began to think of the day ahead, and more immediately of the practicalities of preparing for his second night sleeping aboard his hopefully temporary home.

- CHAPTER TWENTY -

Tuesday, 16th April

HAVING SAID A rather formal goodbye to each other in the gravel-lined carpark outside the Maltsters pub, Tanner watched Jenny climb into her car to begin her journey home, before heading over to his temporary floating retreat.

After shoehorning himself into bed, for the second night in a row he found himself being lulled by the rhythmic sound of water, as it gently lapped against the hull of the boat. He didn't stir again until the following morning, when the sound of his phone's alarm brought him out of another deep, dreamless sleep.

He trudged to and from the marina's shower block, made himself a coffee and dressed in his creased suit, and by just after half past eight he was driving in towards Wroxham Police Station to begin his second day working for Norfolk Constabulary.

His intention was to be at his desk by a quarter to nine, but heavy traffic over Wroxham Bridge and beyond slowed his progress. It was only when he was stop-starting his way up the road towards the station that he worked out the reason. Parked on the kerb directly outside the station was a large white news media van with 'BBC East' displayed on the back.

Beyond that, a small group of reporters had gathered. Although the van wasn't blocking the road, judging by the way everyone was slowing down to take a look at what it was doing there, it was fairly obvious it had caused the long tailback.

Turning in to the almost full car park, acutely aware he was being both filmed and photographed, he noticed that not only was Jenny's car already there, but so was Burgess's and just about everyone else's. With the sudden feeling that he was late, he parked up and hurried inside, doing his best to ignore the small gaggle of reporters as he did so.

The main office bustled with activity.

Instinctively, Tanner looked round for Jenny, but her desk was empty. Remembering they'd moved her the evening before, he was relieved to see her now familiar dark brown leather coat and handbag slung over the chair next to his.

Assuming she was making herself a coffee, he nudged past her chair to get to his own desk. He'd only just sat down and turned his computer on, when she emerged from the kitchen carrying two mugs.

Reaching the desk, she asked, 'Milk, no sugar?'

'Er, thanks, Jenny,' he said, taking the one he was being offered. 'But how did you..?'

With a flirtatious smile, she replied, 'You look like a milk, no sugar sort of a guy. And I assumed you'd be needing one after spending another night on board that boat of yours.'

Returning her smile, he said, 'Actually, I slept really well!'

'Liar!'

Feeling like he was back in the school playground,

he retorted, 'I did!'

Examining his face, she frowned and said, 'I'm not convinced, I'm afraid. But I suppose you'll just have to prove it to me one day,' and gave him a highly suggestive wink.

Tanner could feel himself blush, something else that reminded him of being back at school. Jenny was nothing if not forward, and he took a sip from his coffee, hoping she hadn't noticed.

Fortunately she seemed to have other things on her mind, as she leaned in towards him and asked, 'Did you hear?'

'Hear what?' he answered, in a similar hushed tone.

'The post mortem report's come back.'

Unsure why they were whispering, he leaned forward himself and asked, 'What did it say?'

'I don't know, but Burgess is holding a station-wide briefing at nine o'clock.'

Curious to know why nobody had told him, Tanner glanced down at his watch, and seeing that it was about one minute to, said, 'So we were right then!'

'Looks like it!'

At that moment they saw Barrington come marching out of his office, heading over towards the white board at the end of the room. There he was joined by Burgess. After a brief consultation, during which it looked as if Burgess was being instructed by Barrington as to who was going to say what, and when, Barrington turned to face his audience. 'May I have everyone's attention, please?'

Almost immediately the various conversations subsided, and everyone looked to where Barrington and Burgess were standing, both wearing similar expressions of stern resolution.

In a commanding voice that carried effortlessly to the back of the room, Barrington began his address.

'I'm sure you're all aware by now that yesterday afternoon the body of a young woman was found in the River Thurne, just down from Thurne Dyke Mill. We've yet to formally identify her, but the full post mortem report has now come in, and it's not good, I'm afraid. According to our forensics medical examiner, Dr Johnstone, the probable cause of death was asphyxiation from strangulation, not drowning as was first thought.'

Barrington paused for a moment to allow a few whispered remarks to circumnavigate the office, before continuing.

'She'd also received a serious blow to the top of the forehead, caused by some sort of blunt instrument. Dr Johnstone believes this was too severe to have been caused by her tripping over and hitting her head. The angle of the indentation also suggests that she was struck from above, which again is not consistent with someone having tripped. He does believe, however, that she was struck on the head *before* being strangled, which leads to the theory that her death was very much intentional.' To help clarify this statement, Barrington added, 'Had she been the victim of a mugging, then it would seem unlikely that the assailant would remain at the scene to strangle her until she was dead.'

Barrington deliberately paused to let that sink in.

'Unfortunately, there is another aspect to this young woman's death which is even more disturbing.'

The office fell into a hollow, expectant silence.

'Dr Johnstone believes that she was sexually assaulted, but that it took place post mortem.'

As virtually everyone in the office began talking at the same time, Jenny leaned in to Tanner to ask, 'I assume that means someone had sex with her *after* she'd been killed?'

Tanner replied with a single nod, before they turned their attention back to the front of the office.

Raising his hands for quiet, Barrington continued, 'Detective Inspector Burgess will be leading the investigation, under my command of course, so I'll now hand over to him.'

Burgess was about to take over the briefing when he heard Barrington say, 'But before I do, due to the serious nature of this crime, I just want to add that Detective Inspector Tanner will be working alongside him.'

Burgess shot Barrington a look of vehement disbelief, before finding Tanner's face in the audience and scowling at him.

It was fairly obvious to Tanner, and to everyone else, that Burgess hadn't been included in that decision, although in fairness, neither had Tanner. But he could see why Barrington had decided not to tell Burgess beforehand. Doing so would have given him the opportunity to change Barrington's mind on the subject, as had happened before.

Looking around at his two detective inspectors, Barrington said, 'I assume you're both OK with that?'

Neither Tanner nor Burgess was particularly happy with the decision, Burgess considerably less so than Tanner, but the way they'd been told left them little choice but to accept with a gracious nod and a forced smile.

'One more thing,' said Barrington.

As Burgess began to wonder if he was ever going to be allowed to speak, Barrington went on, 'It's highly likely that this investigation is going to attract considerable media interest. As many of you will have seen on your way in, there's already a BBC East news van parked outside. God knows how they heard about it so quickly, but anyway, I hope it goes without saying that under absolutely *no* circumstances are any of you allowed to talk to them about this case, or any other news organisation for that matter! I also expect you to be discreet when discussing the case with family and friends. And no mention of it is to be made on social media in any shape, manner or form. We all know what a small community the Broads is, and there will be enough rumours flying around without you lot adding to them. Is that understood?'

Barrington glared around the office at everyone as they all either nodded their understanding or verbally agreed.

'Right,' said Barrington, turning to Burgess. 'Carry on.'

'Thank you, sir,' acknowledged Burgess, and took a step forward.

'Our first priority is to identify the body. There was no ID found on her, neither were there any tattoos or other distinguishing marks. The only things we found were some items of jewellery: wedding and engagement rings, one earring and a necklace. Now, as many of you know, a young woman of similar age was reported missing yesterday morning, which DI Tanner and DC Evans have been looking into.'

Directing his attention towards Jenny, Burgess asked, 'Has there been any further news on that since yesterday?'

After glancing over at Tanner, as if seeking permission to answer, Jenny looked back at Burgess to say, 'Not yet, sir, no. As you know, we showed the necklace and earring to the husband yesterday, but he was unable to confirm that they belonged to his wife. The wedding and engagement rings still haven't come back from the medical examiner's office, so we need to chase those up. As far as I know, the husband is still checking with family and friends. We'll give him a call straight after this to see if he's had any luck.'

'OK. Let me know what he says.'

Sensing he was about to move on, half raising his hand, Tanner asked, 'Shouldn't we invite him in to see if he can identify the body?'

'Only if we had a good enough reason to believe that it's his wife,' replied Burgess.

'But...don't we?' questioned Tanner.

After a conspiratorial glance over at DCI Barrington, which led Tanner to believe they'd discussed the idea prior to the briefing, Burgess came back, 'Had he been able to recognise the jewellery, then maybe, yes, but at the moment, the only similarities are that both women are of around the same age.'

'Along with sharing the same hair and skin colouring, and the fact that the woman died at around about the same time as our missing girl was last seen.'

Entering the discussion, DCI Barrington said, 'I think there's also a concern that the husband may not be able to identify the body due to the state of physical decomposition.'

That was at least a fair comment, but Tanner knew from experience that it wouldn't prevent someone close to the victim from being able to make a positive ID, no matter how upsetting it would be for them to do so, and with that in mind he asked, 'But wouldn't it be helpful to try? The alternative would be to ask either him or her parents for the name of her dentist, or to start a search for samples of her DNA.'

Since reading through the post mortem report with DI Burgess twenty minutes earlier to discover to his horror that it was going to be a full-on murder investigation after all, Barrington had been desperately hoping that the dead girl wouldn't turn out to be the daughter of John Lambert; but just because he didn't want her to be, unfortunately didn't mean that she wasn't. It would clearly be better for them to find out, one way or the other, and the sooner they did, the sooner they'd be able to bring the matter to a close. So going back on what he'd agreed with DI Burgess before the briefing, he said, 'OK, you'd better ask him if he's willing,' and turned back to Burgess.

Accepting the fact that he was probably going to have to allow Simon Richardson to try to identify the body, Burgess let it go. 'One thing that's yet to be mentioned is that we've been lucky enough to have recovered a sample of semen from inside the victim, and due to the sexual element of this attack, there's a very high probability that it belongs to the assailant. DS Cooper and DS Gilbert, I'd like you to start talking to every known sex offender in the area, at least those who've displayed an interest in women. Find out where they were on Saturday night between the hours of ten and eleven, and then ask them if they know of anyone with any unusual preferences, necrophilia in particular. Also, run a search for the same through the Police National Database. See if any live nearby, or have recently moved into the area.'

Half raising his hand again, Tanner asked, 'As a sample of semen's been found, shouldn't we collect DNA from Simon Richardson?'

'Are you suggesting he's a suspect?' questioned Burgess.

'If the body does turn out to be his wife, then I'd put him at the top of the list!'

Grudgingly, Burgess said, 'OK, but only if he identifies her as being his wife.'

After nodding his acknowledgement, Tanner asked, 'I don't suppose anything came back on the jewellery we sent over to forensics last night?'

Burgess wasn't even aware it had been sent over, but neither had he thought to ask, and in the light of recent developments, he knew that was an oversight on his behalf. Not wishing to raise attention to it, even though he knew Tanner must have sent them over without asking permission first, he said, 'Er...not yet, no.'

'And how about the blood sample we collected from underneath Wroxham Railway Bridge?' asked Tanner again. In light of the post mortem's findings, he knew it was now potentially a key piece of evidence. 'If it matches the blood of the victim, not only will it give us the murder scene, but as it's along the route we believe our missing girl took after work on Saturday night, it could give us a positive ID on the body as well.'

Inwardly, Burgess was beginning to fume with embarrassed indignation. This new DI from London seemed to be permanently outthinking him.

Keeping his anger in check, Burgess simply decided to proceed on the basis that he knew about both the jewellery *and* the blood having been sent to forensics, and so with an indignant glare, replied, 'I'm fully aware of that, thank you, Tanner! But again, I've heard nothing back on either the jewellery or the blood, so I suggest you make it your priority to chase them up.'

Burgess deliberately paused for a moment, before continuing.

'OK, that's just about it, but before you go, there's one more thing that came up in the post mortem. Regrettably, Dr Johnstone also discovered that the murder victim was pregnant. '

Everyone turned to stare at the person sitting next to them.

'He's estimating she was about midway through; somewhere between fourteen to twenty-seven weeks.'

In the silence that followed, Jenny whispered over to Tanner, 'Why didn't Richardson tell us?'

It was a very good question, and immediately cast a doubt in Tanner's mind that the murder victim was their missing person; otherwise her husband would surely have mentioned it at their very first meeting.

The significance of the news wasn't lost on DI Burgess either, and with a thin, vengeful smile aimed directly at his counterpart, he asked, 'I assume your missing woman wasn't?'

It was now Tanner's turn to look stupid.

'I, er…' he began, and after glancing briefly over at Jenny, said, 'Nothing about it was mentioned by her husband, no.'

'I see,' said Burgess, relishing the moment. 'And don't you think he would have done, had his wife been halfway through her pregnancy?'

With honest humility, Tanner replied, 'I must admit that I'd have thought he would have, yes.'

Feeling as if he'd won the day, and knowing full well that DCI Barrington was standing right next to him, watching his new DI being humiliated in front of the whole office, as he felt he himself had been a couple of minutes earlier, Burgess said, 'Well, maybe you can ask him about it when he comes in to look at the body of a pregnant women who it doesn't sound like he'd have seen before in his entire life!'

Leaping to Tanner's defence, Jenny called out, 'There is another alternative, sir!'

'And what's that, DC Evans?' asked Burgess.

'That he simply didn't know that she was!'

'Is that really very likely - that a husband wouldn't know his wife was halfway through her pregnancy?'

'Maybe not,' replied Jenny, 'But it's still a possibility.'

With a dismissive wave of his hand, Burgess said, 'Well anyway, if you're going to drag him to the morgue to take a look at her, maybe you can ask him on the way?'

Another pause followed, before Burgess called out, 'Right, that's it for now. Make sure you report back to me the moment you hear anything; and remember – no talking to the press!'

- CHAPTER TWENTY ONE -

THE BRIEFING OVER, Tanner and Jenny spent a few minutes discussing how best to go about asking Simon Richardson to help them identify the body. They knew they'd have to do so with both tact and discretion, because if it did turn out to be his wife, he'd naturally become a suspect in her murder, potentially the prime suspect. In that situation, it would become vitally important that they didn't give away information that could have a bearing on any future case made against him. So apart from deciding to withhold the details of her death to him, they decided to extend that to her pregnancy as well, at least until he'd viewed the body and they'd know if he was going to be a suspect or not.

The phone call went surprisingly well. Tanner told him nothing more than a body had been found that met the description of his wife, and that they needed his help to identify her. When he asked if they thought it was her, Tanner answered truthfully in that at that stage they didn't know.

After he agreed to help, Tanner arranged a time to meet him, gave him the address of the Norfolk Coroner's Office in Norwich, and that was that. Richardson didn't ask any more questions and remained calm throughout the conversation.

He arrived looking like he'd been awake half the night. It was evident he'd not shaved that morning, and his hair looked greasy and unwashed.

Tanner and Jenny had been shown where the body was going to be presented by one of Dr Johnstone's assistants, and they'd been waiting for him in reception.

Seeing him walk in, they stepped over to greet him. Tanner said, 'Mr Richardson, thank you for agreeing to come in. I know that this is difficult for you, but unfortunately it *is* necessary.'

In a quiet, unassuming voice, Richardson said, 'I understand, but…do you think it's her? Jane? I-I mean, my wife?'

'To be honest, Mr Richardson, at this stage we simply don't know, which is why we've asked you to come in.'

'Right!' he replied, and forced himself to stand up a little straighter, as he mentally prepared for the task ahead.

When he looked as ready as he could be for such a task, Tanner said, 'If you could follow me,' and led the way through to where the body had been prepared for viewing.

The room they entered was cold and sterile, with hard grey tiled walls and a cold grey floor. In the middle stood a long stainless-steel table on top of which was the outline of a body, draped from head to foot in a single white linen sheet. Behind that stood Dr Johnstone's assistant.

Tanner had been in similar rooms all too many times before, overseeing similar events, but this time it felt different. The last time had been when he'd been called in to formally identify his own daughter, which lent a more personal perspective to something that used to be just a formality.

With Jenny deliberately staying back beside the door, Tanner and Richardson stepped forward until they were standing alongside the table. Tanner turned his head to look at the man beside him, whose gaze was already fixed on where the face was hidden by the linen sheet.

'If you can, simply tell us if she's your wife or not. That's all we need to know.'

'I understand.'

Tanner nodded to the assistant, who reached over, took hold of the corners of the linen sheet, and gently pulled them back to reveal the woman's head.

Whoever had prepared the body for viewing had done a good job. Her skin was smooth and clean, less bloated than when Tanner had first seen her. And with her eyes closed and her hair brushed back, Tanner could more clearly see the resemblance to the photograph they had.

With his voice cracking as if he'd not uttered a word in years, Richardson said, 'It's her.'

'Are you sure?'

'It's definitely her,' he confirmed, still staring.

Tanner took a moment to study the man's face.

Behind his glasses, Richardson's eyes remained fixed, unblinking. His skin had lost its colour, his nostrils flared and he was biting down on his bottom lip. Tanner had seen the expression all too many times before. It was a confused mixture of shock, regret, desperation and loss. He'd even seen it on his own reflection staring back at him from his bathroom mirror, after arriving home that night, nine months before. It was a look which meant Simon Richardson cared deeply about what had happened to his wife, and Tanner knew that it was a difficult combination of emotions to fake. However, it didn't mean that he'd not had something to do with her death. The majority of the murder cases Tanner had been involved in were the tragic result of domestic disputes that had simply got way out of hand. And although there were times when the surviving partner attempted to cover up what had happened, there'd inevitably be that same look after the truth had come out.

With that very much at the forefront of his mind, Tanner thanked the assistant and gently led Richardson out of the room.

Once back in the corridor, with Jenny once more alongside, Tanner said, 'Thank you for doing that, Mr Richardson. I know it wasn't easy.'

But there the social pleasantries had to end. The man was now a suspect in a murder investigation. Consequently, after pausing for a moment, Tanner asked, 'You mentioned you were away at the weekend, playing golf. Do you mind telling us where that was, exactly?'

'Of course, yes, but didn't I already tell you?'

'You told us you were playing golf, but you didn't tell us where.'

'Oh right, I was at–' He stopped, and stared at Tanner. 'You don't think that I – I did *that* to her, do you?'

'For now, we simply need to eliminate you from our enquiries, that's all.'

'So you're saying that she was...?'

'All I'm prepared to say at the moment, Mr Richardson, is that we don't believe her death was accidental. Now if you could tell us where you were playing golf last weekend, that would be helpful.'

His eyes flickered briefly between Jenny and Tanner, before he said, 'I was at The Manor Resort. It's on the north coast, about an hour's drive from here.'

'For the whole weekend?'

'I was taking part in a golf tournament. It was a two-day event.'

'And where were you staying.'

'At the club. The Manor Resort is a hotel as well as a golf course.'

Glancing at Jenny to make sure she'd made a note of that, Tanner turned back to ask something he'd been wanting to know since he'd found out that morning.

'Were you aware, Mr Richardson, that your wife was pregnant?'

Richardson's head snapped around towards Tanner. As his face flushed with raw emotion, he stated, 'Of course I knew she was pregnant!' With tears welling up in his eyes, he added, 'Why wouldn't I have known she was pregnant?'

'Because you never mentioned it to us, Mr Richardson, which I must admit we all thought was rather odd.'

'Believe it or not, I don't go around telling complete strangers that my wife's pregnant! Would you?'

'If my wife had gone missing, and the police came round offering to help find her, then I think I would mention it, yes.'

'Well, I didn't! Why, is that a crime?'

'Er, no, Mr Richardson, it's just that it would have been useful to have known, that's all.'

'I see. So if I'd told you, then you wouldn't think I killed her. Is that what you're saying?'

Tanner shifted uncomfortably from one foot to another. The man did have a point. Would knowing she was pregnant have made any difference?

As he began to wonder if he himself would have told the police about such a thing, were he to have been in a similar situation, he asked, 'May I ask if the baby was planned?'

After continuing to glare at Tanner for another second, the resentment that had been etched on his face faded away to be replaced by a hopeless emptiness.

'We'd been trying for years,' he eventually said. 'Ever since we first got married.'

A moment of silence followed, before Tanner said, with genuine sincerity, 'I am sorry, Mr Richardson.'

There was no response to that, nor was any expected.

'There is just one more thing, Mr Richardson. I'm afraid we're going to need you to provide us with a DNA sample, as well as your fingerprints.'

Lost in thought, Richardson stared down at the floor, and barely loud enough to be heard, said, 'Of course, yes, I understand.'

In the silence that followed, Jenny led him away into another room, where she'd arranged for a forensics officer to meet with them.

- CHAPTER TWENTY TWO -

A S THEY CROSSED towards Tanner's XJS, in the far corner of the Coroner's Office carpark, Tanner asked Jenny, 'What did you think about what he said?'

'About why he didn't tell us his wife was pregnant?'

'No, I think that much was true. It was more what he was saying about the weekend.'

'Did you think he was lying?'

'Not so much lying, no. More that he was trying to hide something.'

'Maybe he's just really bad at playing golf,' said Jenny, 'and he doesn't want us to find out!'

Having spent the last few minutes in the same room as a dead body, she was keen to lighten the mood.

But a part of Tanner was still back in the Coroner's Office. Only half of him had heard what she'd said. The other half remained with Jane Richardson's body, wondering if it could have been her husband who'd murdered her.

Pulling out his phone, he said, 'I'd better give Barrington a call, to let him know the result.'

'Shouldn't you call Burgess instead?' she asked.

'I think I'd prefer to tell Barrington. I don't think Burgess will be too happy to find out that his murder victim is now my missing person.'

'I don't think Barrington's going to be too pleased either. Not when the girl's father is none other than John Lambert!'

'No, well, that can't be helped.'

Having added Barrington's direct line number to his phone the day before, Tanner dialled the number and waited.

'Barrington.'

'It's DI Tanner, calling from the Coroner's Office.'

'Right,' said Barrington, sounding as if he was bracing himself. 'How'd it go?'

'Mr Richardson made a positive ID.'

There was a pause on the end of the phone before Barrington said, 'I was afraid you were going to say that. The results came back from that blood sample that you sent over. It *did* belong to the murder victim, so it looks as if you were right. She must have been killed on her way back from the Bittern pub. I've already asked Burgess to get forensics down to the railway bridge, to see if they can dig up anything else. I suppose you haven't told him yet?'

'Not yet, sir, no. I thought I'd better let you know first.'

'OK, well, thank you.' An audible sigh came over the line. 'I suppose that means someone's going to have to tell her parents.'

Silence followed. It was fairly obvious that he was hoping Tanner would put his hand up for the job, and as it was effectively now his case, even though he wasn't officially leading the investigation, he felt obliged to volunteer.

'Jenny and I can head over there now, sir, if that

helps.'

'That would be appreciated, thank you.'

'No problem, sir.'

'When you're there, make sure you ask them how she got on with her husband, and if she had any problem relationships in the past.'

'There's also the possibility that it could have been a kidnap attempt that went wrong, sir.'

'It could well have been, yes,' agreed Barrington, 'but please tread carefully with them. If we're going to get this wrapped up with minimal fuss, we're going to need them on our side.'

'Yes, sir.'

'Did you get Richardson's DNA and fingerprints?'

'We did. He says he was off playing golf at the time she was killed, but someone's going to need to verify that.'

'Email me over the details, and I'll get Burgess to look into it.'

'Maybe we should send someone over to the Bittern Pub as well, sir?'

'I'll mention it to him. And I'll get someone to start checking through CCTV footage of the area. It's possible we might see someone following her home. And we'll need to start a full background check on Jane Richardson.'

'We've already begun that, sir.'

Sounding surprised, Barrington said, 'Right. Good. I'll leave that with you then.'

The call ended, and Tanner looked over at Jenny. 'I assume you're OK coming with me to let the parents know?'

'Of course! I even know where they live.'

'You do?'

'I think most people around here do. They've got what's probably the largest house in Horning. It's on the river's edge, just past the sailing club.'

- CHAPTER TWENTY THREE -

DETECTIVE INSPECTOR PAUL Burgess was having a bad week, and it was only Tuesday. When old "Tommy" Mills had finally retired the month before, that made him the most senior Detective Inspector at Wroxham Police Station. He'd therefore been expecting to be given the lead on all serious crime cases that came in. With the experience he'd subsequently gain, after a few years he'd be able to apply for a Detective Chief Inspector's position, hopefully somewhere not too far away from Norwich. That was the role he'd set his heart on ever since joining the Force. At that level the pay was good, and although there'd be more responsibility, he knew that the bulk of that could easily be passed down the chain, meaning that if anything went wrong, it would be someone else who'd take the fall. Furthermore, there'd be no more "donkey-work". The position of DCI was predominantly managerial, so all he'd have to do would be to sit behind a desk delegating work to his DIs, in much the same way as Barrington did. Having just turned forty, and having been working within the Norfolk Constabulary since graduating from university at twenty-one, that meant he'd been on the Force for nearly twenty years. What he lacked was experience of heading up serious criminal investigations, and he knew he'd need that if he was ever going to be promoted up to a DCI. But when he'd heard a rumour that Tom's replacement was going to be some DI from London, someone who was older and more experienced than him, he began to worry that his career plan was about to be de-railed. As soon as he'd heard, he'd confronted Barrington about it, asking if it was true, and demanding to know why, when just about everyone working at Wroxham Police Station was born and bred in Norfolk. Burgess was so put out by the news that he'd threatened to put in for a transfer, should the guy from London be allowed to join.

However, by that time it was too late. The deal had been done, forcing Barrington to placate Burgess by saying that he'd still consider him to be the station's most senior DI, and would do his best to give him the lead in any serious cases that arose.

By then, Burgess had found out that the new DI had already led numerous serious criminal investigations; but he also knew how hard it would be for Barrington to replace him, were he to put in for a transfer. Very few police detectives wanted to work in areas with such low crime rates as Norfolk, at least not good ones. Most made a beeline straight to the major cities where there were more promotional opportunities.

When the woman's body had been found the day before, the exact same day the new London DI had started, Burgess was beginning to wonder if the gods were playing some sort of cruel joke on him, especially when the report came in that she'd been murdered. At the time, the only saving grace had been that the new

DI was assigned to Missing Persons; but when the blood sample Tanner had sent off to forensics came back as belonging to his murder victim, followed shortly afterwards by the news that a positive ID had been made, then Burgess knew Barrington would be under mounting pressure to have his most experienced officer heading up the investigation, and that wasn't him! He therefore knew that his only chance to keep a hold of the investigation would be to not make any mistakes, and to bring it to a swift and timely conclusion. So when Barrington told him that the body had been positively identified as Jane Richardson, the daughter of John Lambert, founder and CEO of the Lambert Oak pub chain, he'd been quick to agree to all Barrington's suggestions as to what the first steps should be. Had he known that most of them had originally been proposed by Tanner, no doubt he'd have been less compliant.

And so, taking his most experienced team member, Detective Sergeant Craig Cooper, along with him, he drove over to the Bittern Pub to begin interviewing staff, and to identify which one of them was the last to have seen Jane Richardson on Saturday night. He left his other Detective Sergeant, Vicky Gilbert, behind to begin going through the CCTV footage in a bid to find some shots of Jane leaving the pub, and if anyone could be seen following her.

The Bittern was about as traditional as a British pub could get. Thought to date back to 1568, its exterior walls were painted white, and framed with black interlinking wooden beams.

Outside was a large restaurant area that led all the

way up to the river's edge. There, a mooring was provided free for customers for a maximum of two hours.

Inside the pub were dark wooden panelled walls and rich red carpets, which together with a low beamed ceiling gave it a warm, cosy feel.

The pub was well known to Burgess, and most everyone else serving at Wroxham Police Station. It was their nearest local, and was naturally a frequent port of call. It was usually fairly quiet, as it attracted mainly the older generation and young families, so they hardly ever had to attend on a professional level. The only times there was ever even the slightest hint of trouble was during the peak summer months, when the place would heave with tourists. But even then, things would rarely reach the point where the police would have to be called. Visitors coming to the Broads with the intention of getting drunk every night tended to do so either on board a hire boat, or within whatever campsite they were staying at. Today, still before the Easter rush, there weren't many customers.

Behind the bar stood a tall, good-looking man, probably in his late twenties. He had closely cropped black hair with a long fringe that half-covered his dark brown eyes. A tight fitting short-sleeved white shirt showed off unnaturally tanned muscular arms and a well-developed torso. His teeth were exceptionally white, and he had a very distinctive teardrop tattoo on the left side of his neck.

As regular customers, Burgess and Cooper had seen him there before, but knew neither his name, nor what his specific job was.

As they approached, the man set down the glass

he'd been drying, gave them an immaculate smile, and said, 'Afternoon, Gentlemen. What can I get you?'

As they took out their IDs, Burgess made the formal introductions.

'I'm Detective Inspector Burgess and this is Detective Sergeant Cooper.'

The barman shifted uneasily from one foot to the other. 'We're not in any trouble, are we?' he asked, in an anxious tone.

'Not at all, no,' replied Burgess. 'We're actually looking for some information about a lady called Jane Richardson.'

'What about her?'

'So, you know her then?'

'Of course. She's the manager.'

'So we've been told. May I ask when you saw her last?'

'Me? Not since Friday. She *is* supposed to be in this morning, but so far, no sign!' As he said that, he gazed around the virtually empty bar with an amused smirk.

'So, you weren't working here on Saturday then?'

'Normally I would have been, but I had the weekend off. Why?'

Ignoring his question, Burgess asked, 'I don't suppose you have any idea who would have been last to see her, before she left on Saturday?'

'Not a clue, sorry.'

Burgess paused for a moment. 'Is she particularly close to anyone?'

'What, here? Hardly! Not with any of us at any rate.'

'She doesn't get on with the staff?'

'She doesn't socialise with us, if that's what you mean.' Leaning over the bar towards them, keeping his voice down, he added, 'To be honest, she's always been a bit up herself. Her dad owns the pub, you see. We reckon that's the only reason she got the job.'

'I see,' said Burgess, and pretending to join in with the local gossip, looked around and asked, 'Do you know of anyone in particular who she *didn't* get on with?'

But the barman didn't seem to fall for it, and with a suspicious look, pulled himself away from the bar and said, 'No! Look, why're you asking all this stuff, anyway?'

'How about *you*?'

'How about me, what?'

'Did *you* get on with her?'

'I've just told you that, didn't I?'

Burgess studied his face for a moment. The fact that he'd taken a sudden defensive stance when being asked about his relationship with the woman who was his boss was worth noting.

After glancing at DS Cooper, Burgess continued, 'May I ask your name?'

The man seemed to hesitate for a moment before he answered, long enough for Burgess to know that he'd probably thought about whether he'd be able to get away with not telling them.

'Stephen.'

'Stephen…?'

'Perry.'

'And what do you do here, Mr Perry?'

'I'm the bar manager,' he said, unable to prevent himself from glancing down at the notebook DS Cooper was writing in.

'And you say you weren't here on Saturday?'

'That's right.'

'So, where were you then?'

'Nowhere special. I had the weekend off, that's all.'

'I see. And whereabouts do you live, Mr Perry?'

'Horstead. It's just up…'

'I know where Horstead is, thank you,' stated Burgess, and held the bar manager's gaze for a moment longer. He really wanted to speak to the person who'd last seen Jane Richardson, and although the barman standing before him was looking increasingly anxious, that in itself wasn't unusual. Few people enjoyed talking to the police. Just about everyone had something to hide. Moving on, he asked, 'Is there someone we can talk to who would have been working here on Saturday night?'

Looking relieved that the attention was finally being taken off himself, Perry gave that some thought. 'I'm not sure. Probably someone in the kitchen, but I can check the staff roster if you like.'

'That would be useful, thank you,' replied Burgess. He watched Perry step over to a nearby computer terminal, and added, 'Actually, if you could print out a full staff list, that would be appreciated.'

- CHAPTER TWENTY FOUR -

WHILST BURGESS WAS being kept busy at The Bittern, Tanner and Jenny arrived outside two black wrought iron gates which served as the elaborate entrance to the Lamberts' residence in Horning. In the middle of the two gates were the initials J and L, painted in gold. Beyond, they could see an impressive two storey detached house with whitewashed walls and white shuttered windows. Between the ground floor windows was a carefully-spaced series of polished chrome flower pots, from each of which arose identically shaped fern trees.

Seeing an intercom attached to the top of a brushed chromed post to his immediate right, Tanner wound down his window and reached out to press the buzzer.

After a moment a thin metallic female voice came back. 'Yes?'

Leaning his head out of the window towards the intercom, Tanner called, 'Norfolk Police to see Mr and Mrs Lambert.'

'What's it about?'

'It's concerning their daughter.'

There was no response, but a moment later they heard a clunking sound followed by the low electric hum of the gates as they parted.

As soon as they'd opened wide enough, Tanner

eased his XJS through the gap and followed the circular gravel drive around, eventually parking behind two gleaming cars, an Aston Martin Vanquish and a brand new Range Rover Vogue SE, both black, and both so clean they looked as if they'd just been wheeled out of a showroom.

By the time they eased themselves out of the XJS, which up against the Aston Martin and the Range Rover looked even more dated and dirty than usual, the front door had already been opened.

In the doorway stood an attractive but formidable looking woman with sculpted cheek bones, dark blue eyes, a regal nose, a hard angular chin and thick chestnut brown hair, which cascaded down over her shoulders. The length of her body was covered in an elegant grey cashmere jumper, which she clutched tightly around her waist with folded arms.

'So?' she called out, the moment Tanner closed his door. 'Have you found her yet?'

Hearing her sharp, patronising tone, Tanner was already regretting having volunteered for the job. He'd forgotten how obnoxious the rich could be, especially when they came face to face with the police.

Before he said anything, he thought he'd better make the formal introductions. As they crunched their way over the gravel drive, up to the front door, he said, 'Detective Inspector Tanner and Detective Constable Evans. Could we come inside?'

Ignoring both IDs and the policeman's request, with her arms still folded, the woman said, 'You haven't answered my question.'

Stopping where he was, Tanner put his ID away to ask, 'Are you Mrs Lambert, the mother of Jane

Richardson?'

'Of course! Who did you think I was?'

'Is your husband in too, by any chance?'

'He's on his stupid boat.'

'And when will he be back?'

'He hasn't *gone* anywhere! It's moored up at the back of the house.'

Hoping that would mean Mr Lambert would be able to join them, Tanner asked again, 'May we come inside?' He'd no intention of breaking the news of their daughter's death whilst standing on their porch steps, and if at all possible, it was always better to tell parents such tragic news when they were together.

'Have you found her or not?' she demanded.

'We have news,' Tanner conceded, 'but we'd prefer to be able to come in to discuss it with both you and your husband.'

'Very well!' she said, with a heavy sigh, and disappeared inside, leaving Tanner and Jenny to make their own way in.

As they stepped into the hall, from somewhere towards the back of the house they heard Mrs Lambert bellow, 'JOHN! WE'VE GOT VISITORS!' and then, 'You'd better come through. My husband won't be long.'

Following the sound of her voice, they entered a luxurious kitchen which stretched over the entire width of the house. In the middle was a large island surrounded by dark brown wooden cabinets and a cream marble worktop. The far wall was nothing but glass, allowing for a clear, unobstructed view of a freshly mown lawn which stretched all the way down to the River Bure. There, moored up at the end was a white motor yacht which was so big, they could hardly see the river beyond.

Tanner and Jenny watched as a heavy-set man began to climb down from the boat onto the hard standing. He had a weathered tanned face and wiry grey hair, and was wearing blue jeans which looked a little on the tight side, along with a navy blue jumper and an open necked office shirt.

As they watched him lumbering his way up the lawn, staring down at the grass as he did so, Mrs Lambert asked, 'Can I get you anything to drink? Tea? Coffee?'

'Thank you, no,' replied Tanner.

As the big man entered the kitchen through one of the glass doors, Mrs Lambert said, 'It's the police, darling. They've finally got some news about Jane!'

'And about bloody time too,' he mumbled. Stopping next to his wife, he glared at the two police officers. 'Well, where is she then?'

Tanner hesitated.

This was the hard part.

'Mr and Mrs Lambert, I'm afraid to tell you that at around one o'clock yesterday afternoon, the body of a young woman was found in the river, near Thurne Dyke.'

Neither parent said anything. Both just continued to stare at him.

'Today she has been positively identified as your daughter, Jane Richardson.'

A cold hard silence followed.

With a faltering voice, Mrs Lambert eventually said, 'You must be mistaken. Our Jane isn't… She's just run off with somebody, that's all!'

'I'm afraid her husband formally identified her body this afternoon.'

'That idiot! Well, he's wrong! Plain and simple!'

'Supporting evidence has also been found.'

'Evidence? What evidence?'

Tanner took a moment before continuing. The fact that they weren't prepared to believe what he was telling them was very normal. Denial was the first of several stages of grief, something he was all too familiar with. But murder could never be described as normal, and as with Jane's husband, he was careful to say only as much about her death as was necessary to convince them.

'We found some of her blood along the towpath under the railway bridge, just outside Wroxham, which we believe was the route she took back from work on Saturday night.'

'You're honestly suggesting that our daughter was stupid enough to trip over, and fall into the river? She doesn't even drink! Did you know that?'

'It looks like someone may have been there with her. Someone who wished her harm.'

'You mean she was…?'

'I'm very sorry, but it looks like she was unlawfully killed, yes.'

Unable to take her tear-filled eyes off Tanner, Mrs Lambert slumped onto one of the high chairs that surrounded the island. The fact that her daughter was dead seemed to have finally penetrated the barrier of her conscious mind.

The oppressive silence that followed was broken by the breaking voice of the father.

'Do you… do you know who did it?'

'It's too early to say, but I can assure you that we're...'

Mrs Lambert spat out, 'It was that husband of hers, wasn't it?'

'As I was saying,' continued Tanner, in a calming voice, 'it really is too early to say, but we are doing everything we can...'

Rising from her chair, Mrs Lambert continued her accusation. 'It was him! I know it was! He *never* loved her, not like we did!'

'Mrs Lambert...'

'Have you talked to him yet?'

'We have, but...'

'Then you know how much he resented her. God knows why she married him. He wasn't even man enough to get her pregnant. We had to pay for them to go to an IVF clinic, and half the time he didn't even bother to go with her. They were supposed to have their final meeting there during Jane's lunchbreak on Saturday, just to make sure the baby was...'

She stopped mid-sentence, her eyes widening as she remembered that her daughter had been pregnant. It was left for her husband to ask what they already knew, but didn't want to believe.

'The baby?'

Tanner looked first at the father, and then the mother, and shook his head.

Having this confirmed was simply too much for them to bear. Mrs Lambert sank back onto the seat, covering her face with her long bony fingers and broke down in noisy sobs.

Beside her, her husband gripped the edge of the marble worktop, staring down at his hands, tears falling from his eyes.

Tanner and Jenny stood quietly, waiting for the right time to speak.

Trying to regain some of his composure as he wiped the side of his face with the back of his hand, Mr Lambert said, 'If there's anything we can do to help, please don't hesitate to ask.'

Seizing the opportunity, Tanner asked, 'Did your daughter know of anyone who may have wished her harm?'

Sniffing loudly, Mrs Lambert looked up and said, 'You mean, apart from her husband?'

'Ruth, *please!*'

'What? You know it was him, just as well as I do! He only married her for her money. Everyone knew it – everyone except you, of course! And now he's killed her *and* her baby. And I suppose that means he's going to inherit her entire estate? Well, not if I have anything to do with it, he isn't!'

Pushing on, Tanner asked, 'Have you ever had any threats yourself, ransom demands or anything.'

Mr Lambert turned back to him. 'You think someone may have been trying to kidnap her?'

'It's certainly something we're considering, yes. Has anyone tried anything like that before?'

'Nothing like that, no. I've always been mindful to keep Jane out of the public eye, for that very reason.'

'What about boyfriends?'

'You mean, before Simon?'

'Either before or during.'

Ignoring the inference that she may have been having an affair, Mr Lambert said, 'Well, she's had some of course, but none who've caused any trouble, nothing serious at least.'

'Would you be able to tell us how we'd be able to get in touch with them?'

'With her old boyfriends?' questioned Mr Lambert, looking at his wife for help. 'I can hardly remember their names, let alone where they all live!'

Sliding off her chair, Mrs Lambert crossed the kitchen floor to stare unseeing out of the window, clutching her cashmere jumper around her.

Sensing the time had probably come for them to go, Tanner said, 'We'd better leave it there. I am truly sorry for your loss, Mr and Mrs Lambert, but I can assure you that we're doing everything in our power to find out who did this to your daughter.'

Mrs Lambert let out a huff of disgust. 'Then I suggest you'd better hurry up and arrest that husband of hers, hadn't you!'

- CHAPTER TWENTY FIVE -

I N THE HALLWAY, as Mr Lambert held the door open for them, he said, 'You must forgive my wife. She's never really got on with Simon.'

'And how about you?' Tanner asked, stepping outside.

'Me and Simon? Well, I must admit that I wasn't too keen at first, but Jane always seemed to like him.'

'What was the relationship like between them?'

'Generally good, I think. I know they had issues when she couldn't get pregnant, but I don't think that was necessarily Simon's fault, and they seemed to get back to normal pretty quickly when we heard that the IVF treatment had worked.'

'Do you know the name of the clinic they used?'

'It's called Buxton Manor. It's not far from here. Just over Ludham Bridge, on the way towards Barton Broad.'

Tanner checked to make sure Jenny had made a note of that. 'Mr Richardson mentioned to us that he and Jane led relatively separate lives, despite the fact that they were married. Would you say that was true?'

'I know they had their own sets of friends, and that Simon would occasionally go away to play golf with his. Jane was always fiercely independent, a bit like me, I suppose.'

As John Lambert seemed so composed, Tanner thought it was a good time to get one of the formalities out the way. 'We'll need to arrange to take DNA samples and fingerprints, from both you and your wife, at some point.'

'Is that really necessary?'

'I'm afraid it is, yes. But it's just a formality, for purposes of elimination, to help us identify evidence found without wasting valuable time. Shall I send a forensics officer around, or would you prefer to come down to the station?'

'The former, obviously!'

Tanner and Jenny said goodbye once more, and headed back to the car.

- CHAPTER TWENTY SIX -

A S TANNER EASED the car around the circular drive towards the wrought iron gates, Jenny asked, 'Do you think it was Richardson?'

Tanner thought for a moment. 'We'll have to see how his alibi stands up, but it certainly sounds like he's got a motive.'

'Inheritance money?'

'Uh-huh,' he nodded. 'In my experience, people do some very stupid things when large amounts of money are involved.'

'But why would he wait until she was pregnant? If he was going to kill her, you'd have thought he'd have done so before, given the effort and expense involved in IVF. Why put himself through that unnecessarily?'

It was a good question, one which naturally led Tanner to think of another possibility.

'Maybe it's not his own child.'

'That would make sense,' said Jenny. 'If they were having IVF treatment, maybe he was the one who couldn't have children, so they had to resort to using someone else's sperm.'

'Which could be why he didn't think it worth mentioning to us when we first spoke to him.'

'It's even possible that she'd decided not to tell him that the baby wasn't his, though that would involve the collusion of the IVF clinic.'

'And when he found out, knowing at the back of his mind he'd inherit a small fortune, he went and...'

As they waited for the gate to open, Tanner and Jenny stared at each other.

In less than a minute, the idea of Simon Richardson being the prime suspect for the murder of his wife had changed from vaguely possible to highly probable.

Bringing them back down to earth, Tanner said, 'But it's still going to depend on his alibi, and for a conviction we'd need some sort of physical evidence to link him directly to the murder.'

The gates were fully open, and as they drove through he added, 'I suppose we'd better get back to the station, to see if there's been any developments. But before we do that, I suggest that we take a quick look at this IVF clinic. What was it called again?'

Referring to her notes, Jenny replied, 'Buxton Manor. I think I know where it is.'

'If we can have a quick chat with them, then at least we'll be able to find out if the baby was Richardson's. If it *was* someone else's, then I think that may explain why he decided not to wait until she'd had it.'

- CHAPTER TWENTY SEVEN -

BUXTON MANOR WAS an imposing 18th Century manor house set within an acre of beautifully landscaped gardens. It had magnolia painted walls, lead-lined windows and a steep thatched roof, one that had lost its pristine yellow sheen many years before and was now an uninspiring dull grey colour.

The house itself had served as a discreet private medical centre for a little over six years, providing a wide range of services, IVF treatment being one of them.

At the end of the gravel drive, Tanner carefully parked between a midnight blue Aston Martin Rapide and a sultry black Bentley Continental.

Removing her seatbelt, Jenny said, 'Someone's making some money!'

'Someone, as in, not us!' remarked Tanner.

As he pushed open the Jag's heavy door, it creaked loudly, as if in protest at having to rub shoulders with two such opulent modern cars.

Opening her own door, Jenny said, 'You may want to put some oil on that.'

'On me, or the door?' questioned Tanner, groaning as he heaved himself out.

'I suppose that depends on if you enjoy being

covered in oil whilst someone tugs at your handle,' said Jenny.

The second she'd said it, she knew it was too much, even by her own standards.

'Sorry about that. It just sort of…slipped out!'

But Tanner was becoming increasingly used to her highly suggestive, borderline inappropriate remarks, and came back with one of his own. 'With it being covered in oil, I'm not surprised!'

Grateful he'd not taken offence at the remark, which if not unprofessional, was most definitely unladylike, she gave him an appreciative smile, and together they crunched their way past a couple of more average-looking cars, up to Buxton Manor's main entrance.

Inside the manor was very much in keeping with the outside. It had a low ceiling with exposed wooden beams, and although Tanner wasn't tall enough to hit his head on them, he found himself instinctively stooping to make sure that he didn't.

Even the wide reception desk seemed to be designed to fit with the rest of the building, as it had been carved out of dark mahogany; and where one would normally find medically-themed posters lining the walls, instead were elegant landscape paintings of the Norfolk Broads, in a variety of different views.

From behind the desk, a round-faced young woman with a mass of permed blond hair welcomed them with a professional smile.

Pulling out their respective IDs, Tanner asked, 'Could you tell us who manages your IVF department?'

'Dr. Khatri is our IVF and gynaecology specialist. I assume you don't have an appointment?'

'I'm afraid not, no.'

'OK. Hold on. I'll see if he's free.'

She picked up her desk phone, pressed a button for a line and a moment later said, 'Sorry to bother you, Dr. Khatri, but there are a couple of police detectives at reception asking to see you.'

A short pause followed, before she said, 'OK, thanks. I'll let them know.'

Replacing the receiver, she looked up at Tanner and said, 'He'll be down in about ten minutes. Would you like a coffee while you wait?'

Noticing that there was a pot of filtered coffee standing on a table just behind the reception desk, for a change Tanner accepted the offer, and turned to Jenny. 'Coffee?'

'I wouldn't mind.'

Unsmiling, the receptionist pushed herself up from her chair to prepare the two coffees, asking, 'How'd you like it?'

'Milk, no sugar,' replied Tanner.

'Same for me, thanks,' added Jenny.

The receptionist passed the two white cups and saucers over the top of the desk. Then, looking from Jenny to Tanner, she leaned forward, and in a low conspiratorial tone asked, 'I don't suppose you're here about that murder that was on the telly this morning?'

With the strong sense that the woman was the type who felt it was her civic duty to tell everyone about everything and anything, embellishing whatever it was in the process, Tanner thought it best to lie.

'Oh no, nothing like that.'

Exchanging glances between them, keeping her voice low, she asked, 'But I assume you are here for…professional reasons, and not because you two are…?'

The two police detectives gave each other an embarrassed glance, before Tanner stated, 'It's police business! Nothing more. And nothing of any great importance.'

'Well, that's fortunate, for you at least.'

Glancing around to make sure that there was nobody else in reception to overhear what she was about to say, she went on, 'You know, I can't help but feel sorry for the couples who do have to come here for IVF treatment. It must be dreadful for them, not being able to have children, and everything.'

Neither Tanner nor Jenny felt even remotely comfortable being included in such a delicate conversation, and attempted to show their disinterest by looking away whilst drinking their coffee.

'Of course, it's never been a problem for me,' she continued, seemingly oblivious to just how inappropriate the two police officers felt such a conversation was. 'I fell pregnant within a few weeks of me and my husband deciding that we wanted to start a family, and I'm already expecting our second!'

As she said that, with one of her hands resting over her lower abdomen, she asked, 'Would you like to see some pictures?'

Without waiting for a response, she picked up her smartphone and began frantically swiping at the surface. 'I've got some in here somewhere,' she said, smiling proudly. 'Yes, here they are!'

After she'd stared down at the screen with a look of

maternal pride, she was about to show Tanner and Jenny when a side door opened and in walked a stick-thin middle-aged Asian man with hollow cheeks, sunken brown eyes and greying black hair.

From over the tops of their coffee cups, Tanner and Jenny gave the man a look of social desperation, but he didn't immediately look at them. Instead he approached the desk, leaned over the top of it and whispered, 'Are these the two police officers?'

Hiding her smartphone, the frumpy-looking receptionist replied, 'They are, yes.'

He turned to greet them. 'You'd better come through, but I've only got a few minutes.'

Tanner and Jenny abandoned their cups on top of the desk, thanked the receptionist for the coffee, and hurried over to where the door was being held open for them.

- CHAPTER TWENTY EIGHT -

ENTERING A DARK wood-panelled office, they were shown to two old dining chairs set before an antique writing desk, one which had a worn green leather writing surface bearing an open laptop.

Taking his own seat, clasping his hands on the desk the man said, 'Right, so, I'm Dr. Khatri. I'm the lead consultant for the Gynaecology and IVF department. How may I help?'

Tanner said, 'We're here to investigate the death of someone who we believe to be one of your clients, a Mrs Jane Richardson.'

There was a long pause before he responded by saying, 'I'm sorry, but did you say that Jane Richardson is *dead?*'

'I'm afraid so,' confirmed Tanner.

With his obvious surprise turning to a look of disbelief, the doctor asked, 'But...how? I-I mean, I only saw her on Saturday!'

'We believe she was killed later that evening, on her way back from work.'

'My god! How awful!'

'Yes.'

'And how do you think I'd be able to help?'

'We've just been to see her parents. They told us

that Mrs Richardson and her husband had been coming here for IVF treatment, and that the treatment was successful.'

'That's correct, yes. The meeting on Saturday was the final one.'

'Did her husband attend that meeting?'

'Not that one, no.'

'Did he miss many of them?'

'He did have a tendency to.'

'Is that normal, for the husbands not to attend?'

'I'd say it's a little unusual, but he's hardly the first. Believe it or not, some men still seem to be of the opinion that reproduction is primarily the responsibility of the woman, and so they don't feel it's necessary for them to come along.'

'Does it depend on who's the cause of the problem?' asked Tanner, feeling forced to confront his own thoughts on the subject.

'Not really. Even if the problem lies with the man, they're often unwilling to accept it.'

'And in the case of the Richardsons?'

Dr Khatri frowned at him. 'You're asking me if they were here because of Simon or Jane?'

'I am, yes.'

'Well, unfortunately, I'm unable to answer that question; it's strictly confidential.'

'I understand,' Tanner said, 'but this *is* a murder enquiry.'

'And what can that possibly have to do with the death of Jane Richardson?'

'We feel it may have a bearing on motive.'

'Motive?'

'That's correct.'

'Are you seriously suggesting that Simon murdered his wife?'

'At this stage we're simply trying to establish if there is a motive for such a possibility.'

'Why on earth would he do that? She was eighteen weeks pregnant!'

Treading carefully, Tanner said, 'We're wondering whether the fact that she was pregnant could be a motive, if he never wanted her to be.'

'But that's hardly likely though, is it!'

'Why?'

'Why would he have gone to all the trouble and expense of having IVF treatment if he didn't want it to work?'

'We don't know, but we do know that they didn't pay for it. It was financed by Mrs Richardson's parents.'

'But, even so!'

Deciding to move the conversation along, Tanner asked, 'I assume that in some cases, when the man is found to be the problem, that the sperm from another man has to be used?'

'In some cases, yes, of course, but in those circumstances IVF wouldn't be the correct course of action for them.'

'So you're saying that that wasn't the case here?'

'I'm not prepared to say either way, but my previous answer should be enough for you to work that one out for yourself.'

'So, Simon *was* the father of the baby?'

Instead of answering, the doctor simply stared at him.

Realising he wasn't going to say more, Tanner

looked over at Jenny and said, 'I think we can take that as a yes.'

Pushing his chair out from his desk, Dr Khatri stood up and said, 'If that will be all, I have another appointment.'

Having learnt what they'd come to find out, Tanner got to his feet. 'Thank you for your time, Dr Khatri. We'll show ourselves out.'

- CHAPTER TWENTY NINE -

BACK OUT IN the carpark, having managed to slip past the receptionist without saying goodbye, Jenny said, 'At least we know that Richardson was the father.'

'Which I think makes it less likely he killed her,' replied Tanner. 'Not after she became pregnant. Anyway, for now I suggest we head back to the station and see if there have been any developments.'

As they pulled their respective seatbelts on, Jenny suggested, 'How about we pick up something to eat on the way? There's a garage just down the road.'

Glancing down at his dashboard, Tanner saw that not only was it gone half past twelve, but that the needle of his petrol gauge was resting on the red.

'No problem,' he replied. 'I could do with some petrol as well, and a coffee.'

'Not at the same time, I hope!'

Smiling, Tanner reversed out of his parking space, and was soon turning out of Buxton Manor, back onto the road.

Five minutes later he pulled in to the garage and drew up alongside the nearest free pump.

As soon as the car stopped, Jenny undid her seatbelt, and grabbing her handbag, asked, 'Can I get you a sandwich?'

'That's kind of you, thanks. A ploughman's, if they've got it.'

Leaving him to fill up the car, she crossed the forecourt and headed inside.

Even before he'd finished filling up, she was coming out again, her hands empty.

Replacing the pump's nozzle back in its cradle, Tanner said, 'Don't tell me they've run out of coffee?'

'You'll never guess what's happened.' she said, with breathless excitement. 'They've arrested Simon Richardson!'

'Seriously?'

'Seriously! It's on the local news!' and she gestured inside the garage shop.

'I've got to see this,' said Tanner, nudging his way past her.

Just above the tills, hanging down from the ceiling, was a small flat-screen TV, tuned in to the BBC local news, where a sombre-looking male reporter was talking to the camera, directly in front of Wroxham Police Station. At the bottom of the screen, next to the title LATEST NEWS, the strapline said, *Man arrested in connection with local murder inquiry.*

Entering the garage behind him, Jenny said, 'When I was here, they were filming Burgess leading him inside, in handcuffs. They must have discovered something when we were out.'

'No kidding!' exclaimed Tanner. 'But even so, it's far too soon to make an arrest, surely!'

They watched the TV together in silence for a while longer, before Tanner reached for his wallet. 'Let me pay for the petrol, then I suggest we get back to see what's been going on.'

- CHAPTER THIRTY -

CREEPING DOWN THE heavily congested road towards Wroxham Police Station, it soon became apparent that the news of what was now a high-profile murder investigation had spread. Three media vans were parked awkwardly on the kerb opposite the station, the one from BBC East having been joined by Channel 4 and Sky News, and they'd done so in such a way that cars coming into Wroxham from the other direction were being forced to steer around them.

As Tanner indicated left into the station's carpark, he could see a dozen or so reporters milling about on the pavement, directly outside the station, some with large TV cameras held down by their side, others with stills cameras hanging around their necks. All of them were keeping an eye out for something to film. The sight of Tanner's Jaguar XJS turning in must have been unusual enough for them, as many began focussing their lenses on the car.

None of them seemed to know who the people inside the car were, or if they had a direct involvement in the investigation, so even though they continued to film and take pictures, the officers were saved from having to fend off any questions.

With Jenny hurrying in his wake, Tanner headed

straight for Barrington's office. As he did so, Burgess, who was up near the white board at the far end of the room, caught his eye and gave him a self-satisfied smirk.

I've got no idea what you're smiling about, thought Tanner, as he knocked on Barrington's door.

At the invitation to enter, he turned to Jenny. 'You'd probably be best off waiting out here.'

'No problem at all!' she said, adding, 'Good luck!' before turning to head back to her desk.

He stepped inside, sneaking a glance over at Burgess as he did.

Closing the door behind him, he said, 'Sorry to barge in, sir, but I heard the news that DI Burgess has arrested Simon Richardson.'

'He has, yes,' confirmed Barrington, staring absently at his computer monitor.

'Don't you think that was a little premature, sir?'

'His alibi didn't check out.'

'But we still need some sort of physical evidence to link him to the murder before we can charge him.'

Glancing up at Tanner, with the same look of smug self-satisfaction that Burgess had earlier, Barrington said, 'Burgess got that as well. We had a positive match on the semen found inside the victim. According to forensics, it belongs to Simon Richardson!'

Tanner stopped. He'd completely forgotten about the sample they'd recovered from Jane Richardson's body, and a match with her husband would be the physical evidence they needed to begin legal proceedings against him. However, despite that, he still felt it was too soon. As far as Tanner was concerned, it would have been prudent to have built a watertight case before having placed him under arrest.

But there was something else as well, something that didn't feel right, and it took him only a second to realise what that was. The forensics medical examiner had said that the victim had been sexually abused *after* she'd been murdered. The idea of having sex with someone who was already dead was such a disturbing thing, even by rapist standards, and Tanner couldn't think of any reason for Richardson to have done it. On top of that, he must have known that in doing so he'd be leaving physical evidence at the scene which would link him directly to the murder.

Keeping that to himself for now, Tanner said, 'I still feel it's too soon to arrest him, sir. In my experience, cases like this are rarely so clear cut.'

'Well, I think we can count our blessings that in this case, it is, especially as more media arrived shortly after you left, followed soon after by a call from Head Office.'

'But we've yet to go through her emails and social media accounts. There could easily be another man in her life. And did anyone check the CCTV footage?'

'I appreciate your concern, Tanner, but CCTV cameras were checked, and they clearly showed her leaving the Bittern pub at the stated time, with nobody following her.'

'And what about Richardson's alibi – has that been thoroughly gone over?'

'DI Burgess phoned them himself. As it turned out, not only wasn't he a member of the golf club, but he hadn't even signed on as a guest, and his name didn't appear in the tournament's results.'

'What about the hotel he said he was staying at?'

'What about it?'

'Did Burgess check with them?'

'I've no idea, but the bottom line is that not only has he lied about taking part in a golf tournament, his semen was found inside the victim! I'm not sure how much more evidence you'd need!'

'I appreciate that, sir, but the medical examiner said that the victim was sexually assaulted *post-mortem*. Why would he have wanted to have sex with his own wife after he'd killed her, knowing that in doing so he'd be leaving behind the one piece of evidence that would tie him to her murder?'

'Clearly the man has some serious mental issues, which shouldn't come as too much of a surprise really; after all, he had just strangled the poor girl to death.'

There was a knock at the door, and a young PC poked his head in.

'Sorry to disturb you, sir, but there's a call for DI Tanner. It's John Lambert.'

'He must have heard the news,' observed Tanner.

Concerned that his new DI might be tempted to voice his doubts over the arrest, especially to the suspect's father-in-law, Barrington instructed, 'Put the call through to my line. DI Tanner will take it in here.'

Whilst they waited for the call to come through, Barrington said, 'Now listen, Tanner, I appreciate your concerns, but now's not the time to raise them with Mr Lambert, is that understood?'

As Barrington's desk phone began to ring, Tanner said, 'Of course, sir.'

Barrington paused for a moment before pushing the phone towards him, but before letting go of it, he said, 'I'd better put it on speakerphone,' and pushed the relevant button.

Leaning in towards it, Tanner said, 'Detective Inspector Tanner speaking.'

'It's John Lambert. I just heard the news.'

Tanner decided that even though he wasn't allowed to voice his doubts over the arrest of the man's son-in-law, he could at least do his best to play it down, so he said, 'We've brought Simon Richardson in for questioning, yes.'

'The news said that you'd arrested him for the murder of my daughter!'

Seeing Barrington nod over at him, Tanner replied, 'I can confirm that we have.'

'I see,' came Lambert's reply. 'I must admit that I wasn't expecting that to have happened so soon. Are you sure it's him?'

With Barrington glaring over at him, Tanner took a moment to work out his answer.

'Evidence has been found that does implicate him directly.' He decided to include a caveat. 'But I should mention that I'm not the one leading the investigation.'

Barrington scowled over at him, but Tanner ignored his obvious objection by adding, 'Detective Inspector Burgess is taking the lead on this one.'

Lambert said, 'That sounds like you don't agree with him?'

Noticing that Barrington's fists had clenched on top of his desk, and that his scowl had turned into more of a snarl, Tanner thought it best to avoid the question by saying, 'DI Burgess has been working for Norfolk Constabulary for a number of years, whereas I've only recently joined.'

'That doesn't answer my question!'

Knowing it would have repercussions, Tanner bit the bullet and said, 'Personally, I'd have waited a little longer to check through the evidence before making an arrest.'

Barrington shoved his seat away from his desk, stood up and began pacing up and down behind it. If Tanner had been on the phone to anyone else, he'd have interrupted the conversation, but as nobody had told Lambert that his conversation wasn't being held in private, he felt unable to do that.

Aware that he was disobeying a direct order, Tanner added, 'I'd only have done that so we could have had the chance to dot the I's and cross the T's, and maybe to discover more in the process. But saying that, what we've found already *is* substantial.'

'But is it enough to convict him?'

Speaking more to Barrington than Lambert, Tanner replied, 'It's not about whether or not we can convict him, Mr Lambert, it's about making sure we have the right man!'

'Of course,' conceded Lambert, 'and for that reason I sincerely hope you have! Out of respect to my daughter's memory, and the health of my wife, I don't want this attracting any more media attention than it already has. And if you've gone and charged the wrong person, on behalf of my son-in-law, I'll be filing a lawsuit for both wrongful arrest *and* character defamation. So for the sake of your Detective Chief Inspector Barrington, I sincerely hope this Burgess character you mentioned *has* got the right man!'

Without saying goodbye, Lambert ended the call.

In the silence that followed, Barrington slunk over to the window and peered out through the horizontal blinds towards the car park behind which the journalists seemed to be lying in wait. His rage at Tanner for telling Lambert that they'd acted prematurely had been replaced with the grave concern that he may well be right.

When Burgess had told him that not only had Richardson's alibi failed to check out, but also that his DNA matched the semen found inside the victim, Barrington had jumped at the chance for them to make an early arrest. The hope had been that doing so would extinguish media interest, as they rarely had an eye for good news, only bad. He also thought it would earn him praise from Head Office. However, if they were to discover that they'd got the wrong man, instead of extinguishing media interest it would ignite it, and Head Office would be more likely to demote him than offer him a promotion. Worse still, if his actions led to a lawsuit being filed against Norfolk Constabulary, then it was likely that his job, possibly his entire career, would be on the line.

There was another knock at the door, closely followed by the head of Detective Inspector Burgess, wearing what now seemed like a misplaced expression of smug contempt.

'Excuse me, sir. I just thought I'd let you know that Simon Richardson's solicitor has arrived, so DS Cooper and myself are about to go down to begin the interview.'

Heading back to his desk, Barrington said, 'About that, Burgess. Come in for a sec, will you?'

As any trace of a smile fell from Burgess's face, he stepped inside, closed the door, and with a venomous glare directed at Tanner, said, 'Of course, sir.'

'We've just had the suspect's father-in-law on the phone,' began Barrington.

'You mean, Mr Lambert?' Until that moment, he'd always thought of John Lambert as being the murder victim's father, not their prime suspect's father-in-law.

'He was expressing his surprise that we'd made an arrest so soon.'

'Well, yes, sir, but as we agreed –'

'And Tanner here is suggesting that it may have been prudent to have waited, at least until we could build a stronger case against him.'

After once again glaring at Tanner, Burgess continued with what he'd been about to say.

'But as we agreed, *sir*, the combination of him not playing golf as he claimed he was, and that his semen was found inside the victim, is enough to not only arrest him, but to charge him as well!'

Barrington blurted out, 'You haven't gone and charged him, have you?'

'Well, no, sir, but for the life of me I can't see why we shouldn't!'

Entering the discussion, with diplomatic tact, Tanner said, 'And I'd have to agree with you, if it wasn't for the semen.'

Staring over at him, Burgess said, 'But that is the main evidence we have against him!'

'Perhaps, but I suspect it could also be what proves him to be innocent.'

'But...' began Burgess, before turning to Barrington and saying, 'I'm sorry, sir, but he's not making any sense!'

'I'm merely suggesting,' continued Tanner, 'that it does strike me as being a little odd that he'd set out to deliberately kill his wife, and once he'd done so, by not only hitting her over the head, but by strangling her as well, he'd then decide to claim his conjugal rights, so leaving behind the one piece of evidence that would guarantee his conviction!'

Burgess was stunned into silence, leaving Barrington to clarify what Tanner had said. 'The suggestion is that he wouldn't have wanted to have sex with her after she was dead.'

'It would be unusual, sir,' confirmed Tanner.

'Unusual maybe,' agreed Burgess, 'but hardly impossible, especially for someone who'd just murdered his wife with his bare hands! Maybe that's what turns him on - having sex with dead people! For all we know, maybe she'd been refusing to have sex with him, and that was how he'd decided to get his own back, by screwing her when she was dead!'

'If that was the case,' interjected Tanner, 'then I'd have thought it more likely he'd have done so whilst she was still alive, so she'd see him doing it.'

'Yes, but *you're* not him though, *are you*?'

'And with respect, neither are *you*!'

With Burgess looking as if he was about to launch himself at Tanner, and with Tanner seeming to be happy to defend himself against such an attack, Barrington said, 'All right you two, that's enough!'

But Tanner still had one more thing to say, and turning to Barrington, added, 'And a jury only needs a seed of doubt to overturn a conviction, sir.'

As Burgess stared at him in some desperation, Barrington thought for a moment before answering. 'I'm afraid Tanner's right. We're going to need more if we're going to charge him.' Glancing down at his watch, he added, 'And we have less than twenty-three hours. After that, we'll need to apply for an extension if we're going to keep hold of him, which may not be granted. Even if it is, it would only serve to drag this out for another two days, which is something we simply can't afford to do!'

As Barrington considered his two DIs, he asked, 'What else have we got, apart from his dodgy alibi and the semen?'

'We've checked the CCTV footage,' said Burgess, 'but there was nothing there. It just showed the victim leaving the pub on her own. I've also spoken to most of the pub staff, but they only confirmed what the CCTV footage showed.'

'What sort of relationship did she have with them?'

'Well, she was the manager, so probably as you'd expect. I think a number of them resented her, thinking that she'd only got the job because her dad owned the pub, but nothing more than that.'

'Anything else?'

Silence followed, during which Burgess looked as if he was struggling to think of something to add. Eventually he said, 'The bar manager did appear to become very defensive when we questioned him about his relationship with the victim, certainly more so than anyone else did. At first I thought it was because something had been going on between them.'

'You think this bar manager may have been having an affair with Jane Richardson?'

'At the time I did, yes, sir. But DS Cooper was under the impression that Jane Richardson wouldn't be his type.'

'How do you mean?'

'He thinks the bar manager is gay, sir.'

'Gay?' repeated Barrington, as if he'd never heard the word spoken out loud before.

'Yes, sir. He had a very distinctive haircut, along with a tear-drop tattoo. And although I didn't notice it at first, he was also wearing eye-liner.'

'And that makes him gay, does it?'

'When combined with his general demeanour, I'd say it does, yes.'

'Right. And is *any* of this relevant?'

'Only in that we didn't think he'd have a personal interest in Jane Richardson, despite the way he became defensive when being asked about her.'

'So, not really then?'

'Well…'

Before Burgess had a chance to say anything else that Barrington considered to be a complete waste of his time, he interrupted him. 'So, what's next?'

Looking as if he was unsure as to his meaning, Burgess said, 'We need to interview the suspect, sir.'

'I was thinking more along the lines of what we can do to shore up the case we have against him?'

Once again, silence followed.

Assuming that Burgess didn't have any more ideas as to how to go about doing that, Tanner re-entered the discussion.

'I think it would be a good idea to find out what Mr Richardson was wearing the night she was killed, sir. Shoes as well. We could then get forensics to check them over for signs of blood, or soil from under the railway bridge. I suggest we should also go through the victim's text messages, emails and social media accounts, to see if there's any mention in there about them having argued recently. It would then be a good idea to follow that up by speaking to her friends. Maybe she'd told one of them something in confidence. We also need to take a look at her Will, sir,' he continued, 'and to find out how much she was worth. When I spoke to her parents, there was the suggestion that she had a substantial estate that Richardson would be due to inherit.'

Tanner glanced over at Burgess, who was staring at the wall behind Barrington's desk with tightly pursed lips. For the second time in as many days, Tanner realised he'd probably managed to make his contemporary look as if he didn't have a clue as to what he was doing. But this time around, it hadn't been his intention, and he couldn't help but feel guilty for having done so.

From Barrington's perspective, it was becoming increasingly obvious that Burgess simply wasn't up to the task of leading such a high-profile investigation. However, he knew making Tanner the lead now would only serve as humiliation, which would probably force Burgess to put in for a transfer. He had no experience of investigating murder, but he was a good DI nonetheless, and a difficult one to replace. Consequently, Barrington knew they were going to have to continue as they were, with Burgess leading and Tanner supporting.

Making a point of glancing down at his watch, Barrington said, 'OK, Burgess, I suggest you begin interviewing the suspect, but before you do, get DS Gilbert to arrange for forensics to head down to his house. We need his clothes and shoes.'

'It may be useful for them to have a look for the

murder weapon as well, sir,' suggested Tanner.

'He's most likely to have ditched it,' said Barrington, 'but it's worth a look, I suppose. Maybe you and Jenny could join forensics and have a look for yourselves?'

'I was hoping she would be able to start going through Jane Richardson's personal data, sir.'

'OK, well, fair enough.'

'And I was hoping to be able to sit in on the interview with Mr Richardson.'

Glancing over at Burgess, Barrington asked, 'Any objection?'

Seeing the look on Burgess's face, Tanner added, 'I'd only be looking to sit in.'

Still staring at the wall, without any outward sign of emotion, Burgess said, 'Whatever you think best, sir.'

Realising Burgess had resorted to sulking like a five year-old, Barrington let out a heavy sigh. 'It probably *is* for the best, yes, Burgess. If the two of you can annoy him as much as you seem to be able to annoy me, you'll probably have him signing a written confession within the first five minutes!'

'What about DS Cooper, sir?' asked Burgess, still hoping he wouldn't have to have Tanner joining him for the interview.

'You can send him down to the house to supervise forensics. Make sure he looks for anything that could have caused that injury to the victim's head. And after DS Gilbert's arranged for forensics to go down there, get her to start digging into Jane's finances. If she is worth a small fortune, we need to know.'

Seeing Burgess nod his understanding, Barrington ended the meeting. 'Right, that will do. Let me know how you get on with our Mr Richardson. If you tell him what we've already got on him, hopefully he'll own up to it, and that will be that!'

- CHAPTER THIRTY ONE -

THE INTERVIEW ROOM at Wroxham Police Station was like most: small, nondescript and windowless. Its furniture consisted of nothing more than four chairs and a table pushed up against a wall. On the table sat a square black box which was the station's relatively new digital recorder, a time-saving device that allowed interview recordings to be accessed remotely through Norfolk Constabulary's intranet.

Simon Richardson was seated at the far side of the table, deep in conversation with a wiry, bald-headed man who stood up to introduce himself as the two detectives entered.

'I'm Clive Percival. I've been appointed to represent Mr Simon Richardson.'

'Thank you,' said Burgess, and gestured for him to resume his seat, making a note of his name on the case file he'd brought with him.

In the silence that followed, Burgess reached over the table and pressed a small red button on the front of the recording device, underneath the letters REC.

Taking the chair closest to the recorder, Burgess leaned in towards the machine. Referring to his notes, he said, 'We're here to interview Mr Simon Richardson of 1, River View Lane, Wroxham, in connection with the murder of Mrs Jane Richardson of the same address.' Checking the display on the front of the digital recorder, he continued, 'The time is 13:22 on Tuesday, 16th April. Present in the room are Mr Simon Richardson, his legal representative Mr Clive Percival, Detective Inspector Paul Burgess and Detective Inspector John Tanner.'

Without looking up from his file, he added, 'Mr Richardson, you have been arrested on suspicion of the murder of your wife, Mrs Jane Richardson.'

'This is insane!' muttered Richardson under his breath, clenching his hands together on the table in front of him so tightly that his knuckles had turned white.

Ignoring him, Burgess read out his rights.

'You do not have to say anything, but it may harm your defence if you do not mention when questioned something which you later rely on in court. Anything you do say may be given in evidence.'

Looking up, first at the solicitor, then at his client, Burgess asked, 'Do you understand why you've been arrested, and the allegations that have been made against you?'

'What, that I murdered my wife?'

'You don't have to admit to it, Mr Richardson,' said Burgess, with a malevolent smile. 'Unless of course you want to.'

Looking back at him with defiant disdain, Richardson said, 'Yes, I understand that for some moronic reason you seem to be under the impression that I murdered my wife, despite the fact that I didn't, *obviously*!'

'And you understand your rights under caution?'
'I do.'

Pleased to have the legal formalities out the way, Burgess asked, 'May I ask, for the record, where you were on the night of Saturday, 13th April, between the hours of ten and eleven o'clock?'

'I've already told you this,' he replied, before pointing at Tanner and adding, 'Well, I've already told *him*!'

'For my benefit?' requested Burgess.

'I was away for the weekend.'

Picking up his pen, Burgess said, 'And where was that again?'

'It's called the Manor Resort.'

'That's right. And you said that you were playing golf there, is that correct?'

His eyes flicked between Burgess and Tanner, but he said nothing.

'Sorry, but was that a yes or a no?'

'I was there, if that's what you mean,' he eventually said.

'Playing golf?'

Shifting uncomfortably in his chair, he eventually answered, 'I'd intended to.'

'Forgive me, but does that mean you did, or you didn't?'

'It means exactly what I said. I'd intended to.'

'So you went there, but you didn't actually play?'

'That's correct.'

'I see,' said Burgess. 'I hope you don't mind me asking, but why did you go somewhere to play golf, but not actually play?'

'It's simple,' he shrugged. 'When I hit a few practice balls on Saturday morning, my shoulder started to play up, so I thought it would be sensible not to push it.'

'So you came straight home then?'

'No, I decided to stay.'

'For the whole weekend?'

'I'd already paid for the accommodation, so I thought I might as well.'

'But if you weren't playing golf, what *did* you do for the entire weekend?'

'I watched, as a spectator. That's not against the law, is it?'

'I'd have to check,' said Burgess, pretending to make a note of it. 'But that aside, what's of interest to me is that you told my colleague here that you were away playing golf for the weekend, when you clearly weren't.'

'And as I've just explained, it had been my intention to.'

'But you didn't?'

The question was left unanswered.

'I'm going to be completely honest with you, Mr Richardson. I already knew that you didn't. I knew that because when I spoke to The Manor Resort golf course earlier today, they had no record of you having played there, that weekend or any other.'

Richardson shrugged again. 'As I said, I didn't play.'

'And never had?'

'Not there, no. But I did stay there though. You can check with the hotel if you like.'

'We will, thank you.'

Allowing the room to fall into an oppressive silence, Burgess took a moment to check through his notes before asking, 'I assume you're aware of who your wife's father is?'

'Er…let me guess. Santa Claus?'

'He may as well be, judging by how much money you're likely to inherit, now that your wife – his daughter – is dead.'

'I wasn't aware she was worth anything.'

'Really,' muttered Burgess, disingenuously.

'I wasn't! I mean, I assumed she would be when her parents…'

'Were dead?'

'Passed away,' he corrected, 'but not before then.'

Burgess returned to reading through his notes.

After about a minute of nobody speaking, Richardson asked, 'How long is all this going to take?'

'We've only got a couple more questions, Mr Richardson.'

'Well, would you mind hurrying up then? Unlike you, it would seem, I do have things I need to be getting on with.'

Still perusing his notes, Burgess asked, 'When was the last time you had sexual relations with your wife, Mr Richardson?'

'I beg your pardon?'

Looking up, Burgess said, 'Sorry, didn't you hear the question?'

'I heard the question all right!'

'So, when was the last time you had sex with your wife?'

Staring over at his solicitor, Richardson asked, 'Do I have to answer that?'

'I assume the question has some bearing on the accusation being made against my client?' queried the solicitor.

'It does,' replied Burgess.

Leaning in towards Richardson, the solicitor said,

'You don't *have* to answer, no, but as it's already been explained to you, it could harm your defence if you…'

'It's not that,' interrupted Simon. 'It's just that it's got nothing to do with them!'

'Then it's entirely up to you.'

He thought for a moment, then said, 'I'm sorry, but I'm not prepared to answer that.'

'Was it on Saturday night, by any chance?'

'What do you mean, was it on Saturday night? Of course it wasn't on Saturday night! I've already told you! I was nowhere near the place on Saturday night!'

'I see. So you know where she was murdered then?'

'What?'

'You just said you were nowhere near the place where she was murdered, so I'm forced to assume that you know where that was.'

'I didn't mean that! I meant that I was nowhere near *here*, as in the Broads!'

'So you didn't know she was murdered under Wroxham Railway Bridge, which I understand is just down the road from where you live?'

Richardson seemed momentarily stunned, and it took him a moment or two to reply, which he did with quiet reserve.

'I didn't know that, no.'

'Going back to the last time you had sex with your wife,' continued Burgess. 'When was that again?'

'To be honest, I can't remember.'

'So, not recently?'

'As I said, I can't remember.'

'But you do know that it definitely wasn't on Saturday night?'

Stepping in, the solicitor said, 'May I remind you,

Detective Inspector, that asking the same question over and over again is a well-documented oppressive interview technique used by police the world over. It may well work in other countries, but here in the United Kingdom, any evidence obtained by using it will be deemed inadmissible in court. Consequently, if you continue to question my client along the same lines, it won't make any difference whether he answers you or not!'

'Forgive me,' said Burgess. 'I was just curious to know how it was possible for your client's semen to have been found inside the murder victim, his wife, after she'd been dragged out of the River Thurne on Monday, if the last time he'd had sex with her was so long ago he couldn't remember?'

As Richardson stared at Burgess, his solicitor couldn't help but to lower his head to stare down at the table.

'But… I didn't…'

'Kill her, or have sex with her afterwards?'

'Afterwards? What do you mean, *afterwards*?'

'Afterwards, as in after she was beaten over the head, strangled until dead and then raped.'

'But that's…'

'…utterly disgusting and only something a seriously deranged individual would do? I'd have to agree with you on that one. So you're saying that you didn't, then?'

'Of course I didn't!'

'Even though your semen was found inside her?'

Exchanging desperate glances between his solicitor and the Detective Inspector, he blurted out, 'Look, I've no idea how my…my… got there, but it wasn't me! I didn't…put it there!'

'And of course there's the fact that she was murdered just down the road from where you live, and not forgetting that you're in line to inherit what we've been led to believe is a substantial sum of money.'

'As I've already explained, I was nowhere near the place. I was…'

'*Not* playing golf. Yes, so you said.'

'But I…'

With a victorious grin aimed squarely over at the solicitor, Burgess said, 'I think we can call that lunch, don't you?'

Before the solicitor or anyone else had the chance to say anything, Burgess leaned over toward the digital recorder and said, 'The interview is suspended for one hour. The time now is exactly 13:37.'

As Burgess and Tanner got to their feet, Tanner couldn't help but be impressed. Burgess may not have been up to the task of leading a murder investigation, but what he lacked in that department he certainly made up for in his ability to interrogate a suspect.

- CHAPTER THIRTY TWO -

IMMEDIATELY AFTER THE interview, Burgess and Tanner met briefly with Barrington again, when it was agreed that Burgess should remain at the station, ready to resume the interview with Simon Richardson, hopefully whilst being fed information as it came in. Tanner was to head up to The Manor Resort to confirm Richardson's new alibi, that he had been there, but hadn't taken part in the golf tournament. Jenny, meanwhile, was to stay behind to continue the monotonous, time-consuming task of ploughing through Jane Richardson's electronic communications, looking for anything that could suggest a motive for her husband to do what by then they all believed that he had. At the far end of the room, DS Gilbert was left to do her best to delve into the victim's finances, whilst DS Cooper went over to the marital home to coordinate the forensics unit Gilbert had requested earlier.

For Tanner, driving up to The Manor Resort on his own gave him the perfect chance to clear his mind. It had been his idea that Jenny should stay behind. There'd been a significant amount going on since his arrival at Wroxham Police Station only the morning before, and he needed some quiet meditative time to begin processing it all. Having an attractive Detective

Constable sitting next to him, a girl he was already beginning to have feelings for, was hardly going to help.

The hour-long drive through low undulating landscape proved to be just what he needed, and by the time he reached his destination he felt mentally refreshed.

The Manor Resort was housed in an impressive 18th-century Palladian mansion house, with four Romanesque pillars standing at the top of a flight of shallow stone steps to mark the building's entrance, offering commanding views out over the golf course and the Norfolk coastline beyond.

Reception was a high-fronted desk set in one corner of a vast open space with a polished marble floor, a sweeping double-staircase and a lofty ceiling. Behind the desk sat two attractive young ladies wearing the Resort's uniform of purple jackets over crisp white blouses. One of them was serving a guest, but as Tanner approached, the other looked up, smiled and asked, 'May I help you?'

As her voice echoed around the reception area, in a bid to be discreet, Tanner pulled out his ID and said quietly, 'My name's Detective Inspector Tanner from Norfolk Police. I was hoping to find out about someone who may have been here to play golf last weekend.'

With a fixed smile, and as if she'd said it a hundred times before, the girl said, 'This is The Manor Resort hotel. The golf course is next door. If you follow the road around, you'll see a sign for the entrance on your left.'

'But this is where visitors stay who are here to play

golf?'

'Naturally, yes.'

'Then I wonder if you could tell me if a man called Simon Richardson was staying here on Saturday night?'

After a moment's consideration, she said, 'The name does sound familiar. Hold on, let me check for you.' A few clicks of the mouse later, she said, 'Did you say Mr Richardson?'

'Simon Richardson,' confirmed Tanner.

'He checked in on Friday. Room 14.'

'And when did he check out?'

'On Sunday,' she replied, in a curt but professional manner.

Tanner heard the sound of the entrance door opening behind him, and turned to see a well-dressed elderly couple enter the hotel and approach the desk.

Having also seen them, the lady asked, 'Is there anything else I can help you with?'

All he'd so far discovered was that someone called Simon Richardson had checked in on Friday and checked out again on Sunday, something he could have found out by simply phoning them up. 'I don't suppose you can remember what he did when he was here?'

With a scowl of rebuke, she said, 'It's not our job to keep tabs on our guests!' and glanced behind him at the waiting couple.

'But you remember him, though?'

She stared blankly at Tanner, clearly wanting him to leave so that she could deal with the paying customers.

Reading her thoughts, Tanner leaned forward, engaged eye contact with her, and in a quiet but firm voice, said, 'This is a murder enquiry!'

That seemed to get the girl's attention, and seeing her colleague was now free, she called her over. 'Sarah, could you attend to Mr and Mrs Winterbourne? Thankyou.'

As the old couple smiled and stepped over to other side of the reception desk, the girl was now free to focus on the questions being asked of her by the Detective Inspector. 'He came in carrying all his golf clubs, if that helps.'

'Do you know if he left at all, on Saturday?'

'From what I remember, he spent pretty much the entire time in his room, and only came down for dinner.'

'Are you sure?'

'I can't be one hundred percent certain, no.'

'But you were on duty at the time.'

'I do afternoons and evenings, yes. Guests are free to come and go as they please, obviously. But I did have the impression that he'd be the type who'd be looking to spend the weekend in his room.'

'What makes you think that?'

Glancing over at her colleague, and seeing that she was fully engaged with dealing with the old couple, she leaned forward slightly and said, 'I don't think he was alone.'

'He was here with a woman?'

She shook her head meaningfully. 'He was with a friend. A *male* friend.'

'You mean, you think he's gay?'

'Well, I'm fairly certain his friend is, at least. Fake tan, whitened teeth, exceptionally good-looking, definitely wearing eyeliner, and with a weird haircut - shaved sides with a long fringe; it's a particular style.

He also had a small teardrop tattoo on his neck and, well, he just had that sort of look about him.'

Realising she'd just given the same description of the bar manager from the Bittern pub as Burgess had when they'd been speaking to DCI Barrington, Tanner asked, 'Do you know his name, by any chance?'

'I can look it up for you.' Returning to her screen, a moment later she said, 'Mr Stephen Perry. He took the adjacent room, number 16, but our cleaner said it was hardly used.'

As she said that, he pulled out his phone, and after thanking the receptionist, stepped away from the desk and put a call through to Jenny.

The moment the call was answered, he said, 'Jenny, it's Tanner. How's everything going?'

'Nothing much has happened really,' she replied. 'Burgess has been in and out a couple of times with the suspect, but he doesn't seem to be getting anywhere. And DS Cooper called in to say that he didn't find anything that he thought could have been used as a murder weapon, but forensics have taken away Richardson's clothes and shoes. The only person who's had any luck is Vicky.'

'Vicky?' asked Tanner, unfamiliar with the name.

'Sorry – DS Gilbert. She was finally given a warrant to access Jane Richardson's financial accounts, and it would appear she's worth a considerable sum.'

'How much?'

'We don't know, exactly, but her trust fund matured when she was twenty-five, and that was worth over five million, most of which is tied up in stocks and shares. On top of that, she owns a twenty-five percent share in her dad's company, and has over £120,000 cash in her bank account, which makes you wonder why she was bothering to work at the pub.'

'Probably learning the ropes, with a view to taking over the business,' replied Tanner. 'Anyway, can you do me a favour?'

'No problem.'

'Can you go into the system and see if Burgess has left a note on there saying what the bar manager's name is – the one at the Bittern?'

'OK, hold on.'

About a minute later, she asked, 'Do you mean Stephen Perry?'

'Yes, him! We're going to have to have a word.'

'With the Bittern's bar manager?' she repeated, sounding confused.

'Stephen Perry, yes! I've discovered that our Simon Richardson is correct in saying that he was staying at The Manor Resort hotel, but he wasn't there alone.'

'He was there with the bar manager from the Bittern?'

'Uh-huh,' confirmed Tanner. 'They had adjacent rooms, one of which was hardly used. I'd therefore have to say that there's a very real possibility that the two of them planned it together, especially now we know how much Jane was worth.'

There was a pause from the other end of the line, before Jenny said, 'There's also another possibility that's probably worth considering.'

'What's that?'

'That Stephen Perry planned it on his own. If he'd found out how much his boyfriend's wife was worth, and that Richardson was going to inherit her estate, then he'd certainly have a motive. All he'd have to do would be to marry his boyfriend, and he'd be set for life. And without wanting to sound crude, he'd have had access to Richardson's semen as well.'

'Thanks for that, Jenny.'

'But it's true though, isn't it?'

'No doubt it is, but why would he want to inject his boyfriend's semen into his dead wife?'

'Maybe it wasn't about the money,' mused Jenny. 'Maybe Richardson had just told him that his wife was pregnant, and that he wanted to make a fresh start with her?'

'Meaning that they were going to have to stop seeing each other.'

'So Perry decided to frame him for his wife's murder.'

'And with Stephen Perry being the only person who'd be able to corroborate his alibi,' added Tanner, 'all he'd have to do would be to confirm that Richardson had been with him, but that he just happened to pop out on Saturday night.'

There was a momentary pause, before Jenny asked, 'What d'you want me to do?'

'I suggest you relay this conversation to Burgess. Then I think we need to ask Barrington if it's OK to bring Stephen Perry in for questioning. Actually, no. I'd better ask him. But there's no doubt that we need to find out what he knows.'

'No probs,' agreed Jenny.

'Anyway,' continued Tanner, 'I'm heading back now, so I should be there in about an hour or so.'

- CHAPTER THIRTY THREE -

AS SOON AS he finished speaking with Jenny, Tanner put a call through to DCI Barrington, during which it was agreed that Stephen Perry should be brought in for questioning. Even if he was able to corroborate Richardson's alibi, the hotel was only an hour's drive from Wroxham, and it wouldn't have been difficult for either one of them, or even both, to have left the hotel unnoticed.

It was agreed that DS Cooper should take Jenny down to the Bittern, along with a couple of uniformed police constables, to find Perry and bring him in. Burgess was to remain at the station, keeping the pressure firmly on Richardson. That way, by the time Tanner returned from the Manor Resort hotel, Stephen Perry would hopefully be ready for Burgess and Tanner to begin the interview process.

Arriving back at base, Tanner was just in time to see a police car pull into the carpark, immediately followed by a dark blue Audi A5.

He paused to watch, as amidst a storm of flash photography, a tall tanned young man with a long fringe, wearing skinny-fit black jeans and a black military style jacket, was helped out of the back of the police car and escorted inside the station, smiling and nodding over at the journalists.

Seeing Jenny emerge from the Audi along with DS Cooper, ignoring the journalists' shouted questions, Tanner headed over to join them.

'So that's the barman from the Bittern?'

'Uh-huh,' she replied. 'And he didn't exactly come quietly either. He refused to co-operate, so we had no choice but to arrest him, only for him to begin accusing us of police brutality, gay-bashing *and* unlawful arrest.'

'He doesn't seem to be too upset now, though,' observed Tanner.

They looked over at him.

He was clearly doing everything possible to court the attention of the journalists, and had begun shouting, 'This is how Norfolk Police treats gay people! By arresting them!'

'Let's hope he's as vocal when being questioned,' said Tanner, as he followed Jenny inside.

Once in the reception area, Perry was handed over to the duty sergeant for formal processing, during which time he was advised to take legal counsel, and that if he didn't have a solicitor, one could be provided free of charge. But he declined, saying that he'd nothing to hide.

Eventually he was led into the station's second interview room, where he was soon joined by Burgess and Tanner.

With the digital recorder on, and the legal formalities complete, Burgess began the interview.

'You do know you're allowed to have a solicitor present, don't you?'

'As I told the other guy,' Perry said, flicking his fringe out of his eyes, 'I've got nothing to hide.'

'As long as you understand your rights, that's fine by me. So, where shall we start?'

'How about by explaining to me what I'm doing here, other than you've got a thing against gay men, of course?'

Ignoring the question, Burgess asked, 'Where were you on Saturday night, between the hours of ten and eleven?'

'I was in bed with Simon Richardson.'

'I see. And where was that?'

'At the Manor Resort hotel.'

Burgess paused for a moment, before asking, 'Where did you two first meet?'

'At the Bittern. He'd come in occasionally at lunchtime, when Jane first started working there. He'd tell everyone that he'd come to see her, but he told me later that he only showed up to see me.'

'How long ago was that?'

'About a year, give or take.'

'And when did you start seeing each other?'

'It was a few months later, I suppose. He was making it very obvious that he fancied me, so I asked him out, and it went from there.'

Burgess paused, thought for a moment, and then asked, 'How often did you go off together for the weekend?'

'Only about once a month. We would have gone away more, but he said that he was too busy; that, and his wife would become suspicious.'

Stopping to refer to his notes, Burgess deliberately allowed the room to fall into silence. After about a minute or so, he looked up and said, 'When we first spoke, you said you knew that Jane Richardson's father owned the pub. Did you also know that he was the founder and CEO of the Lambert Oak pub chain?'

'We all did. He came in and told us, when Jane started working there.'

'So you know John Lambert then?'

'Most people around here do, don't they?'

'And when did you find out how much Jane Richardson was worth? Was that before or after you asked her husband out on a date?'

'Oh, I see what you're getting at now. You think that because I'm gay, I therefore must be mentally ill. Consequently I wouldn't think twice before murdering my boyfriend's wife, just because her dad's rich.'

'I wasn't talking about her dad, I was talking about Jane Richardson. Did you know she was worth over five million pounds?'

'I do now!'

'Did you before?'

'Surprisingly, it didn't come up in conversation, no.'

'I see. So you're honestly trying to tell me that of all the men living in the Broads, you just happened to fall for the one married to a woman who's worth over five million pounds?'

'Unfortunately, all the men who live in the Broads aren't gay, which does narrow the field down. Most men who live here are homophobic retards, like you!' With that, he gave Burgess a self-amused smirk.

'So you're not bothered who you go out with, as long as they're gay?'

'Well, it does help.'

'And rich, of course, or in this instance, married to

a woman who is, especially after you realised that were his wife to die, your boyfriend would get the lot. You'd then only have to marry him and you'd become an over-night multi-millionaire.'

'I think you've been watching a little too much TV, detective.'

Burgess took a moment to collect his thoughts and review his notes. As he did, Tanner picked up a pen that was on the desk, and leaning over towards Burgess, he encircled a word he'd seen on the report.

Understanding what Tanner meant, without looking up, Burgess asked, almost casually, 'Did you know Jane Richardson was pregnant?'

Perry froze, then looked first at Burgess, then at Tanner.

Glancing up from his notes, Burgess asked, 'May I take that as a no?'

'You're lying,' said Perry, as he studied Burgess's face.

Looking down again, Burgess turned over a page before adding, 'Between fourteen to twenty-seven weeks, according to the post-mortem report.'

'I'm afraid I don't believe you, detective. Simon would have told me if she was.'

'But he *did* tell you, didn't he?'

'I just said that he didn't!'

'Just before he told you that he'd decided to make a fresh start with his wife.'

'This is stupid!'

'And therefore he wouldn't be able to see you anymore.'

'As I said, I didn't know!'

'And that's when you realised two things; that if his

wife was pregnant, Simon must have been screwing her behind your back, and secondly that you were about to lose not only him, but all his wife's money as well. And that's when you decided to take revenge by killing her and making it look like your boyfriend did it.'

'And how would I make it look like Simon did it? I suppose I bashed her over the head with one of his stupid golf clubs?'

'Actually no. We found traces of your boyfriend's semen inside his wife. Apparently, it had been inserted there after she'd been killed. And as, according to your testimony at least, he was at the Manor Resort at the time of her death, it only stands to reason that it was you who got hold of a sample of his semen – how you did that I don't wish to know – drugged him, drove back down to Wroxham, killed his wife, injected his sperm into her, and headed back to the hotel just in time to give him another blowjob!'

Perry sat back in his chair, and as he folded his arms, he grinned at Burgess and said, 'This is great! I should've brought popcorn!'

'So you're denying it then?'

'Well, I'd love to own up to it, of course; I mean, who wouldn't? But the problem is, as I mentioned at the beginning, I was with Simon all night. And as he wasn't drugged, but was wide awake at the time you're referring to, he'll be able to vouch for me.'

'Ah, but will he though, especially when he's given a choice of either owning up to having murdered his own wife, or saying that he mysteriously fell asleep at nine o'clock on the Saturday night, just after you'd sucked him off, and didn't wake up till the following morning?'

'But I didn't do it!'

'So it was your boyfriend then?'

'It wasn't him either!'

'Well, it must have been one of you! Unfortunately, there's no other way his semen could have ended up inside his wife after she'd been murdered unless one of you deliberately placed it there. And knowing that it would directly incriminate him if he'd been the one to do so, then it must have been you!'

'Well, it wasn't!'

'So you planned it together then, so providing yourselves with the perfect alibi!'

'Of course not, and I can prove it!'

'You can prove it?' repeated Burgess. 'Excellent! Now I'm the one who should've brought popcorn.'

'It's on my phone. The one you took off me when you dragged me in here.'

'And what's on your phone that can prove your innocence?'

'About a hundred-odd photos and videos. And they'll all be date and time stamped. If you look at them, I think you'll find they'll prove that Simon and I *were* at the Manor Resort hotel on Saturday night, and that neither of us left!'

- CHAPTER THIRTY FOUR -

ABOUT HALF AN hour later, after Stephen Perry's phone had been checked for the images and videos mentioned, Tanner and Burgess were standing in front of DCI Barrington's desk again.

Having just explained to him that both their prime suspects had an alibi supported by material evidence, which would be virtually impossible to fabricate, and even more challenging to disprove in court, and that their only part in the whole thing had been that Simon Richardson was a closet homosexual, who'd been having a clandestine affair with the bar manager from the Bittern pub, they were bracing themselves for Barrington's response.

At first, Barrington neither said nor did anything except to glare at them, as his face slowly filled up with blood. Eventually, with a calm but menacing voice, he said, 'Is this some sort of a joke?'

Not daring to look at him directly, but staring at the back wall instead, Burgess said, 'I'm afraid not, sir.'

'You're honestly standing there telling me that after all *that*, Richardson and that gay-boy friend of his are innocent?'

'It does look that way, sir, yes.'

'Both of them?'

'Both of them,' confirmed Burgess.

'But…what about the semen?'

'At this stage, we don't know how that got there, sir, but Simon Richardson and Stephen Perry were definitely in bed together at the Manor Resort hotel at the time of her death, so we can only conclude that it must have been placed there by someone else.'

'Do you have any idea how stupid this is going to make me look?'

'I can only apologise, sir,' said Burgess.

'You can *only* apologise?' repeated Barrington.

'Er, yes, sir.'

'So you're not going to bother to find out who actually did it?'

'I-I didn't mean that, sir.'

'Well, that's what it sounded like!'

Burgess decided not to respond to that.

Barrington glared at Burgess for another moment or two, then pushed his chair away from his desk, stood up and marched over towards his window. There he peered out through half-closed blinds at the reporters beyond, who were still milling about on the pavement, just behind the carpark's low red brick wall. None of them looked as if they were going anywhere.

'So I suppose we're going to have to let them go,' he said, with obvious reluctance.

'We are, sir, yes,' replied Burgess.

'OK, but I don't want them walking out the front. I can't afford to have them holding an impromptu press conference, telling the world that the only reason they were arrested is because they're gay! They can be driven back to their homes from around the back. And use a police van - no squad cars! I don't want that lot seeing them leave. Understood?'

'Yes, sir,' replied Burgess, 'but they're bound to talk to the press at some stage.'

Spinning around, Barrington said, 'I'm fully aware of that, thank you, Burgess, but not immediately after they've been released, and not directly outside my police station, not when half the country's press is assembled, ready to dote on their every word.'

'Yes, sir.'

Resuming his seat, Barrington scowled at Burgess and Tanner. 'So, what's your next step? I suppose you're going to arrest Mr and Mrs Lambert, only to find out that they were having a sleepover with the Royal Family at the time?'

Forced to ignore Barrington's glib sarcasm, Burgess said, 'To be honest, sir, we're not sure.'

'You're not sure,' repeated Barrington, with a look of disdain.

Shifting his weight from one foot to the other, Burgess said, 'Er, not really, sir, no.'

Barrington turned to Tanner. 'How about you?'

'Personally, sir, I think the case rests on the sperm sample. It was clearly placed there intentionally, and if not by either Simon Richardson or Stephen Perry, then it must have been another person.'

'No kidding!'

'I suggest we look into the possibility that Richardson has been having an affair with someone else. Perry said during his interview that the only reason why he was only able to go away for the weekend once a month was because Richardson was busy. But if his wife worked half the weekend, it's difficult to see what he'd have been busy doing, unless it was spending time with another man, or maybe even a woman. So I suggest we begin a background check on Richardson, to see if there's any sign of him seeing someone else, and go from there. Meanwhile, it may be worth speaking to his neighbours, to see if they've either seen or heard him entertaining any other visitors. As he works predominantly from home, with both Stephen Perry and his wife at the pub, it would be a relatively straightforward process for him to invite other people around.'

'OK, do it! But before you let Richardson go, I want forensics back at his house. See if they can find any prints of anyone other than him and his wife. And get them to check his car as well!'

'Yes, sir.'

'And you'd better delay releasing Stephen Perry. The longer we can hold off on the press finding out that we've just been forced to release our two prime suspects, the better!'

- CHAPTER THIRTY FIVE -

I T WASN'T UNTIL gone nine o'clock in the evening that forensics finished dusting for prints in Simon Richardson's house. Barrington had left work long before, leaving Tanner, Burgess and Jenny to frantically search through Richardson's electronic communications, desperately looking for some evidence that he'd been recently seeing someone on the side, someone other than the bar manager from the Bittern.

Whilst they did that, Cooper and Gilbert drove down to ask the couple's neighbours if they'd seen anyone, male or female, making regular visits.

When the electronic records yielded nothing, and with none of the neighbours having seen any cars pull up or people arrive frequently, other than the house's owners, Barrington was eventually forced to give the order to release both Richardson and Perry, with full knowledge that they didn't have a single other suspect in mind to replace them.

However, the Chief Inspector's plan for them to leave unnoticed by the press backfired in a quite dramatic fashion. Although Richardson was more than happy to leave by the back door, and to be driven discreetly to the end of his road in the back of a police van, Stephen Perry refused point-blank. Instead, he marched out the front door, straight up to the awaiting press, and spent a good ten minutes ranting and raving about how he and Simon Richardson had been wrongly accused of murder, and the only reason they'd been arrested in the first place was because they were in a homosexual relationship together.

For the journalists who'd been waiting outside since that morning, with nothing more to show for it other than a series of no comments and some pictures and video of two unknown men being led inside, this news was an absolute godsend. Furthermore, it happened just in time to make the live feed to the 10 o'clock evening news.

For just about everyone else involved, it was the very worst thing that could happen.

For Simon Richardson, it meant that everyone now knew he was gay, something he'd been desperate to hide since he was a teenager. That was why he'd asked Jane to marry him, so that he could blend in with society without anyone ever finding out. It was also the reason why it had been so difficult for them to have children. He'd never been able to find her sexually attractive, and it had been a real struggle for him to become aroused enough in her presence for them to have sexual intercourse.

For Jane's parents, the news came as a humiliating slap in the face. To find out on the national news that their son-in-law was not only gay, but had been cheating on their murdered daughter with another man, sent Ruth Lambert into a demonic rage, which ended up in her breaking down in torrents of tears and locking herself in the bathroom.

John had never seen her in such a state, and became

so concerned that she might attempt to take her own life that he called for the family doctor, who came straight away. When he managed to persuade her to unlock the bathroom door, he gave her a heavy sedative, and John was able to help her to bed.

It was only after she fell asleep, and the doctor left, that John felt able to vent his own fury, which he did by putting a call through to his solicitor. The Norfolk Constabulary, and especially DCI Barrington, were going to pay, literally, for having brought so much public humiliation to him and his family.

But Barrington didn't have a chance to think about how John Lambert was going to react to the news. As soon as the bulletin aired, he received a call from his immediate superior, Superintendent Phillip Whitaker, demanding to know just what the hell he thought he was playing at, arresting not one but two people for the murder of John Lambert's daughter, only to then release them without charge, and in such a public manner. The situation seemed so desperate that Barrington felt forced to lie to him, saying that another arrest was imminent.

Barrington then phoned Burgess, demanding to know exactly why he'd allowed Stephen Perry to go anywhere near the press, let alone hold his own impromptu press conference right outside Wroxham Police Station, when he'd given him strict instructions not to.

Burgess, in his defence, said that once they'd released Stephen Perry, short of somehow convincing the local magistrate to slap a gagging order on him, they had very little control over what he did, or who he decided to talk to about the case and his relationship with Richardson.

Barrington became even more upset when he learnt that neither Burgess, Tanner, nor anyone else at the station had managed to find a single other person, male or female, who'd been having an intimate relationship with Simon Richardson, intimate enough at least to actively encourage him to provide them with a sample of his semen.

With the case at a complete dead end, an exasperated Barrington told them all to go home, but to be at work first thing the next day, at which time he expected Burgess to brief his team on a new plan going forward.

- CHAPTER THIRTY SIX -

Wednesday, 17th April

MUCH LIKE EVERYONE else, Tanner left Wroxham Police Station feeling drained and frustrated. Their work over the past two days had resulted in nothing more than the announcement that the husband of a murder victim was gay, and that he'd been having an affair with another man. As far as the investigation was concerned, they were right back where they'd started: with the body of an attractive young woman, about halfway through her pregnancy, who'd been beaten over the head, strangled, raped, and then dumped into the river. And the only clue as to who'd been responsible led to two people who had a rock solid alibi.

At the start of the day, Tanner had been hoping to ask Jenny out for a meal again, maybe somewhere different; but not now. It was clear leaving work that neither of them had an appetite for doing so. All they wanted to do was to go home and get some rest; and after dining alone at the Maltsters pub, that was exactly what Tanner did, making sure he'd set his phone to go off twenty minutes earlier than usual before falling into another deep, dreamless sleep.

It wasn't his alarm that woke him up. It was a phone call about five minutes before it was due to go off, from the very person he'd woken up thinking about.

'Tanner, it's Jenny. Are you awake?'

He blinked the web of sleep from his eyes. 'Just about.'

'Burgess just called me,' she said. 'Another body's been found!'

Disturbing images of his daughter crowded Tanner's mind.

'Are you still there?'

'Sorry. Yes,' he replied, fighting to shake off the memories.

As his brain cleared, and feeling more awake, he asked, 'Whereabouts?'

'A carpark in Irstead. It's at the northern end of the Broads.'

'Does it look like it's connected?'

'All Burgess told me was that it's another woman, to call you, and to head up there. I know where it is. Do you want me to pick you up?'

'That would be useful, thanks.'

With the early roads devoid of traffic, it wasn't long before the Golf's headlights were illuminating the fluorescent yellow jacket of a uniformed police constable, stomping his feet in a bid to keep warm, with his collar zipped all the way up to his nose.

Recognising first her car, and then Jenny behind the steering wheel, he stood to one side to direct her into a small public carpark.

Through tendrils of mist illuminated by the car's

headlights, they could see that the entire far section of the carpark had been cordoned off with a line of blue and white police tape. Before that, an ambulance waited with two police cars and three other vehicles, one of which Tanner recognised as belonging to DI Burgess.

After Jenny had parked, they made their way over towards another yellow-jacketed PC.

He held up the police tape for them, and as they ducked underneath, he nodded over towards the river, saying, 'The body is on the slipway.'

Tanner saw there was a narrow concrete sloping ramp that led down into the river, presumably used to launch and retrieve small sailing craft, like single-engine powerboats and dinghies.

Standing on the edge of the slipway, facing down the slope with his hands buried deep in his pockets, the figure of DI Burgess was silhouetted against the surrounding mist.

Hearing someone approach, he glanced around.

When he saw Tanner and Jenny, he looked surprisingly pleased.

'What've we got?' asked Tanner, as he approached, although by that time he could already see.

At the base of the slipway, half-submerged in the river, lay the crumpled body of a blood-soaked young woman, her pale white face staring up at them, as if pleading for help.

Kneeling down beside her was someone who was now familiar to him.

'We're not sure,' replied Burgess, looking down at the body. 'Dr Johnstone's just finishing.'

Having heard the conversation going on behind

him, the doctor got to his feet and made his way up the slipway.

As he pulled off a pair of bloodied latex gloves, he said, 'She's in a bit of a state, I'm afraid.'

'How long's she been dead for?' asked Burgess.

'Not long. I'd say around eight hours.'

'Cause of death?'

'Well, she didn't drown, I know that much. And there's no sign she was strangled. I'm fairly certain it was from a single blow to the front of her head.'

'Like the last one?'

'I'd say so, yes. But there's something else, which isn't very pleasant, I'm afraid.'

Burgess, Tanner and Jenny all frowned over at him.

'She's been cut open.'

Staring back towards the body, Burgess said, 'Sorry, but how d'you mean?'

'Her abdomen. It looks as if someone's tried to disembowel her.'

Hearing that, Jenny instinctively lifted her hand to her mouth to ask, 'But…why would anyone do such a thing?'

'I've got no idea,' replied the doctor, and turned to glance back down at her, just as black syrup-like water began lapping against her exposed thighs. 'But at least forensics should have more luck with this one. She's only been partially submerged, as you can see.'

'I assume she wasn't killed here?' asked Tanner.

'I doubt it. There's not nearly enough blood. My guess would be that whoever did this was intending to use the slipway to dump the body into the river. And as there's no sign of any blood anywhere except down at the bottom, she must have been wrapped up in something. That, or she was originally in the back of a car which was reversed down the slope. Either way, I think it's likely that the intention had been for her to have been pushed all the way out into the river; not left like this. So maybe whoever did this was disturbed before he had a chance to finish the job.'

Nodding in agreement, Burgess asked, 'How long till we can have the post-mortem report?'

'Somehow I knew you were going to ask that. I'll push for end of play today.'

Catching his eye, Tanner asked, 'Would it be possible to have an interim report before then? Maybe by late morning?'

'I'll do the best I can.'

The doctor was about to leave, when he turned to say, 'Oh, I nearly forgot,' and reached inside his forensics overalls to pull out a series of clear plastic evidence bags.

Handing them over to Burgess, he said, 'I didn't find a handbag or anything, but I found a mobile phone in her coat pocket. The others are her items of jewellery, all I could get off her at least. Anyway, assuming the phone belongs to her, identifying this one should at least be considerably more straightforward than the last.'

- CHAPTER THIRTY SEVEN -

THERE WAS A buzz in the air at Wroxham Police Station, as the news spread that the body of another woman had been found in the early hours of the morning, with similar injuries to Jane Richardson. The good news was that the mobile phone gave them the means to make a formal identification.

As they waited for an interim report to come through from the medical examiner, Burgess and Tanner went over the details with Barrington in his office, whilst deciding how best to proceed.

Just before ten o'clock, Dr Johnstone emailed the report through.

Ten minutes after that, Barrington led Burgess and Tanner out into the main office to begin a station-wide briefing.

'If I could have everyone's attention!' he called out, as the three of them reached the whiteboard at the far end of the office, now covered in a series of headshots, scrawled marker pen notes and references.

He waited for everyone to settle down.

'As I'm sure you all know by now, on Monday we discovered the body of a young woman who we identified as being Jane Richardson, the manager of the Bittern pub, and who was brutally murdered on her way back from work at around half past ten on Saturday night.

'On Tuesday we arrested two people in connection with the murder, the victim's husband, Simon Richardson, and the man who we later discovered he'd been having an affair with, Mr Stephen Perry. However, despite substantial evidence against them, both suspects were eventually able to produce an alibi that was supported by both video and photographic material, giving us no choice but to release them.

'As of seven o'clock this morning, we have another victim. The full post-mortem has yet to come through, but what we've learnt so far gives us reason to believe that this woman has also been murdered, and most likely by the same person.

'Before I hand you over to DI Burgess, I just want to remind you of the serious nature of these crimes and what it means if they are linked, so I expect you all to give Burgess your continued commitment and support. And I hope it goes without saying that with the media interest in serial killers being as it is, we'll be under the spotlight even more now.

'Over to you, Burgess!'

Taking a step forward, Burgess stared around at everyone in the room.

'As DCI Barrington has said,' he began, 'it looks like we have a double murder on our hands.'

Allowing the room to fall silent, he turned to face the whiteboard behind him.

From a plastic folder he removed a photograph which he posted adjacent to that of Jane Richardson. The new photograph was of a girl in her late twenties or early thirties with dark brown hair, smiling at the camera. In her hand was a glass of red wine, and surrounding her was a group of girls, all of whom looked to be having a great time. The incongruity of that image, given the circumstances, wasn't lost on any of them.

'We've yet to formally identify the body, but at this stage we believe the second victim is Mrs Emily Harris from Great Yarmouth. She was reported missing by her husband this morning. According to him, she went to visit her mother after work yesterday evening, but never returned.'

He looked over at the picture again.

'Emily was thirty-two years old, Co-Founder and Director of Powell Harris Estate Agents, located just down the road from where she lives. She was killed by a single blow to her frontal lobe. The wound is almost identical to that noted on Jane Richardson's head. She was also raped, post-mortem. There's something else as well.'

He hesitated. 'It looks like someone attempted to disembowel her.'

A stunned silence fell over the office.

'We don't know if Jane Richardson suffered the same fate. As you know, she was pulled into the propeller of a reversing boat, so it was impossible to tell, but I don't think we should rule it out.

'Emily's body was found at the base of a slipway in the small village of Irstead. It's believed that she was murdered around eight or nine hours earlier. That gives us an approximate time of death of between ten and eleven o'clock last night. However, we don't believe she was killed where she was found, so the body must have been left on the slipway sometime afterwards. We think the intention was to push her body out into the River Ant, but for some reason that didn't happen, possibly because whoever did this was interrupted. If that is the case, then there's a strong chance that we may have ourselves a witness.'

DS Cooper raised his hand.

'Are there any CCTV cameras in the area?'

'We couldn't see any, no, but it would be worth checking, both in the carpark where the slipway is, and on any approaching roads. Have a look and let me know. And whilst you're there, start going door to door to ask if anyone saw anything unusual last night. Take a couple of uniforms down to help.'

He turned his attention back to the wider group, now listening in grim-faced silence.

'As you've been told, both victims were raped post-mortem. In the case of Jane Richardson, semen was found inside her which belonged to her husband, Simon Richardson. That was one of the main reasons why we arrested him. Semen has also been found inside the second victim. It too belongs to Simon Richardson.'

News of this sent whispered discussions flying around the room.

Raising his hands to placate those in attendance, Burgess called out, 'I know what you're all thinking, especially as he was released only a couple of hours before this happened, and we're not ruling him out - which is why we still have him up on the board as a suspect. We're also keeping his boyfriend, Stephen Perry, up there as well. However, at this stage we think it's more likely that someone else is doing this, deliberately trying to incriminate Richardson; someone who knows him and is holding some sort of a grudge. Due to his sexual orientation, and that both victims were raped, we believe this is most likely to be a man who is gay, or at least bi-sexual. Someone who at some point has had sexual relations with Richardson. It is very possible that whoever did this may have been planning it for some considerable time, so much so that they froze a sample of his sperm. If that was the case, that means that the person responsible could have done so months, if not years before. So our first priority is to look into his past relationships. We need to find out about *anyone* he's had a relationship with. Tanner and Jenny, I'll leave that with you.'

After seeing them nod their agreement, Burgess looked over at Vicky Gilbert. 'We also need to look into Emily Harris. Vicky, if you could begin that process. See if there's anything that connects her with either Simon or Jane Richardson; friends, work, school, anything.

'DCI Barrington and myself are about to issue a statement to the press outside. Nothing fancy, just enough to give them the facts as they stand. Hopefully that will stop them from going away and writing up something about how Simon Richardson was released only to murder again. Obviously we won't be releasing the name of the second victim, not until we've told the husband, and he's been able to formally identify the body. I've chosen the short straw for that, and I'll be heading over to meet with him immediately after we've issued the statement.

'It looks like we have a particularly nasty individual out there roaming the Broads, someone who not only seems happy enough to take the lives of innocent young women, but also feels it necessary to rape and mutilate them afterwards. It goes without saying that we need to work fast. Does everyone understand what they're doing?'

All those in the room nodded their agreement, and as nobody seemed to have any questions, Burgess concluded the briefing. 'As soon as you get anything, let me know. That's it for now.

- CHAPTER THIRTY EIGHT -

THE MOMENT THE briefing finished, Barrington and Burgess headed outside to issue a formal statement to the press, leaving the rest of the team to focus on their various tasks.

Working together, it didn't take long for Tanner and Jenny to discover that before Richardson was married, he'd had a series of clandestine relationships with other men, all the way back to university, even though he'd been working hard to give the outward impression of being every bit the heterosexual male that society seemed more ready to accept. None of his various affairs and sexual liaisons stood out in any particular way. They'd all been either one night stands, or the relationship had only lasted for a few weeks.

What also became clear was that he'd had the idea of using the institution of marriage as a façade to hide his true sexual orientation for some time, certainly long before he'd met Jane. Prior to marrying her, he'd been engaged twice before. Without making the effort to ask him directly about this, they could only assume that he'd gone ahead and married Jane because he felt that there were only so many times he could break off an engagement before questions began to be asked.

As Tanner and Jenny were delving into Simon's past, over at the cluster of desks near the whiteboard,

DS Gilbert waded through Emily Harris's personal files, desperately looking for anything that could connect her to either Simon Richardson or his late wife. Thankfully it didn't take her long to find it, and the moment she made the connection, she raced over to Tanner and Jenny, her auburn curls knocking against her shoulders, to announce, 'It's the IVF clinic! Emily Harris and her husband were using the same one as Simon and Jane. Buxton Manor!'

As Tanner and Jenny stared at each other, Jenny said, 'That's where whoever did this must have got hold of Simon's sperm sample!'

'Which means that the murderer either works there, or has access,' said Tanner.

'Unless someone broke in,' cautioned Jenny.

As they pulled their coats from the backs of their chairs, Tanner smiled at DS Gilbert. 'Good work, Vicky! We're going to head straight over there. If you could tell Barrington and Burgess where we're going, that would be appreciated.'

- CHAPTER THIRTY NINE -

ABOUT HALF AN hour later, Tanner and Jenny were back at the now familiar Buxton Manor, but unlike their first visit, when they were fishing for a motive for Simon Richardson to have murdered his wife, now they were looking for a killer.

Behind the reception desk sat the same outwardly cheerful-looking receptionist, who heard them come in, glanced up, and with a surprised look, said, 'Oh, hello again!'

'Good morning,' said Tanner, with formal politeness. 'Is Dr Khatri free?'

'I doubt it! He's very busy today.'

'I'm sure he is, but please inform him that Detective Inspector Tanner and Detective Constable Evans are here again.'

Giving Tanner the briefest look of defiant belligerence, the receptionist picked up her desk phone.

After a brief conversation, she returned the receiver to its cradle, forced a smile and said, 'He'll be down in a minute. May I get you a coffee?'

'We're fine, thank you,' said Tanner, with brusque dismissal, before turning around to look for somewhere to sit.

Directly behind him sat two young couples, at opposite ends of a row of eight chairs, all nervously leafing through some of the lifestyle magazines that had been arranged with neat precision over a low mahogany coffee table.

Tanner was just about to indicate to Jenny that perhaps they should take a seat themselves, when the side door creaked open, and Dr Khatri's head appeared.

Looking directly at Tanner, in a low voice he said, 'Would you like to come through?'

Back inside his office, with the door firmly closed, directing Tanner and Jenny to take a seat, the doctor asked, 'How can I help you this time?'

Diving straight in, Tanner said, 'Another body was found early this morning.'

Leaning back in his chair, Dr Khatri said, 'I heard on the news. But I'm not sure what that has to do with either myself or the clinic.'

'She's yet to be formally identified,' continued Tanner, 'but at this stage we believe her to be Mrs Emily Harris.'

The doctor showed no immediate sign that the name meant anything to him, and at first did nothing but to continue to stare at Tanner with his dark sunken eyes. But after a moment or two, he leaned forward in his chair, reached over to his laptop and clicked the mouse a few times. 'I assume you already know that she's a client of ours.'

'We do.'

'OK, well, I'm obviously very sorry to hear this. How do you think we can help?'

Deciding to get straight to the point, Tanner said, 'We need to know where you keep your clients' sperm samples; and more importantly, who has access to them?'

'What on Earth do you want to know that for?'

'We've found the same man's semen inside *both* victims.'

'But...wouldn't that suggest it's the same...?'

'That was our original belief, but we now have reason to think that someone is using the sample in order to frame someone.'

'You mean...Simon Richardson?'

Tanner said nothing, but maintained his steady gaze at the doctor. 'So, we need to know where you keep your clients' samples, and who has access to them.'

Sitting back in his chair, Dr Khatri said, 'Our fertility samples are kept in our lab, down in the basement.'

'Who can gain access?'

'It's strictly limited to lab technicians only.'

'It's kept locked, then?'

'Well, not during the day, no, but it is at night.'

'So you're saying that anyone can go in there during the day and help themselves to whatever they like?'

'It's not as easy as that! There's always someone in there, from nine to five at least, and we all have to wear identity tags.' He glanced down to take hold of his own which hung loosely around his neck and held it up for them to see. 'Furthermore,' he continued, 'if someone was to go in there with the intention of stealing a sperm sample, they'd have to know what they were looking for, and how to find it, even more so if it was a particular individual's.'

'So who would such people be?'

'Only our lab technicians, really.'

'What about you?'

'Well, yes, me as well, I suppose.'

'Just for the record, may I ask what you were doing last Saturday night, between ten and eleven o'clock?'

As his eyes widened with horror, he said, 'You can't possibly think it was me?'

'I'm not suggesting anything, Doctor. I'm simply asking where you were last Saturday night.'

With his professional demeanour beginning to show signs of cracking, he said, 'I was at home! I'm sure I was!'

'On your own?'

'Our children have moved out, but my wife will have been there.'

'Nobody else?'

'Who else do you think would have been?'

'I've no idea; it's just that wives don't make great collaborative witnesses, at least not in a court of law.'

'You're not serious?'

Instead of answering, Tanner moved the conversation along. 'Has anyone noticed any samples going missing?'

'Not that anyone's told me.'

'How about break-ins?'

'Again, not that I know of. The building is fitted with a privately managed security system, so I'm sure we'd have known about it if there had been any breaches.'

'Going back to Emily Harris. How long had she been a client of yours?'

The doctor checked the file he'd opened on his

laptop. 'The Harrises first came to see us back in November of last year.'

'Do you know if they knew the Richardsons?'

Continuing to look at the screen, the doctor said, 'If you mean, did one refer the other, then I'm afraid I couldn't say.'

Tanner hadn't meant that, but it had given him another idea.

'Could you tell us who *did* refer them?'

'As I just said, I can't, no!'

'May I remind you that this is a murder enquiry!'

'So you've said, but under absolutely no circumstances am I allowed to start going around telling people who referred who. It would completely undermine the service we offer!'

'I can come back with a warrant.'

'Then I suggest you do that!'

Deciding that it was probably best to change tack, Tanner asked, 'Do your clients ever meet up together, socially?'

'I have no idea what goes on beyond these walls, but I'd have thought that would be unlikely. The vast majority of them come here for privacy and discretion. Fertility problems are hardly something people like their friends to know about.'

'But maybe if they happened to bump into each other in reception?'

'Well, of course it's possible, I suppose, but it would have nothing whatsoever to do with the clinic.'

Tanner knew he was clutching at straws, and decided to call it a day.

'OK, that will do for now. Thank you for your time, Dr. Khatri. But before we leave, we're going to need the names and contact details for everyone who has worked here, going back to when Mr and Mrs Harris first became clients.'

Pushing himself up from his desk, he said, 'If you speak to Susan on reception, I'll ask her to sort that out for you. Now, if you'll excuse me, I have clients whom I've already kept waiting for quite long enough.'

- CHAPTER FORTY -

BACK OUT IN reception, there was only one couple left waiting, there to see Dr Khatri. As soon as the receptionist saw Tanner and Jenny emerge, she asked them to go straight through.

After they'd passed through the side door, she looked over at Tanner and said, 'I understand you'd like a list of our staff?'

'Along with their contact details, yes, please,' replied Tanner, before adding, 'As far back as when Emily and Clive Harris first began coming here.'

After raising an inquisitive eyebrow, the girl said, 'That shouldn't be a problem,' and turned her attention to her computer's monitor.

As Tanner waited, he strolled over to take a look out of a lead-lined window into the carpark, leaving Jenny leaning up against the reception desk.

Pretending to take an interest in some of the leaflets out on display, in a conversational tone, Jenny asked the receptionist, 'So, how long have you been working here – Susan, isn't it?'

'Who, me?' the girl replied, glancing momentarily up from her computer screen. 'Gosh. It's been so long, I'm not sure I can remember.'

'I suppose you must get to know the clients quite well?'

Re-focussing her mind back to the task in hand, somewhat absently she replied, 'Most of them, I suppose. At least the regulars. I can't say I like them very much though. Too stuck up for my taste.'

'I take it you knew Simon and Jane Richardson?'

Abandoning her database search, she stared up at Jenny, and in a half-whisper said, 'Of course! And for Mr Richardson to have been accused of murdering his own wife – that must have been just *awful* for him!'

'Do you know if any of your clients would know each other socially, outside the clinic?'

Returning to her search, Susan shrugged. 'I'd say most of our clients are referred here by their friends. They tend to stick together, that lot. We also offer a ten percent reduction in our fees whenever someone does, which I doubt most of them can turn down.'

'I don't suppose you take a note of who referred who?'

'Yes, of course. We have to.'

'Do you know if anyone referred the Richardsons?'

'Hold on, let me just print this out and I'll take a look for you. But don't tell anyone I did. I'm really not supposed to.'

As the electrical hum of a laser printer began whirring under the desk, it wasn't long before Susan said, 'It was Mrs Ruth Lambert, Jane Richardson's mother. Apparently, she's been coming here for years for other reasons. Long before I started working here.'

'And what about Clive and Emily Harris? Did anyone refer them?'

A moment later, the girl said, 'It was Ruth Lambert again! Do you think that's important?'

Jenny wasn't sure, but one thing she did know was

that she didn't want the receptionist to think that it was, so she dismissed the idea. 'I doubt it. From what I hear, Mrs Lambert knows just about everyone!'

With a knowing smile of conspiratorial agreement, Susan abandoned her computer screen and reached down to retrieve two pieces of A4 paper which the printer had churned out.

Placing them on top of the high desk, she called over to Tanner, possibly a little too loudly, 'I've printed that list out for you!'

Returning to the desk, Tanner picked up the pages and began glancing through the list, making sure that each name had a phone number and contact address beside it.

'And this is everyone who's worked here, since the Harrises had their first consultation?'

'It goes back six months, which is about when the Harrises first came.'

'OK, well, thank you for your help. We'd better be on our way.'

- CHAPTER FORTY ONE -

AS SOON AS they were out in the carpark, crunching back over the gravel towards the XJS, Jenny took out her notebook and said to Tanner, 'Did you hear that Ruth Lambert referred both her daughter *and* Emily Harris?'

'I did, yes, but I suspect you were right when you said that she probably just knows a lot of people.'

'The *right* people, at least,' agreed Jenny.

Approaching the car, she went on, 'Speaking of knowing people, I can't help but think I recognise her from somewhere.'

'Who?'

'The receptionist. Susan Follett.'

'I can't say the name rings a bell.'

'Me neither, but her face does. I just can't remember from where.'

Tanner stopped beside the driver's side door and turned back to look over at Buxton Manor, pulling out his phone as he did.

Taking it off mute, he checked his messages.

'I've had a missed call from Burgess,' he said. 'I'd better phone him, else he'll have a go at me for not bothering to stay in touch.' He pressed the dial button. 'Hi, it's Tanner. You tried to call?'

'That was half an hour ago!'

'Sorry. We've been at Buxton Manor, where the IVF clinic is.'

'Yes, I heard. How'd you get on?'

'We managed to speak to the lead IVF consultant again. Their sperm samples are kept on site, and although they're secured at night, from what I could make out, just about anyone could have access to them during the day. He's provided us with the names and contact details of everyone who's worked there since Emily Harris first came in.'

'What about break-ins?'

'He doesn't think it's likely. They've got a privately managed security system, and he'd have been told of any breaches. I think our focus should be on the staff working there, so I suggest we start having a chat with those on the list of names.'

'OK. Makes sense. I'll let Barrington know. Whilst you've been away, DS Cooper managed to dig up a witness from the Irstead public carpark. Apparently, some guy saw a car reverse down the slipway at around eleven o'clock last night, dump something out the back and drive off.'

'I don't suppose he saw who was driving it?'

'Only that he thought it was a man wearing a hat of some description; either a baseball cap or one of those trendy flat cap things.'

'Nothing else?'

'He was large, but not tall.'

'So, short and fat, then?'

'Something like that.'

'Not much to go on,' observed Tanner. 'Did he at least see what type of car it was?'

'He reckons it was a Ford Focus.'

'Well, they're common enough,' said Tanner, glancing around at the cars in the manor's carpark. 'There's two of them here, for a start.' He gave Jenny a nudge, and pointed over at them.

'What colour are they?' asked Burgess.

'One's red, the other's light blue.'

'This one's supposed to be black, which should narrow things down. Vicky's started doing a search for registered owners of black Ford Focuses living in the Broads area. Hopefully there aren't too many.'

Thinking that there probably were, Tanner didn't reply, leaving Burgess to say, 'Anyway, if you could get yourselves back here, you can start going through that list of names you've got.'

'No problem,' agreed Tanner, 'but it may be worthwhile asking Simon Richardson if he recognises any of them first. If someone working here *is* trying to pin the murders on him, then it stands to reason that he must know them.'

'OK, fair enough. Whilst you're down there, you can see how he's getting on with the press. We had a call from one of his neighbours this morning. The road outside his house has been swamped with reporters. They must have piled down there after we issued our statement. Apparently they've been making a bit of a nuisance of themselves. Barrington was forced to send a unit down to keep an eye on them.'

'We'll get over there now.'

As the call ended, Jenny asked, 'What's the plan?'

'Apparently the Richardsons' neighbours have been complaining about the reporters hanging around. We can run this list of names past him, and make sure they're being kept under control while we're there. But before we go, I'd like to take a very quick look at that Ford Focus over there.'

'What, the red one?'

'Uh-huh. Cooper managed to dig up an eye witness at Irstead. The man says he saw a black Ford Focus dumping something at the bottom of the slipway.'

Following him, Jenny said in some confusion, 'But...that's a red one!' When he didn't answer, she persisted, 'You do know that black isn't *very* much like red, given that it's a completely different colour?'

'I also know that under a florescent street light, a red car will often look black.'

Jenny raised an eyebrow. She'd never thought about it before, but Tanner was probably right.

The car itself was an older model, and looked as if it hadn't been cleaned in a while.

Cupping their hands over their eyes, they began peering inside, when they heard a shrill voice calling out behind them, 'May I help you?'

Spinning around, they saw the receptionist, Susan, standing just outside the entrance, scowling. She had one hand folded over her waist, whilst the other held a smouldering cigarette.

'I don't suppose you know whose car this is?' Tanner asked.

'It's mine! And I can assure you there's nothing wrong with it. It was serviced and MOT'd last month, and it's taxed and insured as well.'

As Tanner and Jenny strolled back towards her, Tanner said, 'It's just that a car matching the description of yours was seen in a carpark in Irstead last night.'

'Well, I'm fairly sure that it's not the only Ford

Focus in the Norfolk Broads.'

'So it wasn't you, then?'

'What would I be doing hanging about in a carpark in *Irstead*, of all places?'

'May I ask where you were last night between the hours of ten and eleven?'

'I was at home, looking after my baby.'

'Can anyone vouch for that? Your husband, for example?'

Without taking her eyes off Tanner, she took a short sharp drag of her cigarette. Breathing the smoke out of her mouth, she replied, 'He's away at the moment.'

'May I ask where?' asked Tanner, as he began reading through the list of names she'd given him earlier, looking for hers.

'If you must know, we separated a while back. I don't keep tabs on his whereabouts.'

Turning onto the second page, he asked, 'So you don't know where he is?'

'That's what I just said, wasn't it?'

'You're name's Susan Follett, isn't it?'

'That's right, why?'

'It's just that you don't seem to have included yourself on the list of employees.'

'I was only told to print out a list of those who have access to the lab, and I don't!'

'Sorry. That must have been a miscommunication.'

'So, you want my name on there as well, do you?'

'Yes, please.'

'What about the girl who covers the desk at the weekends?'

'We need a list of *everyone* who works here, thank

you.'

Discarding her cigarette onto the gravel drive, as she ground it in with the ball of her foot she said, 'Wait here!' and stomped back inside, muttering to herself, just loud enough for Tanner and Jenny to hear, 'I suppose they want me to print out the names of all the bloody cleaners as well!'

As soon as she'd gone, with a wry smile, Jenny said, 'Another happy customer!'

'She's not particularly cheerful, is she?'

'Do you think she missed her name off on purpose?'

'I suppose that would depend on what Dr. Khatri had told her to print out.'

'She's defensive enough, though,' remarked Jenny. 'And I think it's very odd that she smokes.'

'Less common these days, I suppose.'

'I was thinking more because she said she was expecting her second child.'

There was a momentary pause, before Tanner reached for his phone again.

'Who are you calling?' asked Jenny.

Having dialled a number, Tanner didn't answer, but instead held his index finger up to his lips.

'Burgess, it's Tanner again. I was hoping you'd be able to do me a favour?'

On the other end of the line, Burgess paused momentarily, before asking, 'What's that?'

'Can you get someone to do a very quick background check on a Mrs Susan Follett? She's the receptionist here at Buxton Manor.'

'Any particular reason why?'

'She owns a Ford Focus.'

'A black one?'

'Close enough,' said Tanner, unwilling to tell Burgess that it was actually bright red. 'There's something about her that just doesn't feel right. She gave us the impression that she was happily married with one child and another on the way, but we've just found out her husband's left her and she doesn't seem to even know where he is. Jenny also pointed out that she was openly smoking, which given where she works, and the fact that she said she was pregnant, does seem a little odd.'

'OK, I'll get Vicky to look into it. I'll call you back if we find out anything.'

Ending the call, Tanner looked over at Jenny. 'I don't suppose you can remember where you've seen her before?'

'I can't, no.'

'Well, I suggest we ask Simon Richardson about her when we see him. Maybe he knows her from somewhere.'

Hearing Susan Follett return, Tanner whispered, 'And make sure you make a note of her number plate before we leave.'

- CHAPTER FORTY TWO -

DRIVING DOWN RIVER View Lane towards the Richardson's house, the view at the end was in stark contrast to when they'd first been there. Instead of a quiet road leading towards the peaceful serenity of the majestic River Bure, there were now at least four news vans and a dozen or so other vehicles parked along the road, as near to the end as possible, wherever they could find a space.

'Someone's popular,' remarked Jenny.

'Yes, but I doubt Simon's the type who wants to be, at least not for being a rampant homosexual who everyone thinks murdered two women in nearly as many days, one of which was his wife!'

'I suppose Barrington's news conference didn't have quite the effect he was hoping for.'

'Well, no, but in fairness, I'm not sure how it could have. As soon as that lot found out that three hours after Simon was released for the murder of his wife, another woman was killed, they'd have been down here like a shot, no matter what anyone had said.'

As Tanner reversed onto the grass verge behind another car, more than a hundred feet from Simon's house, he added, 'Frankly, I've got no idea what the press thinks they're going to achieve by doing this.'

Knowing that they were about to step into the glare of the media spotlight, Tanner used the rear-view mirror to make sure his hair was straight, or at least not sticking up anywhere it shouldn't be.

As Jenny did something similar using the passenger's pull-down mirror, she said, 'Maybe they think they're going to catch him in the act of popping out to kill someone else? Or maybe they think he's going to hold his own press conference and confess to both crimes, whilst relaying to the world exactly why he did it?'

With a wry smile, Tanner said, 'Who knows?'

He pushed open the XJS's thirty-year old driver's door and heaved himself out.

As he checked his tie and buttoned his single-breasted dark grey suit jacket, he stared down the road towards the awaiting press. 'At least he's going to be in.'

'You never know. He may have given them the slip,' Jenny suggested.

'What, that lot?'

'Not very likely, is it.'

'Not *very* likely, no.'

Tanner paused for a moment, before eventually saying, 'Shall we go?'

As they hadn't moved since they'd stepped out of the car, it was clear that neither of them particularly wanted to, not when half the national press was waiting for them at the end.

'Maybe we should've phoned him up instead?' suggested Jenny.

'Maybe they'll just think we're Jehovah's Witnesses and leave us alone.'

Ignoring her unimpressed look, he led the way down the last stretch of River View Lane.

As soon as they were spotted marching down the road, the press pack began to sit up and take notice. Tanner and Jenny might not be the police officers leading the investigation, but someone must have recognised them as being connected with the case, as cameras soon began to flash.

On the pavement outside Richardson's driveway stood two uniformed policemen, both of whom Tanner recognised.

'Everything all right here?' he asked, as they approached.

'Just the normal, sir,' replied the nearest. 'When we arrived, we found a few journalists peering through the windows and trying to get in round the back, but we soon put a stop to that.'

Tanner took a moment to stare up at the house. Noticing all the blinds had been pulled down, he asked, 'Is anyone even at home?'

'We've not seen anyone, sir, no, but the press seem to think he is.'

'OK. We need to ask him some questions.' Glancing over his shoulder, he added, 'Whilst we do, any chance you could keep that lot under control?'

'We'll do the best we can, sir.'

Tanner and Jenny stepped past them to weave their way between Simon's red Audi TT and his late wife's silver Porsche 911, heading for the front door. As they did, questions began to be shouted out, none of which Tanner had any intention of answering.

Keeping their backs to the press, Tanner rang the

doorbell and waited.

There was no answer.

'He probably thinks we're reporters,' said Jenny.

'Probably,' agreed Tanner, and stooped down, poked his fingers through the letterbox and peered through the gap.

Unable to see or hear anyone, he called out, 'Mr Richardson, it's Detective Inspector Tanner from Norfolk Police. It's nothing serious. I just need to ask you a couple of questions.'

Still nothing.

'Are you there, Mr Richardson? Can you hear me?'

But only silence followed.

'Maybe he *did* slip out the back?' suggested Jenny.

'Or maybe he's done something stupid,' said Tanner, with quiet concern.

He stood back to study the outside of the house again, looking to see if there were any windows open; but he couldn't see any. There was a side gate though, and gesturing towards it, he said, 'We'd better take a look.'

'But…are we allowed to do that? Isn't that his private property?'

'If there's a chance he may have taken his own life, then frankly I don't care if we're allowed or not!'

Returning to the front door, Tanner pushed his fingers through the letterbox again and called out, 'Mr Richardson, if you don't open up we'll have to force our way in!'

Still nothing.

'I don't like this,' he muttered. 'Come on.'

Knowing that their every move was going to be photographed and probably filmed as well, and by as many as thirty journalists representing half a dozen different media channels from around the UK, after he'd told the uniformed policemen what they were going to do Tanner led Jenny over to the side gate.

It was locked, but only by a bolt on the other side, which Tanner was able to reach over to undo.

Once through, he bolted the gate again, and they walked down the side of the house. At the back they found a small patio area featuring a suite of modern-looking black wicker garden furniture, neatly positioned around a square glass coffee table.

The rear elevation of the house had the large kitchen window and the wide bi-folding glass patio door that they'd seen from the inside on their previous visit, neither of which were open. Although the kitchen window was covered with a blind, the patio door had neither blind nor curtain, giving them a clear, unobstructed view inside.

Cupping their hands over their eyes, they peered through the glass doors into the kitchen, but there was still no sign of him.

'He's probably hiding upstairs,' said Jenny.

'Hopefully,' replied Tanner.

Retrieving his phone from his inside pocket, he asked, 'Do you have his phone number?'

After she'd fished it out from her notebook, Tanner dialled and stood on the patio, listening to the phone ring inside the house with a hollow, muted echo. Eventually it was picked up by the answerphone.

Jenny then read out his mobile number, and as Tanner waited for that to be answered, she once again peered through the patio doors.

Frustrated, Tanner said, 'He's not answering!'

'Sir, I think I can see something.'

Putting his phone away, he joined her in peering through the glass doors again.

She pointed. 'There - there's something on the floor, poking out from behind the island.'

'I can't see anything.'

'It just moved, look!'

'Shit!' said Tanner.

Standing back from the doors, he said. 'Call an ambulance! Then call for back up! We need to get that door open!'

'But…what is it?'

'It's a foot! It's someone's foot!'

- CHAPTER FORTY THREE -

TANNER STOOD STARING down at the body of the person he believed was Simon Richardson, but from what was left of his face, it was difficult to tell. What remained of his nose was nothing more than two fractured pieces of bone, jutting awkwardly out through discoloured broken skin. His mouth bore a closer resemblance to a butchered slab of meat, out from which oozed blackened, half-congealed blood. All Tanner could recognise of the man were his eyes, which stared up towards the ceiling. But even they'd taken on a look of macabre horror, as each of the pupils had been eclipsed by dark circles of haemorrhaged blood, leaked from ruptured vessels deep underneath.

From the time they'd first seen the body behind the kitchen island, it had taken them over ten minutes to gain entry to the property. Initially Tanner had attempted to smash the double-glazing of the patio doors, then the kitchen window, but had failed to crack either.

By the time they'd been able to gain entry by breaking in through the front door, and had surged through the house to the kitchen, any signs of life the body had displayed earlier had long since ebbed away. But from the moment they looked down at what was left of the body, one thing was certain. It was no suicide.

'Jesus Christ!' exclaimed Tanner, as he tore his gaze away from what was left of Simon's face.

Jenny, however, found herself transfixed by the sight of what lay before them. 'Who could have done such a thing?'

'I've no idea, but whoever it was, he must have let them in through the front door. I can't see any other way they could have gained entry. And it must have happened before the press turned up this morning. There's no way they'd have missed someone walking out the front door after having just done this!'

'Maybe they had a key, and came in through the patio?'

Turning to look over at it, Tanner said, 'The key's still in the lock. They wouldn't have been able to lock it from the outside. No! Whoever did this walked straight in through the front.'

The sound of an approaching siren brought Tanner's mind to more urgent practical matters.

Glancing over at the two uniformed police constables who'd helped break down the door, both of whom were now staring breathlessly down into what was left of Simon's face, he said, 'Assuming he's dead, and for his sake I almost hope he is, this is now a murder scene. I need the two of you out of here and the place cordoned off beyond the driveway, all the way round the boundary fence at the back. The press need to be kept as far back as possible, and make sure the road outside is kept clear of traffic. When you've done that, we need witness statements from the neighbours. Did any of them see anyone coming in or out last night, and if they did, we need a description. And if that's an ambulance approaching, send them round the back. I don't want any more people than necessary traipsing their way through the house.'

Despite having received their instructions, neither one of the two constables moved. They just continued to stare down at the man's shattered face.

'Sometime today, if you please!' said Tanner, almost shouting.

Apologising, they began stumbling out. As they did, he saw one of them grab hold of the kitchen door.

'And don't touch anything, for Christ's sake!'

His phone began to ring.

'It's Burgess,' he said. 'I'd better take it.' Before doing so, he said, 'Could you get that patio door open, and then make sure everyone comes in through the back, *not* the front? And then get a forensics team down here.'

Pleased to see her pulling on a pair of latex disposable gloves before doing so, he answered the phone.

'Tanner.'

'It's Burgess. What's going on?'

'We've found Simon Richardson,' he said, glancing back down at the body and muttering, 'at least I think we have.'

'Is he dead?'

'I'd say so.'

Seeing Jenny open the patio door just in time to usher in a couple of paramedics, Tanner stepped to one side to allow them through. 'We've begun cordoning off the area and are in the process of asking the neighbours for statements. Some paramedics have arrived, and DC Evans is putting a call in for forensics.'

'So, you think he was murdered then?'

'That's a definite yes, I'm afraid.'

There was a long silence from the other end of the line before Burgess asked, 'Any ideas?'

Tanner stopped for a moment. Burgess had never asked for his advice before. He hadn't even asked for his opinion. It was clear to Tanner that this was a sign that the DI was beginning to struggle, although that should hardly be a surprise. This was only Burgess's first murder investigation, and it had so far produced three victims, all of which were connected in some way, the most recent of whom having been, only the day before, the prime suspect.

'I think this one is going to come down to motive,' replied Tanner. 'Maybe he found out something that someone didn't want him to know. Although, judging by the injuries he's sustained, it may have been a revenge attack, possibly by someone who thought he'd murdered one of the victims.'

'Just a sec,' said Burgess, 'I've got Vicky waiving something at me. Hang on.'

'OK, no problem.'

While he waited, he looked over at Jenny who was just coming off the phone, out on the patio.

Stepping back inside, she asked, 'What's happening?'

Tanner shrugged back a reply, just as Burgess came back on the line.

'You still there?'

'Yes, still here.'

'Right, we've got some news on that receptionist

you asked us about – Susan Follett.'

Raising an eyebrow over at Jenny, Tanner said, 'Go on.'

'You said she's a married mother with one child.'

'Uh-huh.'

'Well, she's neither! She's never been married and there's no record of her having had any children.'

'She's been lying to us then.'

'There's something else as well,' continued Burgess. 'Vicky's just found out that about five years ago, she and Simon Richardson used to be engaged!'

'Really?' questioned Tanner, with genuine surprise.

'Looks like it. He was the one to call if off, and at the very last minute as well.'

'Sounds like we'd better go down and have another chat with her.'

'I think you need to bring her in for questioning,' said Burgess, 'especially in light of what's just happened to her ex-fiancé.'

'And if she doesn't agree?'

'Then you'll have to arrest her!'

'Without any evidence?'

'There's enough!'

'I'm sorry, Burgess, but there's nothing! I'm happy to go down and have another chat with her, but I'm damned if I'm going to arrest her; not until we have some actual physical evidence, something that can connect her with at least one of the murders.'

With Burgess's voice tightening with anger, he said, 'I suggest we see what Barrington has to say about that!'

'Then I suggest you go and ask him!'

With that, Tanner ended the call, and glared over at

Jenny.

'Twat!' he said.

'What was all that about?'

'Looks like that receptionist over at Buxton Manor hasn't exactly been truthful with us. She's not married, and she doesn't have any children.'

'Then what were those pictures of, the ones she was going to show us?'

'Probably someone else's,' he replied. 'There's something else as well. Vicky's just found out that she used to be engaged to our late friend over there.'

'Who, Simon?'

'Uh-huh.'

As Jenny stared off into space, she paused for a moment before saying, 'You know, I think I've remembered where I'd seen her before. There were pictures of her with Simon, on his Facebook page, from ages ago, but she was a hell of lot thinner back then.' She looked over at his body. 'So you think she's been trying to frame Simon for the murders by using his semen?'

'It's beginning to look that way.'

'And when she realised he wasn't going to be charged, she came over here and did that to him?'

'What's the expression? Hell hath no fury like a woman scorned?'

'Well, if that *was* her,' said Jenny, 'then she certainly rained hell down on him last night!'

Replacing his phone, Tanner said, 'We'd better be off. Burgess seems to think she's our new prime suspect, and he wants us to bring her in for questioning.'

'You don't sound so convinced.'

'It's not a question of what I think. At the moment we don't have a single shred of evidence to connect her to any of this, and I'd prefer to wait until we do. We've already seen what can happen when you start arresting people for murder without having established a chain of evidence.'

There was a lull in the conversation, before Jenny asked, 'So, what are we going to do?'

'We're going to have another chat with her. I'll be very interested to hear what she says when we tell her that we know she lied to us about marriage and children, and the fact that she was engaged to Simon, the very man who she must have seen walk into Buxton Manor with another girl on his arm, one who he *did* marry.'

- CHAPTER FORTY FOUR -

TURNING INTO BUXTON Manor carpark, it was immediately obvious that something was missing.

'Her car's gone!' stated Jenny.

Seeing that it was after half past five, Tanner said, 'She's probably finished for the day. I'll pop inside and see if anyone knows where she is. You may as well wait here.'

Once inside, it was clear something wasn't right. There was nobody behind the reception desk, the phone was ringing without being answered, and there were no less than three couples occupying the waiting area, some looking as if they'd been there for some time and their patience was wearing thin.

Glancing over the top of the reception desk, Tanner saw a nearly full cup of coffee beside the keyboard, one with a single mark of lipstick. Reaching over, he placed his hand around the cup.

It was stone cold.

Just then a voice called out from over to his left. 'Mr and Mrs Jackson?'

As one of the three waiting couples began gathering up their belongings, the man mumbled, 'And about bloody time too.'

Looking over to see who'd called their names, and

seeing a middle-aged woman with greying blond hair standing beside the side door, Tanner asked, 'Excuse me, but I'm looking for Susan Follett?'

'Aren't we all!' exclaimed the lady.

'She's not here then?'

'She is not, no! She walked out about two hours ago, and without even bothering to tell anyone!'

Thanking her for her time, Tanner raced back out into the carpark and sprinted over to his car.

Opening the door, he said, 'She's gone!'

'What, *gone* gone?'

'She walked out just after we left. You *did* make a note of her number plate, didn't you?'

'I did.'

'OK, give Burgess a call. Tell him what's happened, and ask him to put out a radio call for her, or her car. Then ask him for her address. If she's about to do a runner, hopefully she'll stop by her house first.'

- CHAPTER FORTY FIVE -

WITHIN A COUPLE of minutes of making the call, they had Susan Follett's address, and were on the way up to Bodham, a small town nearly an hour's drive north from Buxton Manor, where she was supposed to have rented a flat.

The flat in question was on the ground floor of a two-storey red brick ex-council estate, one of many thousands that were offered for sale under the right-to-buy scheme of the 1980s.

As they parked directly outside the flat, a number of the local residents began looking over to see who'd turned up.

Stepping out of his XJS, Tanner couldn't help but feel conspicuous. He often did when driving around council estates. Although his car was well over thirty years old, it was still a Jag, and vehicles of such pedigree weren't often seen parking up in such places.

'There's no sign of her car,' observed Jenny.

'No, but we'd better see if anyone's at home.'

Walking up to the old white PVC front door, Tanner rang the bell and waited.

An empty chime rang out inside, but there was no response. A voice eventually croaked out from over to their right, 'She ain't in!'

Turning, Tanner saw a woman who looked older

than she probably was glaring at them from the next door down. Squirming on her hip was a red-faced, grubby-looking six-month old baby, who seemed intent on breaking free in order to reach something on the concrete path.

'Sorry?' asked Tanner, even though he'd heard what she'd said.

'You're looking for Suze, right?'

Assuming she meant Susan Follett, Tanner replied, 'We are, yes.'

'Well, as I said, she ain't in.'

'When did you see her last?'

'She ain't bin 'ere for days!'

'I see. I don't suppose you know where she might be?'

With a blank stare, the woman said, 'Not a clue, sorry!' but in a way which made it sound like she wasn't.

Tanner wasn't at all surprised by her apparent lack of cooperation. It must have been abundantly obvious that they weren't there for a social visit, and anything else must mean trouble.

Realising that there was probably only one way they were going to get anything even vaguely useful out of her, Tanner pulled out his ID and said, 'I'm Detective Inspector Tanner, and this is Detective Constable Evans, Norfolk Police. We're just looking to ask Susan a couple of questions, that's all.'

'No problem.'

'So, do you know where she is?'

'Nope!' she replied, and grinned at him.

Replacing his ID, Tanner decided to take a different tack.

'OK, how about this. Either you can start trying to be a little more helpful, or we'll arrest you for obstruction of justice? We'll then be able to have this exact same conversation from the comfort of a holding cell.'

As the baby on her hip began to whine as well as wriggle, the woman said, 'You can try Fen Marsh Mill, if you like.'

'Fen Marsh Mill?' repeated Tanner.

'That's what I said.'

'And what would she be doing there?'

'How'm I supposed to know? She goes there often enough though, for weekends and the like. She owns it, at least she says she does. Her mum left it to her when she died – not that it's done her much good. It's in a right state. She can't afford to do it up, and nobody wants to buy it, so it just sits there, rotting.'

After thanking the woman for her time, and heading back to the car, Tanner asked Jenny, 'Do you know Fen Marsh Mill?'

'Of course! It's a well-known landmark, like all the old mills. I didn't know it was privately owned though.'

Starting the engine, Tanner asked, 'Would you be able to direct me?'

'I've only seen it from the river before. It's at the top end of the Ant. I've no idea how to get there by car though! Hold on, let me take a look,' and she pulled out her phone, and scrolled to its map application.

Tanner put his seat belt on and waited.

It wasn't long before Jenny said, 'It's actually not far from Buxton Manor. But I can't see any way we'll be able to get there by car. Our best bet will be to drive to *here*,' she said, pointing at the screen, 'and to then get a boat over the river.'

'There's no way to get there from the other side?'

'No, look. It's right in the middle of Reedham Marsh. We'd have to go to Irstead Street, here, and then walk all the way round. It would take hours!'

'OK, but is there going to be a boat there to get us across?'

'I don't know. There's public mooring all the way along the bank, so hopefully there'd be someone there who'd be willing to take us.'

'And if there isn't?'

It was a good point. 'I'd better request a patrol boat to meet us there.'

'And I'd better give Burgess a call to let him know what we're up to.'

- CHAPTER FORTY SIX -

UNABLE TO GET through to Burgess's mobile, Tanner was forced to call Wroxham Police Station instead.

He was put through to DS Gilbert, and skipping the normal pleasantries, he asked, 'Where's Burgess?'

'He's out with Cooper. We had a reported sighting of Susan Follett's car, so they went out to take a look.'

'And where was that?'

'In a carpark opposite Fen Marsh Mill, not far from Buxton Manor.'

'Why the hell didn't anyone tell us?' demanded Tanner, with rising anger. 'I mean, it would have been useful to know, given that we've spent the best part of an hour driving all the way up to her bloody flat!'

'I'm sorry, sir,' apologised Vicky, 'but I think he just wanted to take a look for himself.'

'Well, fair enough, I suppose, but someone could have at least told us!'

As Tanner took a calming breath, Vicky apologised again, leaving Tanner to say, 'Anyway, we're heading that way ourselves. There was no sign of Follett at her flat, and her neighbour told us she might be staying at the mill, which is probably why her car's there. So maybe you can tell Burgess that when you next speak to him?'

'Will do, sir,' responded Vicky.

Ending the call, he glanced over at Jenny. 'Communication's good here, isn't it!'

'I think Burgess is still getting used to you being around.'

'I suppose I've only been here for a few days, although it feels like a hell of a lot longer. So anyway, did you sort out a patrol boat?'

'I did, but they said the nearest one would take about an hour to get there.'

'An hour?'

'They've got to stick to the river's speed limit, same as everyone else.'

'And what's that?'

'Between four to six miles an hour, depending on where you are.'

'Wouldn't it be quicker for them to walk?'

'Not if they had to carry the boat.'

Tanner didn't smile at that one, so she continued. 'Don't worry. I'm sure we'll find someone who can give us a lift over.'

Following Jenny's instructions, it took them just over forty-five minutes to reach the carpark where Susan Follett's car had been spotted. By that time it had gone half past seven, and the sky was becoming increasingly dark.

Turning in, they saw DS Cooper pacing up and down beside the car they'd been looking for. He had his hands buried deep inside his pockets and was staring at the ground, looking as if he'd rather have been somewhere else.

Seeing Tanner's XJS pull in, Cooper slipped his

hands out, stood up straight and marched over to meet them, running a hand through his mousy brown hair as he did, presumably in a bid to straighten it.

As Tanner climbed out, he asked, 'Where's Burgess?'

Looking over at the other side of the river, Cooper answered, 'He got someone to give him a lift over to the windmill.'

'What, on his own?' questioned Tanner, as he joined Cooper in staring rather helplessly out over the narrow stretch of river.

On the opposite bank stood Fen Marsh Mill, its conical red-brick tower rising up from the river's edge. Surrounding its base was a thick bed of reeds, which swayed back and forth in the gentle breeze, whispering to each other as they did. At the top of the mill, blades hung like a broken crucifix, and with the sun beginning its inevitable descent towards the horizon beyond, the dilapidated structure was taking on an ominous dark form against what was fast becoming a blood-red sky.

'He only went to have a look,' replied Cooper.

'But why didn't you go with him?'

'He told me to stay here, in case Miss Follett showed up.'

'And where did you think she was, if her car was parked here?'

'I think we just assumed she'd dumped the car here and done a runner.'

'You do know that she owns the mill, don't you?'

With a confused look, Cooper asked, 'The mill, as in *that* mill?'

'No, sergeant. A completely different one that just happens to look just like it!' Cooper seemed unable to grasp the fact that Tanner was being sarcastic, forcing him to say, 'Yes, Cooper, that one! She inherited the damned thing from her parents.'

'But...we didn't know!'

Looking over at Jenny, Tanner said, 'Come on. We'd better see if we can find a boat that can take us across.'

As the two of them hurried over towards the towpath, Cooper called out after them, 'What about me?'

'You can stay there, in case Follett comes back.'

'But...'

'And call for backup, whilst you're at it!' To Jenny he said, 'If Burgess is stuck inside that mill with Susan bloody Follett, and if she is who we think she is, then God help him!'

- CHAPTER FORTY SEVEN -

REACHING THE TOWPATH, they cast their eyes ahead, along the purpose- built moorings that followed the river around a gradual bend. But what would have been lined with cruising boats during the summer months, with more driving up and down, looking for a space, in mid-April was still eerily quiet, and there wasn't a single boat in sight.

Having walked until they could see round the bend, where the moorings ended, they were about to turn back when they heard the sound of a distant rumble.

'That sounds like one approaching now,' said Jenny, as she peered out along the river through the rapidly diminishing light.

To their left the sun was sinking fast, cold shadows stretching out towards them from the bare-branched trees on the far bank.

A moment later she called out, 'There it is!' just as the sleek pointed nose of a beautiful wooden motor cruiser came into view.

As Tanner looked, he saw a green light appear on the boat's near side, followed by a red light on the other side as it rounded the bend in the river.

Using the torch function on her phone, Jenny signalled towards the vessel.

As it began pulling over to their bank of the river,

they could see the head of an elderly man above the windscreen.

When she thought he was close enough to hear, she took out her police ID, held it high in the air and called out, 'Norfolk Police! We need a lift!'

The head nodded in understanding, and a moment later a voice with a thick Norfolk accent drifted over to them saying, 'I'll bring 'er up alongside.'

As the boat came near to the mooring, the engine first slowed, and then sped up briefly as the aft end was expertly reversed in.

When it was close enough, without waiting for it to stop, Jenny reached out, grabbed hold of the hand rail which ran the length of the high wooden coach roof, and resting a foot on the varnished gunwale, pulled herself on board with practised ease.

Tanner did the same, albeit without the elegant grace his young subordinate had shown.

Keeping a firm hold of the railing, he began following Jenny back towards the cockpit. As he did so, the driver put the boat into neutral, spun the wheel hard to port, engaged reverse again to pull the nose out, and then spun the wheel back round the other way as he shifted the gear back into its forward position.

Over the gentle hum of the engine, he called out, 'Where you head'n?'

'Can you take us over to Fen Marsh Mill?' asked Jenny.

'Aye,' he replied, as a trusting pair of blue eyes sparkled out from underneath a worn tweed cloth cap.

'How about you?' she asked, in return. 'Where are you off to?'

'Head'n for 'orning,' he replied, 'but it's later than I thought.'

'I take it this is your boat?' she asked, out of professional curiosity. Hired boats weren't allowed out on the broads at night, and although it wasn't dark yet, it most definitely would have been by the time he'd reached Horning.

'Aye,' replied the man. Giving the steering wheel a loving pat, as if it were a trusted Labrador, he added, 'I've 'ad this'un for over twenty yare now.'

Jenny wasn't too surprised to hear that. It had become a rare sight indeed to see hired wooden motor boats out cruising the Broads, at least none in such cherished condition.

As they began rounding the bend in the river, Jenny saw DS Cooper still standing beside Susan Follett's car. As they motored around a little more, the tall dark blades of Fen Marsh Mill began to loom into view.

Spying an old wooden jetty at its base, Jenny leaned over towards the driver. 'Could you drop us off there?'

With a nod, he began steering the Broads motor cruiser over towards the far starboard side of the river, whilst easing back on the throttle.

Jenny and Tanner made their way around the front of the coach roof to the side, where they crouched down and waited.

When the bow of the boat was about a foot away from the jetty, the driver shifted the throttle into neutral, spun the wheel hard to starboard, and then placed the throttle into reverse, expertly sucking the rear end of the boat in so that it nudged gently up against the mooring.

Stepping off the boat with practised ease, down

onto a low wooden jetty that creaked in protest as she did, Jenny turned to thank the boat's owner.

As Tanner jumped off to join her, the old man asked, 'D'you want me to moor up?'

'You're OK,' replied Jenny. 'We've got a patrol boat coming up from Ludham. They'll be able to give us a lift back when they get here.'

'Right you are, miss.' He rotated the wheel hard to port and pulled the throttle back to begin reversing out.

Watching him motor away, with Fen Marsh Mill looming up behind them, now just a black silhouette against an ever-darkening red sky, Tanner said, 'Maybe we should have asked him to stay?'

As the boat's engine burbled into the distance, leaving nothing but the sound of the forever-whispering reeds that seemed to be closing in around them, Jenny was beginning to think the same thing, but she didn't say so. Instead, she waved to Cooper, still standing on the other side of the river, and called out, 'We're going to have a look around. Keep an eye out for a patrol boat. It should be here any time now.'

At his nod of acknowledgment, she turned to take in her surroundings. She'd only ever seen the mill from the river, never up this close, and it was far larger than she'd expected.

Hearing something move in the reeds to his left, Tanner whipped his head around to see the outline of what looked to be a rowing boat, moored up at the very far end of the jetty they were standing on, but in such a way that it would be hidden by the reeds from anyone trying to see it from the river.

Pointing at it, in a low voice he asked, 'Do you

think that's what she used to get over here?'

Jenny picked her way carefully over the long-neglected jetty, which creaked and rocked under her feet.

Kneeling down to take a closer look, she noted that although the rope that had been used to tie it to the jetty looked as old as the boat, the knot had been tied recently. Also, the oars which rested inside the boat, with the handles nestled in their pivoting rowlocks, were still wet.

Over her shoulder, she said, 'I suspect so, yes. And it's been used very recently as well. She must be here!'

As Tanner glanced around at Fen Marsh Mill behind them, which was now nothing more than a vast black shadow, in the same quiet tone he asked, 'If she is, then where the hell is Burgess?'

- CHAPTER FORTY EIGHT -

LEAVING THE ROWING boat where it was, Jenny crept back over the jetty to join Tanner, who by then had found more sure footing on solid ground.

As she approached, she tilted her head back to stare up at the giant wooden blades, hanging motionless above their heads.

'There should be an entrance here somewhere,' she said, and began leading the way around the base of the mill.

About a quarter of the way around, she found a small wooden door covered in layer upon layer of flaking white paint. 'Here, sir.'

By then, Tanner was having serious misgivings about going inside. After all, they were contemplating the idea of entering the property of a suspected serial killer unarmed, without even having taken the precaution of wearing stab vests.

'How long until you think that patrol boat will get here?' he asked.

'Maybe ten minutes.'

'OK, then I think we're going to have to wait for them.'

'But what about Burgess?'

'What about him?'

'What if he's stuck inside, with *her*?'

'All the more reason to wait!'

Seeing Jenny's hand still resting on the door handle, he whispered, 'Look, Jen, it's just too risky! She could be waiting for us behind the door armed with God knows what. Let's get back to the jetty and see if there's any sign of that patrol boat.'

Jenny was about to do as Tanner had suggested, when she heard a sound coming from inside the mill.

'Hold on,' she said. 'Did you hear that?'

Tanner didn't reply. He may have heard something, but couldn't be sure.

Remaining motionless, they listened again, but the air was still. Even the breeze that had been blowing through the reeds had fallen away.

From over to the west came the distant sound of a bittern, a rarely heard Broad's wading bird, its booming call carrying over the wet reeded landscape towards them. But that wasn't what Jenny had heard.

After a moment or two's silence, Tanner eventually asked, 'What am I supposed to be listening for?'

'I thought I heard someone calling from inside the mill.'

'Are you sure?'

Then the sound came again, but it was much louder that time.

It was a distinct call for help.

'It's Burgess!' declared Jenny.

'Shit!' said Tanner. She was right. It had sounded like Burgess, which meant that they had no choice, or at least *he* didn't.

Having made the decision, he said, 'OK, I'm going in, but you're waiting out here.'

'Sorry boss, but that ain't gonna happen!'

Seeing the look of firm resolve stamped over her face, Tanner capitulated.

'Fair enough,' he began, 'but I'm going in first, and you *must* stay close!'

Nodding in agreement, Jenny stood to one side to allow Tanner to take her place beside the door.

He turned the handle and eased the door open, just enough to look through the gap.

Inside the mill it was pitch black. The air was cold and damp, and clinging to it was a thick, pungent smell which Tanner instantly recognised. It was the raw stench of decomposing flesh.

Tanner pulled out his phone and turned on its torch app.

With Jenny doing the same, he pushed the door open and checked behind it.

There was nobody there.

Realising he'd been holding his breath, he let it out with relief.

Following the beam of light, he stared around.

From what he could see, it looked as if the mill had been converted into a home at some point. In the middle of the floor was a large rug on which sat two settees; both double. They'd been positioned in an L-shape around a low wooden coffee table, on top of which were a collection of mugs, newspapers and magazines. Along the far wall was a very basic kitchen made up of a simple work surface, a sink, and a bin underneath, crammed full to the point of overflowing. On the work surface was a double camping gas stove, and scattered around that was a mess of dirty plates, mugs, and unopened tins of food.

Looking over to his right, Tanner could see a staircase that led around the mill's conical shaped inner wall, up to a floor above. But there was neither sight nor sound of anyone; no Burgess, no Susan Follett.

Before stepping all the way in, Tanner called out, 'Norfolk Police! Is anyone here?'

They listened to his voice echo out around them, but there was no response.

Tanner whispered, 'We'd better take a look upstairs.'

He pushed open the door a fraction more, and with extreme caution, made his way inside.

Jenny followed him to the base of the staircase, chasing shadows around the mill with their torches as they did.

'What *is* that smell?' questioned Jenny.

Placing his foot on the first of a dozen or so steps, Tanner replied, 'I'm not sure, but whatever it is, I think it's coming from up there.' He shone his torch up at a large rectangular hole that had been cut in the ceiling, to which the staircase led.

Keeping his torch light focussed on the hole, he began making his way up.

When the top of his head was level with the ceiling, he stopped, checking behind him to make sure Jenny was still there. Then, with his heart beating hard inside his chest, he raised his head just enough so that he could peer over the edge of the floor of the room above.

If the smell was bad downstairs, it was far worse up there.

He ran the torch beam around.

In the middle of what was a much smaller room

than the one below were a row of three dark wooden cots, each with slatted sides. He could see that the one nearest to him was empty, but within each of the others was a small blanket-covered bundle.

Apart from an old wooden rocking chair under a small window, and a wardrobe next to a chest of drawers at the other end, he couldn't see anything else.

Having followed the torch's light around the full circumference, he eased himself out onto the floor, before turning to offer Jenny his hand.

Once she'd stepped through the hole and was able to see the whole room, she said, 'It looks like some sort of a nursery!'

'Doesn't it!' agreed Tanner.

Creeping up to the middle of the three cots, Tanner shone his torch inside to stare down at the tiny bundle lying there, wrapped up neatly in a white woollen blanket. For a moment, he couldn't work out what he was looking at. Where he'd expected to see the angelic face of a sleeping baby, instead was an undulating mass of blackness, which glistened as it moved in the light of his torch.

Curious, he reached out his hand to touch it.

The moment he did, a sickening swarm of flies launched itself into the air, hurtling towards his face.

Stumbling back, he lashed out wildly at them, only for them to vanish just as quickly as they'd appeared.

Jenny shone her torch into the cot to see where they'd come from.

Staring up at her from out of the top of the blanket was a tiny baby's head; its skin red and blistered, from out of its nose leaked blood-filled pus, and where its eyes should have been were nothing more than two gaping holes, each one crawling with maggots.

Jenny gagged once, then turned to throw up violently over the floor.

'What the hell is it?' asked Tanner, forcing himself back to the edge of the cot. 'My God! It's…a…'

But he couldn't bring himself to say the word, not out loud.

As flies began returning to what looked like the remains of a foetus, Tanner heard something move, just beyond the third cot.

Tearing his gaze away, he aimed his torch towards the sound. There, hidden behind the last cot was the body of a man, slumped up against the wall, his head resting to one side.

'Burgess!'

Racing over to him, Tanner fell to his knees.

'Jesus Christ! Burgess! Are you all right?'

But it was clear from the outset that he wasn't.

In the light from his torch Tanner could see that blood had soaked his shirt around his stomach, over which his hand lay, and was spreading out around where he sat.

Burgess's eyes flickered open.

Without moving his head, he looked up at Tanner, and with a faltering voice, said, 'The bitch. She stabbed me!'

'You'll be all right, don't worry,' said Tanner, with as much conviction as he could muster.

Pulling his tie from around his neck, he called behind him, 'Jenny! I could do with your help here!'

As he waited for her to come, Tanner laid his phone on the ground so that the light shone up towards the ceiling. With both hands now free, he rolled his tie up before moving Burgess's hand away from where he assumed the knife wound was. Finding a deep gash in his upper abdomen, just below his rib cage, he said, 'This is going to hurt.'

Using the rolled-up tie, he plugged it into the hole.

As Burgess writhed in agony, Tanner called out, 'Jenny, where the hell are you?'

'Over here!' came a woman's voice from out of the darkness. But it wasn't Jenny's.

- CHAPTER FORTY NINE -

TANNER CURSED UNDER his breath. He knew who it was, and he knew what must have happened.

Before replying, he lifted Burgess's hand again to place down on top of the rolled-up tie. As he did so, he whispered gently into his ear, 'Keep that held there, and try not to move.'

Reaching over to retrieve his phone from the floor, he slowly got to his feet, turning around as he did.

Ahead of him, just to the side of the cot where he'd seen the decomposing remains, was Susan Follett, her mass of permed hair tied back behind her head.

Locked in her arms, directly in front of her, stood Jenny.

In the light of his torch, Tanner could clearly see the cold sharp blade of a large kitchen knife resting up against the delicate white skin of Jenny's neck, stained red with what he assumed to be Burgess's blood. His attention was distracted by one of Susan Follett's earlobes, which he couldn't help but notice had been ripped in half. The butterfly-shaped earring they'd found under the bridge must have belonged to her, torn off when she'd attacked and killed Jane Richardson.

Taking in Jenny's face, despite it being as pale as the

moon and etched over with fear, he could see her eyes still held a look of defiant courage.

'Are you all right, Jen?' he asked.

'Oh, she's fine, aren't you, *Jen*?' said Susan, pulling her head back by her hair to stare into her eyes.

'I'm OK,' came Jenny's hesitant response.

'Although saying that,' continued Susan, 'she probably won't be, not after I've opened up her throat, right in front of you.'

'There's no need for that, Miss Follett!' stated Tanner. 'And besides, we didn't come here for you. We came looking for our colleague, DI Burgess, who's still alive. So if you let us go, all three of us, we won't be any more trouble.'

'Have you ever lost someone you love, Detective Inspector?'

The question flashed images into Tanner's mind.

'Your daughter, perhaps?'

How the hell did she know about her?

'You know, personally, I think Jenny here looks just like her, your daughter I mean. Don't you think?'

She must have been doing her own background research, thought Tanner. Probably about all of them. But he wasn't going to let her play mind games with him.

'This isn't about me, Miss Follett. And as I said before, we're not here for you. Our colleague behind me is seriously injured. We need to get him to a hospital. So if you let us go, we'll be able to forget all about this.'

Ignoring him, Susan said, 'I see you've met my children. Aren't they just adorable?'

Adorable wasn't exactly the word Tanner would

have used to describe them, but this was hardly the time to disagree.

'They certainly are, Miss Follett. Now, if you put the knife down, there'll be no more harm done, and we'll be on our way.'

'I'm not stupid, you know!'

'I never said you were.'

'Just because I'm a receptionist, and not some arrogant over-paid doctor.'

'Again, I never said that. I'm sorry if I said anything that may have given you that impression.'

'If anyone around here is stupid, it's *you*!' she continued. 'You didn't think for a single moment that it could be me who'd killed those women. I was even willing to show you pictures of my first-born, the one I took from Simon's so-called wife, but you didn't have the professional good sense to look.'

'Those *things* over there, Miss Follett,' began Tanner, pointing down at the row of cots standing between them. 'You do know that they're dead, don't you?'

Through a malicious snarl, she said, 'How *dare you* say that about my babies!'

'And another thing,' said Tanner. 'They're not yours!'

Susan Follett paused for a moment, before a wide, malicious grin stretched out over her round face.

'Finders keepers!' she eventually said. 'Besides, God didn't want those woman to have children.'

'I see,' said Tanner. 'And he told you that himself, did he?'

'Don't mock me, Detective!' she demanded, bringing the knife hard up against Jenny's throat, so much so that the blade began to dig into her skin. 'If God had wanted them to have children, he'd have blessed them naturally, not forced them to have IVF treatment.'

'But wasn't it God's fault that Simon was a homosexual? That *was* the reason why he dumped you, wasn't it? Because he fancied men, not you!'

'You're even more stupid than I thought!' she stated. 'Simon isn't gay! He only said that to get out of having to spend the rest of his life in prison. It's a shame you didn't see through it, though. If you'd charged him like you were supposed to, I wouldn't have had to kill that other woman.'

'What about Simon?' questioned Tanner. 'What did he do to deserve it?'

'He dumped me! That's what he did! And just two days before we were going to get married. And if that wasn't bad enough, five years later he waltzes into my clinic with that over-dressed tart of a wife hanging off his arm, and he doesn't even fucking recognise me! Oh, I can assure you, he more than deserves to be locked up. As far as I'm concerned, they can throw away the key.'

'That's as maybe, Miss Follett, but did he really deserve to die?'

Tanner watched as a cloud of confusion descended over Susan's face. As it did, the knife she'd been holding up against Jenny's throat dropped down slightly.

'Why would you say that - that he didn't deserve to die?'

With the sudden realisation that not only must it have been someone else who'd killed Richardson, but that this deranged woman standing before him didn't know he was dead, he had an unexpected new card in his hand, and he didn't waste a moment putting it into play.

'Haven't you heard?' he began, as he started to edge his way around the cots towards her. 'Simon's dead!'

Dragging Jenny back, with narrowing eyes, Susan glared at him.

'You're lying!'

'I can assure you, Miss Follett, that I'm not! Jenny and I found his body this afternoon, lying in a pool of blood in his kitchen, just after we left you at Buxton Manor.'

'I'm sorry, detective, but I don't believe you.'

'It's true, Miss Follett. Someone beat him over the head to such an extent that by the time we found him, there was nothing left of his face but an unrecognizable mess of blood and bone. It's all over the news!'

'But...why would anyone want to hurt Simon?'

'Probably because you made the entire population think that he was a psycho nut-job who'd not only killed his wife, but Emily Harris as well!'

'I only killed that bitch of a wife of his to make him pay for what he'd done to me! And that other one would've been fine if you'd locked him up like you were supposed to!'

'Either way, Miss Follett, Simon *is* dead! And he is because of what *you* started!'

As it began to sink in that someone *had* killed her ex-fiancé, a man she was evidently still desperately in love with, tears began to fill up her eyes. 'No, Detective Inspector. His blood is on *your* hands, not mine!'

With Jenny's eye's widening with fear, Susan gripped the knife so hard that her knuckles turned white. As she yanked Jenny's head back again, with a demonic grin, she whispered, 'And now I'm going to make *you* pay!'

- CHAPTER FIFTY -

SENSING WHAT SHE was about to do, Tanner launched himself at her with a primal yell.

Time seemed to expand into a never-ending single moment.

He watched as Jenny's cheeks flushed.

Her eyelids closed as she blinked, the tears behind them spilling out onto her cheeks.

The deranged receptionist had begun to draw the blade over her throat.

Seeing Tanner approach, Susan took an instinctive step away from him. But there was nothing for her to step on to.

As they'd been talking, Tanner had been steadily steering her towards the gaping black hole in the floor.

Losing her balance, she let go of the knife, trying to grab hold of Jenny instead.

But Tanner got to her first.

Taking hold of an outstretched arm, he heaved her back from the brink, leaving Susan to fall through the hole, tumbling on to the top of the stairs before going over the side to land hard on the floor, some ten feet below.

Realising she was safe, Jenny began to sob, openly and unashamedly.

With one hand on her shoulder, Tanner stared deep

into her eyes, a look of anxious torment stretched out over his face.

Seeing his concern, she tried to reassure him by saying, 'I'm OK! I'm OK!'

But Tanner wasn't looking at her face anymore. He was staring just below it.

With all that had happened, Jenny hadn't felt the razor-sharp blade of Susan's knife as it was drawn over her neck, opening up her jugular vein, out of which blood as black as the night was now cascading.

Seeing where he was looking, she placed her hand where Susan's knife had been. Feeling the sticky warmth of her blood pouring over her hand, with the smell of iron thick in her mouth, she lifted it up to stare.

As realisation hit her, her legs buckled, snapping Tanner out of his hypnotic state.

He dropped his phone, the torch light went out, and the mill was plunged into darkness, all but for the delicate light of a rising moon, glancing in through the mill's narrow upstairs window.

In one swift movement, he dragged her over to the nearest wall, propping her up against it.

As she stared up at him, he threw off his coat and jacket.

Ripping the buttons from his shirt, he tore it off, wadded it up, and pushed it against the open wound.

Watching as she held it in place, with tears filling up his own eyes, he stared down at her and said, 'Don't you worry, Jenny, you're going to be OK!'

With just the flicker of a smile, she looked deep into his eyes and asked, 'Promise?'

Bundling her up in his arms, in one swift movement he got to his feet, and as he began carrying her towards the stairs, he looked down at her again. 'I promise!'

- CHAPTER FIFTY ONE -

GRATEFUL FOR THE moonlight, as quickly as he dared, Tanner carried Jenny down the staircase.

There was no sign of Susan Follett, neither there nor on the floor beneath, but at that time he hardly cared. His only interest was in getting Jenny safely down without falling.

Reaching the lower level, he raced over to the door, prised it open with his foot, and ran out to the river, just in time to see the patrol boat Jenny had called earlier begin mooring up alongside the old wooden jetty.

Breathing hard, he sprinted over to them, calling out, 'I'VE GOT A WOUNDED OFFICER HERE!'

One of the uniformed men inside the boat leapt out to help him, whilst the other dived inside the small cockpit to retrieve the first aid kit.

With Jenny still cradled in his arms, Tanner sank to his knees, telling the first officer, 'It's her neck. It's been cut.'

But it was obvious where the wound was. The shirt Tanner had used to staunch the flow of blood was heavily stained.

Joining them on the jetty, the second officer wasted no time in pulling a large dressing pad out from the first aid kit and tearing it open. When it was ready, with Tanner supporting Jenny's head, in one swift movement the first officer removed the shirt as the second officer replaced it with the dressing pad. As he held it in place, the first officer found a roll of gauze and began winding it around her neck, so holding the pad in place.

A single blast of a siren shattered the stillness of the night.

A police car had entered the carpark on the other side of the river, its flashing blue lights ricocheting off the mill behind them. The first officer glanced up at Tanner and said, 'She must have lost a lot of blood. We need to get her to a hospital. If you can carry her to the boat, we'll take her to the other side. The squad car can take her from there.'

Tanner was desperate to stay with her, but remembering that Burgess was still inside the mill, and was possibly still alive, putting his professional responsibilities before his personal feelings for Jenny, he said, 'OK, but as soon as she's in the squad car, I need you back here.'

Before handing her into the boat, Tanner took a moment to look down at Jenny's face. Alarmed to see her eyes were closed and that her skin was as white as the moon, and hoping to God she hadn't slipped away whilst they'd been bandaging her neck, he said, 'Jen!'

With a huge surge of relief, he saw her eyes flutter open.

'We've stopped the blood, Jen, and we're taking you to a hospital. You're going to be OK!'

But although the corners of her mouth turned upwards in response, it was clear that she was far from being OK.

'Quick, take her!' he said, passing her over.

As the two police officers lifted her into the boat, Tanner stood up and faced the other side of the river. Seeing Cooper standing there with the two police officers who'd just arrived in the car, he called out, 'Jenny's coming over in the patrol boat. She needs *urgent* medical attention!'

Cooper yelled back, 'We'll take her to Wroxham Medical Centre. It's not far.'

'OK, but get the squad car to take her. I need you over here. Burgess is still inside. He's been badly hurt, and I'm going to need help getting him down.'

As the patrol boat left the jetty heading for the far bank, Cooper asked, 'What about Susan Follett?'

Tanner paused for a moment, before saying, 'I think she's still inside as well.'

- CHAPTER FIFTY TWO -

WITHOUT WAITING TO see the patrol boat reach the other side, Tanner turned and ran back towards the mill.

Standing outside the still open door, he pushed it inwards with his foot to peer into the cold, silent interior. Without his phone, he couldn't see as much as before, but the light from the moon flooding in through a small window to his right was enough for him to have a good look around.

There was no sign of Susan Follett that he could see, but for all he knew she'd retrieved her knife and was lying in wait for him.

After straining both his eyes and ears for another couple of seconds, unable to see or hear anything, he was about to go in when he remembered that he'd not looked behind the door. But he had neither the inclination, nor the courage, to do so now. Instead, he slammed it back until the inside handle hit the wall behind it.

There wasn't room for anyone to hide there; certainly not Susan Follett.

Without wasting another moment, he launched himself inside, bounded up the stairs, past the cots with their putrid remains, and over to where he'd left his fallen colleague.

Dropping to his knees, he looked down at where Burgess sat.

His head had rolled forward, and his eyes were staring vacantly down at his lap.

With one hand, Tanner lifted his head up, using two fingers of the other to push up against the side of his neck.

His skin felt cold and loose. There was no sign of a pulse.

'Burgess!' he called, turning his head around so that he could stare into his eyes. But although open, there was nobody inside looking back at him.

Tanner stared down at where he'd been stabbed. Burgess's hand wasn't resting over the wound anymore. Instead it lay upturned in a dark pool of blood on the floor beside him. Held loosely in the palm of the hand was Tanner's rolled up blood-soaked tie.

Tanner placed his index finger against his wrist.

Nothing.

From downstairs he heard Cooper calling out, 'Hello! Tanner? Are you in here?'

'I'm upstairs,' he shouted, but his voice lacked the urgency of before. Although he'd need to wait for a medical expert to confirm it, by that time Tanner knew that Burgess was dead.

- CHAPTER FIFTY THREE -

THE SOUND OF Cooper's footsteps clattering up the windmill's wooden stairs was soon followed by more. Glancing over his shoulder, Tanner saw Cooper had been followed by the two uniformed policemen from the patrol boat.

As the three of them picked their way past the macabre cots, using their torches to stare briefly into each as they passed, Tanner stood up to take a step away from Burgess's crumpled body.

Cooper shone his phone's torch down at Burgess, propped up against the wall, still staring at his own outstretched legs.

'Is he...?' Cooper began, but didn't finish. He didn't have to. They all knew what he'd been about to ask.

Before answering, Tanner hesitated. Although every fibre of his being declared that Burgess was dead, he didn't want to say so. Not out loud. Doing so would only make it seem more real. There were also more practical matters to consider if he was – that this had become yet another murder scene, and any attempts made to help him would only serve to contaminate the physical evidence. Tanner knew who'd done it, there was no question about that, but he hadn't witnessed her do so. Consequently, a jury would need as much physical evidence as possible to secure a conviction of first degree murder.

Hearing the distant wail of an ambulance approach, searching for words, Tanner eventually said, 'I-I don't know. He was stabbed. I plugged the wound, as best I could, but…'

The uniformed policeman knelt down beside Burgess's body. Without touching him, he leant over, and using his torch, shone the light directly into Burgess's eyes. After withdrawing the beam he waited, just for a moment, before shining it back.

'There's no pupil dilation,' he said.

Using the torch again, he looked first at the wound, then at the upturned hand, still loosely holding Tanner's rolled-up tie.

'I'd say it's probably best we wait for the ambulance,' he eventually said. 'The external bleeding looks as if it's stopped, but with a stab wound, the internal bleeding will be significant. If we were to move him, it would probably only make it worse.'

After shining his torch once more into Burgess's face, he looked up at Tanner and said, 'But if I was to be honest with you, I'd say we're too late.'

- CHAPTER FIFTY FOUR -

B Y THE TIME Tanner retrieved his jacket and his phone and emerged from the mill, a number of vehicles had arrived on the other side of the river, including two squad cars and an ambulance.

With flashing blue lights dancing over the surface of the river, Tanner watched as two paramedics and a number of other police personnel were ferried over by a patrol boat driver, one of them he recognised as being DCI Barrington.

Approaching the jetty to meet him, after waiting for the paramedics to climb out, Tanner watched as Barrington stepped off the boat saying, 'I heard the news. How's Burgess?'

'It's not good, I'm afraid, sir.'

'Not good as in...?'

Tanner didn't answer him directly, but instead said, 'We're going to have to get the whole area cordoned off.'

'Shit!' said Barrington.

The moment he said it, he remembered his position, and that he *had* to be more respectful. So he quickly added, 'I am deeply sorry to hear that.'

'Me too, sir,' replied Tanner. 'We may not have seen eye to eye all the time, but he certainly didn't deserve that.'

'No,' agreed Barrington.

Taking a nervous breath, Tanner asked, 'Any news of Jenny, sir?'

'Nothing yet. All I've heard is that she's been taken to Wroxham Medical Centre. That's about it.'

As Barrington stared up at Fen Marsh Mill, he asked, 'What about Susan Follett?'

'We haven't been able to find her. She fell down the stairs, just after she cut Jenny's…, but then she seemed to vanish. I've got Cooper and another officer looking for her now, but I don't think she's in the mill.'

Remembering the hidden rowing boat, Tanner peered along the jetty. It was still tied up, and he pointed to it. 'We think she used that boat to get herself over the river, but as it's still here, she must be this side, somewhere.'

Barrington surveyed the surrounding reeds. The wind had dropped to nothing, and they were standing tall and still in the cold night air.

'There's something else as well, sir,' continued Tanner. 'Inside the mill.'

'What's that?'

'Cots, sir. Three of them. And inside two of them are…' Tanner stopped as he searched for the most appropriate words to describe them. 'I believe they are the unborn children of Jane Richardson and Emily Warren. Follett must have surgically removed them. She had them wrapped up in blankets, as if they were new-born babies.'

'Jesus Christ!' said Barrington, with a look of absolute horror.

'She admitted to killing Jane and Emily, but I don't

think she killed Simon. When I asked her about it, she didn't even seem to know he was dead.'

'She didn't kill him.' stated Barrington. 'Forensics found fingerprints plastered all over him and the kitchen, and DS Gilbert just told me on the way over here who they belong to.'

- CHAPTER FIFTY FIVE -

ABOUT AN HOUR later, having returned to his boat to retrieve a fresh shirt and tie, Tanner brought his XJS to a halt outside the imposing black wrought iron gates that marked the entrance to the Lambert's residence in Horning.

Before reaching for the intercom button, he stared down at the empty passenger seat. He took a moment to say a silent prayer that Jenny would be OK. As he did, the squad car that had followed him there pulled up behind him, its orange indicator stabbing at the night, but thankfully not the blue roof lights.

Tanner lowered his window, leaned out and pressed the intercom button.

It wasn't long before a man's metallic voice responded.

Recognising it, Tanner said, 'Mr Lambert, it's Detective Inspector Tanner. Could you open the gates, please?'

There was a pause, before John Lambert replied, 'It's very late, Detective. Can't you come back another time?'

'I'm afraid it can't wait.'

'Well, I'm sorry, Detective, but I think it's going to have to.'

'You need to let us in, Mr Lambert, and you need

to do so now. If you don't, you could be facing a charge of obstruction of justice.'

The intercom fell silent, before Tanner heard a familiar clunking sound and the gates started to whir open.

As Tanner began driving in, motion sensor lights sprang on, lighting up both the drive and the entire front section of the house. There, the same two cars were parked as before, the Aston Martin Vanquish and the Range Rover Vogue, looking even more glamorous in the incandescent brightness of the now spot-lit drive.

With the squad car following, Tanner continued all the way around until he'd reached the front of the house.

As he climbed out of the car, the front door opened, and John Lambert emerged, folding his arms over his chest with resolute firmness.

'What do you want?' he called out, as the squad car pulled up behind Tanner's.

With the two uniformed officers stepping out, Tanner said, 'We need to speak to your wife, Mr Lambert.'

'Well, she's not in, I'm afraid.'

Gesturing over at the two gleaming black cars, Tanner said, 'I assume one of those is hers?'

'Just because her car's here, doesn't mean she is.'

'Then you won't mind telling us where she's gone?'

'I've really no idea. Now if you don't get the fuck off my property, I'll be suing you for trespass, harassment, intimidation, and anything else my lawyer can think of!'

'Mr Lambert, we know what your wife has done. I

suspect you probably do as well. As much as I'm sure you'd like to, unfortunately you won't be able to stop us from arresting her. If you're not prepared to ask her to come to the door, we do have the authority to gain entry to your property to conduct a thorough search, by force if necessary.'

With a look of increasing desperation, John blurted out, 'But as I said, she's not in!'

As Tanner gestured over his shoulder for the two police officers to come forward, Ruth Lambert appeared from behind the door; her face pale, her eyes red.

Resting a steadying hand on her husband's shoulder, she looked at him and said, 'It's OK John. You don't have to do this.'

'But...'

Standing beside her husband, Ruth gazed over at Tanner and said, 'I'm ready to come with you, Detective,' and took a step forward.

Taking a firm hold of her arm, John tried pulling her back. As he did, he glared over at Tanner, saying, 'No! You can't have her! I've already lost my daughter. I'm damned if I'm going to lose my wife as well!'

Resting her hand on his, Ruth turned to study her husband's face.

'I'm sorry, John, darling,' she said. 'I shouldn't have done it. I know I shouldn't have, but I didn't have a choice. I couldn't let him get away with it. Not our Jane. Our precious, beautiful Jane.'

As she prised his fingers from her arm, John lost control of his emotions and began to sob, the hand that had been holding on to his wife now a fist, pressed firmly against his mouth.

Stepping forward, Tanner took hold of Ruth's other arm and began guiding her towards the two waiting police officers.

As one of them began handcuffing her hands behind her back, John screamed out, 'YOU CAN'T LEAVE ME! YOU CAN'T LEAVE ME!'

Tanner stood helplessly by as John sank to his knees, raking his fingers back through his hair. He didn't have the heart to tell him that his wife had murdered an innocent man. Simon Richardson hadn't killed their daughter, no matter what the press may have said. No doubt he'd find that out soon enough, as would his wife. But it wouldn't be him who'd be telling them.

Hearing the police car's doors close, Tanner tore his eyes away from the distraught man and climbed back inside his own. Starting the engine, he waited for the car behind to lead the way back out, before following along behind.

As both vehicles waited for the gates to automatically open, Tanner's mobile phone began to ring.

Digging it out from his inside pocket, he answered it by saying, 'Tanner speaking!'

'Hi, Tanner, it's Vicky – DS Gilbert.'

'Yes, Vicky. How can I help?'

'I just wanted to let you know that we've had a call from Wroxham Medical Centre, about Jenny, sir.'

Tanner didn't say anything in response. Instead he just sat there, his heart pounding deep inside his chest.

He stared into the rear-view mirror, looking at John Lambert, still sobbing on the porch.

Is that about to be me? he wondered.

'I just thought you'd like to know that she's going to be OK.'

As he heard the words, a surge of relief swept through his body.

'Are you still there, sir?' asked Vicky.

Before daring to say anything in response, Tanner sucked in a lungful of air which juddered as it went down. After holding his breath for a moment, with forced dispassion, he eventually managed to say, 'That's good news, Vicky. Thanks for letting me know.'

With that, he ended the call.

Seeing the car ahead set off through the now almost fully open gates, he put the phone away, wiped the tears which had appeared from nowhere from his eyes, placed his XJS's gear lever into the drive position, and headed back towards Wroxham.

- CHAPTER FIFTY SIX -

ARRIVING BACK AT the station, through a furious burst of flash photography from the awaiting press, all desperate to catch a glimpse of the handcuffed woman they could see being helped out of the back of the squad car, Tanner followed the two uniformed police officers as Ruth Lambert was led inside.

It was only after he'd watched her being handed over to the desk sergeant, and had completed his arrest report, that he was finally able to make his way back to his Norfolk cabin cruising yacht on Malthouse Broad.

Driving out of Wroxham, over the low bridge, now devoid of traffic, he glanced briefly down at the moonlit River Bure as it slipped gently past. As he did, he found himself thinking about Jenny, wondering when he'd be able to see her, and how long it would be before she was back on her feet.

Would she still be interested in pursuing a career within the police? After all that had happened, he wouldn't be surprised if she decided to call it a day. Half of him hoped that she would, and find herself an office job instead. At least that way she'd be safe. But the other half of him knew that he'd miss her if she did, and doubted she'd still be interested in him were she to decide to leave.

Forcing himself to stop thinking about her, instead he thought about the wooden yacht that was waiting for him, and was surprised to find himself actually looking forward to being back on board. Despite its insanely cramped accommodation and total lack of even the most basic amenities, he was beginning to think of it as a safe haven; one that was far removed from society's seemingly endless storm of dangerous obsessions and cruel machinations, and one which was increasingly beginning to feel like being his new home.

- EPILOGUE -

OVER THE NEXT couple of days, leading up to the busy Easter weekend, Tanner kept close tabs on the situation with Jenny by occasionally asking DS Vicky Gilbert how she was doing. He'd tried to make such enquiries seem as casual as possible, by finding excuses to pass by Vicky's desk, or by deciding to make a coffee whenever she happened to be doing the same. But by the time Good Friday rolled along, it had become fairly obvious, to Vicky at least, that his interest in his colleague's wellbeing was beyond just professional.

During such enquiries he'd learnt that her condition had initially been very much touch and go. The knife wound to her neck had sliced open her main jugular vein. Subsequently she'd lost a huge amount of blood; so much that she'd fallen into hypovolemic shock, just before reaching Wroxham Medical Centre. Fortunately, DS Cooper had had the foresight to call ahead to let them know of the incoming medical emergency, and that warning had probably saved her life.

Despite knowing that she was OK, and that she had started to receive visitors, Tanner decided to wait until Saturday before going to see her himself. He'd delayed his visit for a couple of reasons. For a start, he didn't want to be seen doing anything that could give people the impression that his feelings towards her were anything other than professional; but he also wanted to wait until he could find some suitable gifts to bring with him, one of which proved just a little difficult to track down, and he'd had to buy it from eBay.

With a nervous knock, he poked his head around the door to her private room.

Pleased to see there was nobody else there, he crept inside.

She was asleep, or at least her eyes were closed. The bed she was lying in was angled in such a way that she could sit up, but she must have drifted off.

In the silence he looked round at the various cards and flowers that surrounded her.

After a moment or two he realised he'd better make some sort of noise to alert her to his presence, just in case she woke up to find an uninvited man in her room gawping at her; so he cleared his throat rather loudly and said, 'Hello? Jenny? Are you awake?'

Her eyelids fluttered open.

Seeing Tanner standing in front of her, holding a brown paper bag in one hand and a large plastic bag in the other, she gave him a warm smile, and croaked out, 'Hello, boss!'

Returning her smile, he said, 'I just thought I'd drop by to see how you're doing.'

As she made an effort to sit up properly, whilst making a few self-conscious jabs at her hair, she said, 'I'm feeling much better, thank you.'

An awkward silence followed, as Tanner tried to think of what to say next.

Eventually he placed the plastic bag down by his feet, which allowed him to pull a bunch of purple grapes out of the paper one.

Handing them over to her, he said, 'I brought these for you.'

'Wow!' she said, with wry amusement. 'You shouldn't have!'

'Well, I thought it was the least I could do.'

'You mean, after leading me into a disused windmill for me to have my throat cut open by some deranged psychopathic receptionist? Yes, bringing me grapes probably was the least you could do.'

Having said that, she couldn't help but let a smile play over her lips.

With an ambivalent shrug, Tanner added, 'I brought you something else as well.'

Reaching for the plastic bag by his feet, he pulled out a small rectangular box with the picture of a car on its front.

Handing it over to her, he said, 'It's an Airfix model of a Jaguar XJS.'

Taking it from him, Jenny stared down at it, momentarily stumped for a suitable response.

'I know how much you like my car, so I thought I'd give you one of your own!'

Finally getting the joke, she looked up at him and smiled.

'It's just what I've always wanted, thank you!'

She was about to open it, when Tanner stopped her by saying, 'Actually, it's probably not a great idea to do that. It's a collectors' item, you see, so it's worth more if you *don't* open it.'

'You mean, you bought me an Airfix model of a car that I don't really like very much, and I can't even make it?'

'Well, yes, but I thought you'd enjoy looking at the picture.'

She stared around, looking for somewhere suitable to put it, but with so many flowers and cards, she eventually left it lying in her lap, saying, 'I'll ask the nurse to think of something suitable to do with it.'

Reaching back into the plastic bag, Tanner pulled out a much larger box.

Handing it over to her, he said, 'I brought you this as well.'

'It's…a…2000-piece jigsaw puzzle!' she said, staring down.

'I thought it would help pass the time.'

'Well, at least it's a picture of a boat.'

'A sailing boat as well!' he pointed out.

'Fab!' she replied, and again spent a few moments staring around, wondering where she was going to put it.

'Shall I ask if the nurse can find you a table so you can start doing it?'

'Er…it would have to be quite a large one.'

'Oh, I'm sure they've got one that's big enough.'

'If you mean, like a dining room table, then I'm not sure it would fit through the door.

'Maybe they've got a fold up one you can use. Hold on – I'll ask someone.'

As Tanner made as if he was about to go looking for a nurse, Jenny said, 'Don't worry. I'll just pop it down here, on the floor. Hopefully the cleaners will find it there in the morning.'

They exchanged smiles at their shared sense of humour, then there was a moment's pause, before with a serious expression, Jenny said, 'I heard that Burgess didn't make it.'

'I'm afraid he didn't, no.'

Silence followed, as they both paid their quiet respects to their fallen colleague.

After a while, Tanner said, 'There's a rumour that Barrington might not, either.'

'How d'you mean?'

'I suspect that the powers at be are looking for a scapegoat for what happened to Burgess, and that Barrington is going to be it.'

There was another lull in the conversation.

'I've not heard anything about a funeral,' said Jenny, deciding to leave the discussion about Barrington till another time.

'There's going to have to be an inquest first.'

'Of course. How about Susan Follett. Was there any news?'

'Didn't anyone tell you? She was picked up last night, trying to sneak into her flat.'

'That was stupid of her! Why did she go back there?'

'I've no idea, but if it wasn't for Vicky having had the good sense to arrange for a patrol car to keep an eye on the place, she'd probably have found some way to leave the country by now.'

'Has she been charged yet?' asked Jenny, enjoying the opportunity to talk about work again.

'She has, although she denies knowing anything about what she's been charged with; certainly nothing about the murders of Jane Richardson and Emily Warren.'

'Even though we found their unborn children in that god-forsaken mill of hers?'

With a shrug, Tanner said, 'She even denied killing Burgess. She said that she was forced to stab him out of self-defence. According to her, he tried to rape her! But anyway, there's more than enough evidence for a conviction. The knife she used to try to kill you was the same one used on Burgess. It was also what was used to remove the foetus from Emily Warren.'

'How about the murder weapon. Did anyone find that?'

'We didn't, no. We assumed she must have thrown it in the river somewhere, but there should be more than enough evidence for a jury to find her guilty for the murder of the two women, and Burgess as well.'

Keen to steer the conversation away from work, Tanner changed the subject. 'Any idea when you'll be given the all-clear?'

With her normal presumption, Jenny asked, 'Why? Are you thinking about asking me out on a date?'

Tanner had forgotten about her bold mischievous streak, and it took him a moment to come back with, 'I was actually wondering if you'd like to come sailing on my boat with me?'

'I didn't think you could sail?'

'I can't, no.'

'Or that it was your boat!'

'You're right, it isn't, but the owner's said that he doesn't mind if I take her out occasionally, as long as I can find someone experienced enough to sail her.'

'That would be me, then!' she said, happy to

volunteer.

'That would be you, then, yes!' agreed Tanner.

With a warm, appreciative smile, Jenny said, 'I'd like that, very much. Thank you. The doctor said that I should be able to leave here tomorrow, although I doubt I'll be up for doing much for a while.'

'No, of course.'

'How about next weekend? I'm sure I'll be back on my feet by then. Certainly enough to sail some old Detective Inspector from London around for a few hours, even if he doesn't know the difference between a quant and a rhond hook.'

Admittedly, Tanner didn't know what either was, but standing there, staring deep into Jenny's eyes, he was already looking forward to finding out.

A LETER FROM DAVID

I just wanted to say a huge thank you for deciding to read *Broadland*. If you enjoyed it, I'd be really grateful if you could leave a review on Amazon, or mention it to your friends and family. Word-of-mouth recommendations are just so important to an author's success, and doing so will help new readers discover my work.

It would be great to hear from you as well, either on Facebook, Twitter, Goodreads or via my website. There are plenty more books to come, so I sincerely hope you'll be able to join me for what I promise will be an exciting adventure!

David-Blake.com
facebook.com/DavidBlakeAuthor
facebook.com/groups/DavidBlakeAuthor
twitter.com/DavidDBlake

ABOUT THE AUTHOR

David Blake is an international bestselling author who lives in North London. At time of going to print he has written eighteen books, along with a collection of short stories. He's currently working on his nineteenth, *The Wherryman*, which is the follow-up to *Broadland, St. Benet's, Moorings, Three Rivers and Horsey Mere*. When not writing, David likes to spend his time mucking about in boats, often in the Norfolk Broads, where his crime fiction books are based.

www.David-Blake.com

ST. BENET'S

A DI Tanner Mystery

Book Two

A girl thrown from a church tower, a man sacrificed to Satan, and a priest, murdered at the hands of the Devil.

When the body of an old man is found lying in the ruins of St Benet's Abbey, his throat cut, a knife resting in his open hand, DI John Tanner and DC Jenny Evans are given no choice but to accept a ruling of death by misadventure.

But when the body goes missing from its tomb, after a priest is found nailed to a cross, and another impaled on a stake, everything begins to point back to the murder of a teenage girl, thrown from the top of a church tower, some forty-three years before.

St. Benet's Sample Chapter

- Prologue -

Thursday, 8th July, 1976

CLAIRE JUDSON'S DELICATE bare feet burned against the black sun-scorched path as she sprinted over towards the half-open church door. Once inside, she crouched low, and took a moment to peer around.

The church was empty; at least she thought it was.

There she remained for a moment, basking in the cool stale air whilst relishing the touch of the cold flagstone floor against the soles of her feet.

She'd abandoned her ugly school shoes and the white socks that came with them when she'd been hiding behind a gravestone outside, waiting for the coast to be clear. As painful as it had been to run on the blistering tarmac, the shoes' solid block heels made it impossible for her to walk anywhere without being heard, and silence was imperative. Her clandestine lunchtime rendezvous at the top of the bell tower with her much older boyfriend *had* to remain a secret. The Catholic girls' boarding school that she attended just down the road was well known for its zero tolerance towards pupils having any sort of relations with the opposite sex. If she was caught, she'd be expelled. There was no question about that.

However, with current circumstances as they were, she didn't feel she had much of a choice. The stifling heatwave that had gripped the Norfolk Broads for the last two weeks, as it had the rest of the country, left her in a permanent state of sexual arousal. From the moment she awoke, a thin layer of sweat clung to her, making some of the most sensitive parts of her body stick to the coarse material that made up her hideously unfashionable school uniform.

Not wearing a bra probably didn't help. She'd yet to get used to them. Although they provided her with much needed support, she found them to be insanely uncomfortable, and she was always looking for an excuse not to wear them; the intense summer's heat proving to be the perfect one.

On that particular day, she wasn't wearing any pants either. Gary had asked her not to. After their liaison the previous day, he'd mentioned that the idea of her walking around school without them would be a real turn-on for him. She'd yet to have the chance to tell him, but she was fairly sure that doing as he suggested had aroused her far more.

Since starting school that morning she'd found the combination of the oppressive heat, along with the knowledge that she was secretly strutting around her strict boarding school wearing nothing under her uniform, made thinking about anything other than Gary having his way with her virtually impossible.

It had been purely by chance that their covert encounters had coincided with the beginning of the heatwave. That was also when a deep sense of guilt had started to follow her around school, like an annoying unwanted friend. She'd been brought up to believe that sex performed outside of the holy union of marriage was a sin against God. She'd never understood why, especially after she'd had her first orgasm. How could something that felt so good possibly be against God? Quite the opposite! It made her feel empowered, liberated, alive - at least it did when she wasn't worrying about what would happen to her soul after her mortal existence came to an end. As long as Gary wore a condom, she really couldn't see the harm. The act itself made her feel far closer to God than anything had done before, certainly more than singing insipidly boring hymns, or being forced to listen to never-ending sermons, the sole purpose of which seemed to be to incite perpetual fear of what lay in wait for mankind beyond the grave for all but the most spiritually minded.

Naturally, the Church took offence at the use of contraception as well. Now that *really* didn't make sense! Why ban the one thing that turned sex into nothing more than a harmless act of mutual affection?

But there was one thing that meant what she had been doing with such hedonistic pleasure was most definitely wrong, both in the eyes of God and the law of the land: she was only fifteen. But it was a minor technicality, at least it was in her eyes. She would be sixteen in September, which was close enough.

However, she hadn't been entirely honest about it with Gary. When they'd first met, she'd told him she was eighteen, and that she was about to sit her 'A' levels. In fact she hadn't even done her mock 'O' level exams. In her defence, she *felt* like she was eighteen, and she most definitely looked it. She could probably pass for nineteen, maybe even twenty, or she could if she was allowed to wear makeup and some half decent clothes.

Once she was sure that no-one was there, she padded over the cool flagstone floor towards the narrow door that marked the entrance to the bell tower. Ducking inside, she closed it gently behind her to begin stepping lightly up the narrow stone steps which circled around the outer edge.

As she neared the top, the spiralling stairs became progressively steeper, so much so that with no hand rail, she used the steps in front of her like the rungs of a ladder, placing hand over hand on each as she climbed ever higher.

At last she arrived at the level where the giant domed church bells hung from their massive beams, waiting in patient silence for the next time they were needed. From there, a steel ladder took her up to where the final half-dozen or so wooden steps led out onto the roof.

Breathing hard, her legs beginning to tire, she couldn't help but imagine Gary's smile as he lifted up her skirt.

Directly ahead now was the ancient wooden door that led out to the roof, a band of sunlight filling the gap between it and the frame, like a saintly halo.

A mischievous smile played over her lips as she imagined the door being the entrance to heaven itself. As far as she was concerned, it wasn't far off.

She paused to catch her breath, bracing herself for the intense heat that awaited her. It was supposed to be one of the hottest days since records began, and even though she'd be at the top of a tower over a hundred feet high, she knew it would make no difference. The air would be as listless up there as it was at ground level, as it had been since their very first illicit meeting.

Her breathing may have eased, but her heart continued to pound hard in her chest as she climbed the last of the steps. What she'd been doing with Gary at the top of the very place where she attended Sunday Mass every week was by far the most exciting thing she'd ever done in her entire life.

Inching open the door, she squinted in the sun's glare, and stepped out onto the grey wooden planking.

Gary wasn't there.

He'd normally be waiting for her just beside the entrance, leaning against the stone ramparts, cigarette in hand.

She checked her watch.

She was a little early, perhaps, but she'd never arrived ahead of him before. He only lived down the road, so he didn't have far to come. He was a barman at The Bittern in Wroxham, working the evening shift, and didn't start until three. That was why they were only able to meet during her school lunch break.

From the stairs behind her came the sharp creaking of wood.

Knowing it must be Gary, she decided to strike the exact same pose he always did when she was about to emerge. Without a cigarette, she instead used her free hand to raise up her pleated green skirt, all the way to the top of her legs, exposing her smooth porcelain white thighs along with the perfectly formed curvature of her bum, so giving him proof that she wasn't wearing anything underneath, just as he'd requested.

When she saw the top of his dark head she called, 'Hello stranger!' With amused nonchalance she then turned to gaze out over the village of Horning, shimmering in the breathless heat of the sun, adding, 'What do you think of the view?'

She pictured his wide square shoulders rising slowly up through the roof, and the way he would stop and stare in awe and desire at the half-naked school girl standing ready for his attention.

Turning to smile at him, she was so expecting it to be Gary that it took her a full second to realise that it wasn't. The man who was openly ogling her, and who seemed unperturbed by the fact that she had caught him doing so, was wearing the black cassock of a priest.

Dropping her skirt, flushing in hot embarrassment, she spun to face him, adopting the traditional pose of an innocent young Catholic school girl as she did, legs locked together, her hands clasped in front of her skirt, as if the combination of the two created some sort of impenetrable barrier to her long-lost virginity.

As the man stepped out onto the roof, being careful not to trip over the hem of his cassock, his gaze seemed to linger unduly on her full naturally red lips, and her cute up-turned nose. 'I thought I heard someone creeping around up here,' he said.

Unable to think of anything to say in response, she stared down at her bare feet, attempting to offer the correct level of reverence due to a man of the cloth.

Placing his hands firmly on his hips, in a voice of stern condemnation he asked, 'Shouldn't you be at school, young lady?'

'I am - I - I mean, I should, yes, sorry,' she stuttered, 'but it's my lunch break, you see, so I, er…'

'So you thought you'd sneak up here, did you?'

Claire replied with a single nod.

'To meet someone, I assume?'

She didn't answer.

'Was it Gary Mitchell, by any chance?'

Once more her cheeks flushed, but now with embarrassed indignation.

How the hell did he know about Gary?

As if able to read her mind, the man said, 'Don't worry. I won't tell anyone.'

'You won't?' she asked, lifting her head just enough to send him a questioning look.

'I won't,' he confirmed. Staring deep into her translucent blue eyes, he added, 'As long as you're prepared to do something for me.'

Assuming that whatever that was would involve some insanely boring chore, like having to mop the church floor after school for a week, with an insolent glare she demanded, 'And what's that?'

'Oh, nothing much,' he replied, allowing his eyes to slide down the length of her curvaceous young body. 'My silence in exchange for, shall we say…a kiss?'

'A…*kiss?*' she repeated, incredulous, and began searching his face for a sign that he wasn't being serious.

The intense focus of his eyes, and the salacious grin that now curled his lips, did nothing to allay her fear that a kiss was exactly what he wanted.

Panic began to take hold. There was something about this whole situation that was beginning to make her feel increasingly uncomfortable - the way she'd seen him openly ogling her earlier, and how he'd done nothing to avert his gaze, even when she'd caught him in the act. And to ask for a kiss in return for his silence?

The sense of heightened arousal she'd felt climbing the church tower had now been replaced by one of exposed vulnerability. He'd seen just how naked she was underneath her skirt, and Gary had taught her the effect such knowledge could have on a man.

But a priest?

She stole a glance down at his groin.

Her breath caught in her throat.

Underneath his long black cassock, it was blatantly obvious that the man was fully aroused. But as disturbing a sight as that was, what was far worse was the fact that he seemed to be doing nothing to hide it.

Instinctively, she took a half step back from him, wrenching her eyes away to the enclosed square roof, desperately searching for a way to escape. But she was at the top of a tower, over a hundred feet above the ground. The only exit was the door through which she'd come, and to reach that she had to pass the very man she was becoming increasingly desperate to get away from.

The man glanced down at where her hands remained locked in front of her pleated green skirt, before returning to stare at her face.

As if shocked by the fear he saw written there, he frowned down at her and said, 'My goodness, child, I didn't mean on the lips!'

As a surge of relief flowed through her body, she looked into his eyes to ask, 'You didn't?'

Returning to her what had transformed into a

warm, almost benevolent smile, as if appalled by the very suggestion, he exclaimed, 'Good Lord, no!' His eyes then stopped to rest briefly on her soft inviting mouth, before continuing down the length of her body. Narrowing them at where her hands were again, with a single step forward, he added, 'At least, not on *those* lips.'